His Irish Detective

Summer Devon

Summer Devon

His Irish Detective

Cover by Fantasia Frog

Dedication

***Of course* this one is to you, and it's about freaking time.**
So say *all* of us.
But the paper version is for Jim F. who asked.

There was an old woman had three sons,
Jerry, and James, and John:
Jerry was hung, James was drowned,
John was lost and never was found,
And there was an end of the three sons,
Jerry, and James, and John!

--Nursery Rhyme

CHAPTER ONE

1885 *Kent, England*

"You're looking well." Quade, on a rare visit to the family estate, never knew what to say to his family members. A compliment seemed the sort of comment that would make his older brother happy. And to be sure, Jack did look glossy and self-satisfied. He was the only one of the Marrills who seemed unaffected by the cloud hanging over them. With his white-toothed smile, and fine wool sack coat open to display a new gold watch chain, he was the picture of health and wealth.

"Ha, I should. I've had a fine time in London last month. Without the wife." Jack tipped him a wink.

"Is Mary here?"

Jack rolled his eyes—and Quade understood he'd been expected to give Jack a congratulatory slap on the back or make inquiries about that London visit. But Jack remained good-natured. "I left the dear thing back at the River. She's feeling poorly." The River House was his home, ten miles off—a gift from his in-laws.

The three Marrill men sat in the drawing room, waiting for the butler to bring refreshments. Quade, just arrived from London, would rather retreat to read or perhaps take a walk than eat tea with his glowering father.

"You're better, Father?" Jack asked.

"I'm perfectly well," Mr. Marrill gave him a reproachful glance.

"You've been ill?" Quade supposed that would account for his father's weight loss and new halting gait.

"Nothing of the sort." Mr. Marrill picked up a pile of letters and flipped through them.

Jack caught Quade's eye, wrinkled his nose, and drew his bottom lip over his top, a perfect exaggeration of their father's sternest expression. Quade stifled a laugh.

"What's so amusing?" Mr. Marrill demanded.

Jack winked at Quade, then jerked a thumb in his direction. "Quade made a funny face."

Quade couldn't help smiling at his idiot brother, though he half agreed with their father, who muttered, "Juvenile nonsense."

Jack pulled out a cigar, and their father waved a hand. "Not in here," he said, so Jack sauntered out the French windows to the garden, into the cool, cloudy day.

Their father, now alone in the room with Quade, rose to his feet, and so, of course, Quade did too.

His father scowled. "What's that bulging in your jacket pocket?"

Quade hadn't hidden the partial manuscript properly. He considered lying because he knew his father would disapprove, but was unable to invent anything interesting. He said, "It's from a book about medieval law. I'm compiling the index."

"Sounds dry and dull as…" His father's voice trailed off.

Was he going to say as dry and dull as the grave? As Quade's life? But his father only shook his head. He seemed even more unhappy being alone with his youngest son than usual.

"I'm going to the library. Pray do not forget that we change for dinner," his father said and walked quickly toward the door, though he had that new limp and seemed to be nursing a pain in his side.

"What is wrong, Father?"

A slender man, Mr. Marrill was almost gaunt now, though his graying hair was still thick and his dark eyes as he glanced back at Quade were sharp as always. He muttered something about rheumatism.

"I'm sorry," Quade said. "It's only a recent problem, I expect?"

His father gave a choked sound, an imitation of laughter, but didn't speak again before he left, slamming the door behind him.

Quade went out to see Jack. "Why didn't Father tell me he's been ill?"

"Best ask him about it," drawled Jack.

"I doubt he'd tell me. He seems even less communicative than ever."

"Does he?" Jack still played with the unlit cigar. "He's always been a suspicious old fogey. This and that has made him worse of late."

"What does 'this and that' mean? Is there some new disaster looming over Father or you?"

Jack gave a short laugh, much like their father's. "I'm not sure it's your business." He didn't sneer, merely stated a fact. "You are so removed from our daily lives, d'you see? Neither my confidant nor Father's."

"No," Quade agreed. He didn't often feel the lack of such intimacy with his family. "But I do worry about the old man."

"No need. He doesn't worry about us at all." Jack walked away toward the large garden.

"You seem on edge as well," Quade called after him.

Jack merely waved his cigar in the air. "I shall see you inside."

Quade considered following, but he'd enough of his early years as an unwanted extra trailing after his brothers. And though Jack's thoughtless comment about Quade's place in their family held no malice, it had stung. How childish to allow these snubs or his father's dislike of him to make him sulky. He watched his brother make his way to the hedge bordering the formal garden and wondered again how soon he might return to London.

With a sense of relief at being left to his own devices, Quade returned to the drawing room, where he settled into an overstuff chair and pulled out the loose pages to check over. He clenched a pencil between his teeth as he read through dense, handwritten passages, looking for words that would appear in the index. A notebook lay on his knee, held open with his elbow as he read.

The manuscript, written by a professor, was exactly as his father had described: dry, dull, filled with dates and facts that would put a normal man to sleep. Quade thought the whole thing fascinating. He loved his work and was grateful to be able to drag it along anywhere he went.

A few minutes later, the glass doors to the garden smashed open, and Jack staggered in. His handsome face was flushed and grossly swollen. His hands clawed at his throat, and he emitted a horrible high-pitched wheeze over and over.

Quade dropped the papers and rushed to Jack, who fell to his knees, still making the dreadful noise.

"Help! I need help," Quade shouted over his shoulder at the closed door. "We need help, damnation."

When a servant rushed in at last, Quade ordered, "Fetch a doctor."

Cursing, he knelt next to Jack, undoing his neck cloth and popping the now too tight collar stud with shaking fingers. He pushed aside the flailing hands and begged Jack to try to relax, for surely breathing would come easier if he could only stop moving about so violently.

Suddenly, the room filled with people, pushing Quade to the side and carrying Jack away and up to his room.

Quade followed behind, telling the doctor's assistant all he knew. Even as they rushed up the stairs, the whistling wail issuing from Jack faltered, then ceased. At that moment, Quade understood the only thing worse than that awful noise was silence.

He lurked in the corridor, frozen in horror, until a harsh whisper behind him startled him into taking a step backward. "What have you done?" his father growled.

"Nothing." Quade turned to face him.

"I saw you out there with him."

"Only for a few moments. Then I returned inside. Father, what do you think happened with Jack? I don't know."

His father stared down the dark corridor—no one had bothered to turn on the gaslights yet—then back at Quade, who understood that his father didn't believe him.

The nightmare of a moment was too familiar. Another death? And in this variation of the bad dream, no one believed him. "Truly, I have no notion what happened."

His father shook his head and whispered. "It will be fine. This isn't like the other times. Not at all. The doctor is excellent." He was speaking to himself, so Quade didn't answer. He wanted to agree, but feared agitating Mr. Marrill again.

At last his father made his slow, limping way back down the stairs, and Quade soon followed. An hour—or perhaps years—later, the doctor slowly descended the stairs to the family gathered to wait in the larger sitting room.

Even before he made the announcement, Quade's mother let out a single muffled sob, only one, and sat up straighter.

The words were but a faraway echo of what they all knew. Jack was gone. The doctor said that Jack's heart had failed and the culprit had been an insect bite or sting, though they couldn't find a mark on the body, only a pronounced swollen area on his wrist.

Reverend Peeler, the vicar, had just arrived at the house to offer kind words and prayers to the family. He sidled up to the physician. "Are you quite sure? It's rather cold for insects, don't you think?"

The doctor murmured something Quade couldn't hear, so he inched closer. He could see the skepticism on the faces of the listening gentlemen, his father's friends. Quade's own heart grew heavy with the same suspicion no matter how much he tried to ignore it.

Murder.

Jack was dead. Murdered perhaps? Dead. Murder. Those two words thumped through his head without cessation, but not distracting enough he couldn't hear Reverend Peeler continue in a carrying whisper. "And then there's the other matter. The other brothers, you know, and the cousin. All those deaths… Most peculiar."

Quade's father must not have heard the vicar's gossip, because he didn't order Reverend Peeler from the house.

"An insect sting. No contagion," the doctor announced to the room at large. "He can rest in peace in the chapel."

He was a good man, and a fine doctor. Yet Quade's troubling thoughts refused to be vanquished, and, he suspected, neither would the gossip.

He slipped away from the crowd, went outside, and by the light of a single candle, searched the garden. The cigar lay in the grass, damp from dew and Jack's saliva. Quade gingerly picked it up with a handkerchief. Upstairs in his room, he wrapped it in more layers of cloth, placed it in a box, and pushed the box far into the bottom of his valise.

Jack was laid out on a bier in the chapel, surrounded by pale flowers and candles. Above them, the passing bell tolled in the tower.

When Quade walked down the center aisle between pews to pay his respects, the clack of his boots on the flagstones echoed through the vault of the church. He longed to run, to escape the staring congregation. He considered singing. If he bellowed out a good tavern ditty, it would prove he was a madman, and perhaps they'd say the word outright instead of in whispers. *Murderer.*

Along with the shock, sorrow —the more standard collection of emotions—the single selfish question nagged. Why did he have to be at the hall when Jack died? He was the only person close enough to have helped. He should have done something different, taken some action that might have saved his brother. And now Quade was acutely aware that everyone knew the truth: he was the only one who had been near when the illness seized Jack.

"Jack, are you at peace? Any advice?" he muttered to the gray figure of his brother in an open coffin nearly blanketed in roses to cover the smell. "No, no. You're gone, and my worry is all for me. I apologize. Give my best to the others."

He didn't know what else to say to Jack, nearly nine years his elder and practically a stranger. That cocky smile Jack had flashed only minutes before he'd died seemed to have come from another world, one that had vanished forever with a bee sting. He couldn't lose everything about his brother. Quade fished through sparse memories and landed on the day Jack had pulled out a pocketknife to repair a toy for him. "Thank you for fixing the top. I wish I'd known you better."

Quade's eyes and nose prickled, but he wouldn't reach for the black-edged handkerchief and make that sort of a show in front of the eager spectators in the pews.

He couldn't imagine what Jack would have done if he'd caught Quade in tears. Maybe grin at him, ruffle his hair, then saunter away. Jack hadn't been sour, not like their oldest brother. He'd been the one to laugh, the trickster brother with the lightest heart. A plodder like Quade could never keep up with him, and only recently understood that he hadn't wished to try.

He stared at Jack's white face, and the usual phrases filled his mind. Thirty-three was too damned young to die. That wasn't lively Jack in that coffin, just a badly made imitation.

Quade resisted the urge to pull out his watch to see if he'd stood there too long or not long enough. Time didn't seem to pass the way it had before Jack's death.

Might he turn and make his way to the front row of benches without anyone remarking about his time spent with the corpse of his brother?

They'd whisper no matter what he did or said. Jack was the fourth brother to die.

Quade barely recalled his youngest brother, who'd drowned years ago. The second died in an accident while Quade was home on holiday from the university. The carriage had apparently gone over a narrow bridge during a storm. Another had been found in the woods with a broken neck after his saddle horse returned home without him. Now here lay Jack...and only Quade remained alive.

In the last six years, other male relations had met unfortunate ends. Quade's uncle and cousin died—and the cousin dead after a mysterious assault late at night in a London alley. The only remaining cousin, a small child, lived with Quade's mother and father.

Much of the dead uncle's estate had gone to Quade's father, joining money and lands again, an ever-increasing pile of wealth. And the last son would inherit it all.

Quade could almost hear the thoughts behind the dozens of faces that watched him. *No doubt it's a temptation to put even your own family out of the way for such rich gains, eh?*

He wanted to turn and shout at the lines of people sitting in their finest mourning, insist they speak to his face, say their suspicions out loud. But as he walked to the front, he caught sight of his parents' blank, pale faces, and he recalled again that his indignation or fear of the truth was hardly the point. Jack's widow was still in bed, overcome and doused with laudanum, days after the tragedy.

He took his seat next to his mother, who was ramrod stiff and dry-eyed. Her favorite son dead, yet only that unblinking stare and her set mouth and face displayed the depth of her pain. She wouldn't welcome any touch that might bring emotion to the surface, especially in public, so Quade faced forward, straightened his own back, and raged in silence until it was time to follow his brother's body to the graveyard.

After they returned home, his father summoned Quade to the library. He sat at his desk, folded his bony hands, and proceeded to lay out the details of Jack's will, namely that the money their grandfather had left Jack would revert to the estate since it was still in a trust and Jack had left no male heirs. Quade, standing in front of the desk, his hands at his back, was grateful the conversation was apparently simple and short, with no overflow of emotion. But then his father said, "We're hiring someone to watch you."

Quade didn't understand. His hands dropped to his sides. "Watch me do what?"

"We need someone to keep an eye on you day and night." It sounded like a threat.

"Why? Do you think I'm in danger?"

His father's gaze, usually steady and unflinching, shifted from his face to something in a far corner, and at last Quade understood. The anger filled him like poison and his blood felt thick. "Are you saying I had something to do with Jack's death? Or any of the others? And now you want to make sure I don't go after another victim? You, for instance? My cousin? Is that why you won't allow the boy to be alone with me?"

"Don't be an ass," his father snapped.

He's also furious about all this, Quade realized, and felt an unaccustomed surge of fellowship with his father. This was his father, who couldn't be guilty of murdering his own children or his brother. Quade's father and uncle had been closer than Quade had been to any of his brothers. "I beg your pardon, sir," he said. "That remark was not called for. But Father, please, there must be something happening to us. To Jack and—"

"Jack's passing was due to natural causes." His father rested his hands together, fingers laced, a sign of calm until it grew clear his grip on himself was so tight, his fingernails went white. "As for the rest of it, I have too much on my plate as it is to entertain such nonsense—"

"These deaths of the men in our family. Men and boys," Quade said, thinking of his youngest brother. "I want to understand what is happening. Don't you?"

"*You* have no reason to fear." His father's nostrils flared as if he smelled something unpleasant. "Did I not just tell you that I've hired someone to watch over you?"

The way he said that initial "you" was almost vicious.

Quade heard an accusation in his tone and responded without thinking. "I swear to you, I have no hand in this." He could have been speaking at a wall for all the good it did.

His father shuffled the papers on his desk and seemed to examine them. "This conversation is over."

"That's absurd," Quade said. "The conversation hasn't even begun."

"Do stop enacting a drama for once," his father said. "You have expressed your feelings far more strongly than necessary recently."

What the devil did that mean? When had he ever expressed his feelings to his father or anyone else in the family? At the moment, he was too confused to understand how he felt, much less speak of his emotions.

"I don't understand what you think I might have done. You know I'm not a violent man." Quade took a step closer to the desk. He stopped when his father held up a hand.

The older man began to rub at his temples. "Get out, if you please. I must compose a letter to Jack's lawyer." He apparently couldn't meet Quade's gaze. He hadn't been able to for several years. It wasn't merely to do with the deaths haunting their family. They hadn't had an easy moment since the day his father had gone into Quade's room and discovered a scandalous book by the bed, *Short Essays on Sodomy and Tribadism.* His benign jokes about Quade as a monk also ceased that day.

Quade knew his father well enough to know that the discussion was at an end. But he couldn't simply walk away now.

What was this business about hiring a guard? Or was it a guard? Would his father actually hire a killer to dispatch Quade? Such a bizarre notion, but Quade had no idea what was real and what was invented at this point.

Far better to believe it wasn't malicious action by his father, who'd perhaps hired someone to ferret out the truth. That would be a relief.

But all those deaths…Quade, who didn't usually have leaps of imagination, wondered if his father blamed him and looked for a quiet way to end the matter? He couldn't ignore the possibility he had a target on his own back and anyone might hold the weapon.

"Shall I arrange the person to watch over me?" Quade asked. "I could ask some of the barristers with whom I'm acquainted if they can find a suitable candidate."

"No. I will."

"Do you have someone in mind?"

For a moment, he thought his father would refuse to answer until Mr. Marrill said, "I have the name from our London solicitor, a gentleman named Mr. Sloan."

"That's familiar. Isn't he some variety of wealthy philanthropist?"

His father ignored him. "Mr. Sloan has a business partner, a Mr. Kelly, who has an agency that provides services such as this."

"Protecting victims, or tracking down criminals?"

His father stared down at his hands and didn't answer. Quade wanted to protest his own innocence again. But then again, he was hardly sure if his father was innocent himself.

He longed to believe it was just a series of terrible accidents. Nothing more.

"Perhaps there is only horrible coincidence at work," Quade picked his words carefully, and watched his father. "It could be that there are only victims of fate and not some dreadful scheme. But whether it be men's plans or God's will, I should think you'd want answers as well."

His father looked up and met his eyes. For a moment, he thought his father might agree. Instead he only said, "Enough. Go, please."

Quade wanted to run away and escape his family's woes. No, he wanted to stay as long as it took to discover the truth. At least he had that box in his bag.

He'd send the cigar off to Hemner, an expert who'd written a treatise on subtle poisons that Quade had translated from German. Best not to send from the village post office however. Quade had no desire to rouse any more curiosity or suspicion.

Quade left the Marrill estate less than a week later, unable to bear his father's dislike and suspicions, or, worse, the devastated stare of his mother that he couldn't shift no matter what he said or did. He returned to London and hoped the matter was over. It would never be over, of course, not while his parents and he still breathed and knew the others did not. But that was far too dramatic to say aloud.

A few days after that, he received a letter that a "valet" would be coming to him, and he must hire the man. The man was both obsequious and obtrusive and snooped through Quade's possessions—confirming Quade's suspicions he was under surveillance—but at least he didn't try to push Quade down the stairs or smash him over the head with the heavy umbrella stand.

Quade had done his own snooping and discovered that Patrick Kelly's agency was well regarded. But when he tried to talk to his new "valet," hoping to engage his help in discovering anything about the Marrill family misfortune, the idiot pretended he had no notion what Quade was talking about.

"I'm a servant, sir," he'd said. "Nothing more."

Quade wrote a note to Kelly, demanding to know what the fool Whitmore was up to.

Kelly's answer was polite and said nothing more than that he hoped Whitmore was professional but that he couldn't discuss the matter with anyone other than his client—and he assumed Mr. Marrill knew who had retained his services. Next, Quade wrote to his father, who didn't answer. He considered telling his father what he'd done with the cigar, but wanted to get an answer from Hemner first.

Soon after that, Quade had managed to behave obnoxiously enough to drive off Whitmore, and Quade thought he was safe from anyone else invading his space.

And then the Irishman appeared.

CHAPTER TWO

Colm Kelly woke without a headache. He'd had one before, hadn't he? Yes, and he knew he'd woken more than once. The air smelled of flowers, and the pillow cushioning his head was the softest he'd ever felt. The sheets he lay on were so bright white, his eyes smarted.

A hospital? English hospitals were supposed to be fine establishments, but did they offer their guests four-poster beds and flowers for strangers?

"Mr. Kelly," someone called to him. "Mr. Kelly? He's awake."

"Who's awake?" Colm croaked an answer. His throat felt as if it had been rubbed with broken glass. His arm ached, but the sharp pains over most of his body had diminished.

"You are." Someone stood over him with near-black hair and blue eyes, a familiar sight, though this version of a Kelly relation was a tad darker than usual. He had strong eyebrows that gave him an impatient or mocking appearance. "I'll ask you again. Why the hell did you have my name?" he demanded. He had a most peculiar accent, but Colm had heard it once, perhaps earlier, during a nightmare.

"You've asked me that question before?"

"Yes, and you told me you weren't interested in whatever I had to sell and to keep my filthy hands to myself. You also cursed me in what I assume is Gaelic."

"Ah." The conversation sounded familiar. "When did all this start?"

"They interrupted dinner last night to haul me off to the train station. It's close to teatime now."

Colm shut his eyes, trying to bring up the recent past. "I'm in England," he told the man as he remembered the train. "London?"

"Yes, London, and apparently you're one of my long-lost Irish relatives. Why'd you have to get yourself found?"

That wasn't an English accent. "Why d'you talk funny?"

Someone in the room, another man, laughed.

"I'm American. Crazy fool, you came looking for me and you didn't know that?"

Colm shifted on the bed, trying to sit up, indignant at last. “You’re a Kelly, but I don’t precisely know who you are, ya pisspot.”

“I’m Patrick Kelly.”

Colm examined the well-groomed man standing before him. The Padraig Kelly he knew well didn’t live in an English city. Just last week, during a walk through his little village, Colm had passed the time of day with Patrick. He could see that cousin bent over a horse’s hoof with a file, talking a mix of nonsense and Gaelic to the animal while he worked. He’d offered Colm a drink.

Colm’s longing for the sight of that forge close to his constable’s cottage brought on the nauseating recollection that he’d likely never see it again. Worse, his old friend and relation would likely pretend not to know or see him should they ever met again.The American version of Patrick Kelly stared back. “You don’t have a lot to say for yourself, except did you truly call me a pisspot? That’s quite a mouth you have on you, Colm Kelly.”

Colm considered apologizing, but this seemed to be the sort of man who didn’t like weakness and might take an apology as backing down from a position.

He sank against the huge pillows and admitted, “I’m not myself at all, sir. I’m not sure how I ended up here except, now I remember I had your name and address from my sister. You’ve corresponded with Aileen McConnell?”

“Never heard of her. Why are you here?”

That was a question he hated to think about. After the night from hell, Colm had had just enough money to buy himself a fourth-class ticket to Dublin, harvester’s fare. The steamer packet also included fare to England. The single parting gift he had was that scrap of paper from Aileen, who’d always kept track of family. She’d known about this long-lost family member, though she apparently hadn’t bothered to contact the man herself.

Colm had spent much of the journey to Liverpool huddled on a bench in a far corner of the boat, staring down at Aileen’s note, which was an address in London and a name. Patrick Kelly. This idiot.

The American went on, “You were found sick and passed out on a train.”

"Yes. I'd been injured." Beaten and kicked.

"They summoned me because the only thing you had was a piece of paper with my name."

He sounded angry, and weak as he was, Colm didn't want to hear it from strangers. "I'm sorry I was out of my wits enough to take advantage of you, Cousin Patrick," he said, attempting to put a sneer in his voice.

Patrick actually smiled. He shook his head. "I'm annoyed because I've been forced to have some sort of reunion with a member of the clan that tossed my mam aside as if she were garbage."

Colm's flash of anger was over and gone quickly, as always. "Oh? Her as well? I didn't know. That's my story too."

"Go on." After a moment of silence, Patrick spoke with exaggerated patience. "Tell me what happened. My mother wasn't forced to leave, but I understand you were?"

Colm must have been daft to open that door. "I had to leave my home. After some trouble."

"Ah-ha. Perhaps that explains the black eye and bruises."

"Mm," Colm agreed.

"Go on." Patrick waved a hand. "Why?"

"I was a constable." *Was.* No more dark blue and brass for him. The position of sergeant had occupied nearly every waking minute, covering all those villages, including his own. What could replace that life and that home in a hostile land like England?

"Truly? Royal Irish Constabulary?" His cousin sounded astonished.

"Yes."

"That trouble you got into must have been serious. Why aren't you any longer?"

He felt too discouraged to lie. "I broke the law."

Patrick Kelly growled. "You took bribes?"

"No."

"Rape? Thievery?"

"No, God help me, I'm not an animal. Thank you for your aid, Mr. American Kelly, but now I'll be on my way." Colm pushed down the covers. He was in his own underclothes, and someone had washed and bandaged his injuries.

"Where will you go?" Patrick Kelly folded his arms and stared down his nose, which had clearly been broken at least once. He looked like any roughneck cousin back in County Wexford. No, this relation's eyebrows were thicker and darker—a foreigner after all.

"Not your concern," Colm said.

The other voice spoke up. "You've wanted more family, Patrick, and here you have one as a surprise gift." That was an Englishman, and one from the upper crust—Colm had heard that sort of voice on stage once. The English gentleman continued, "We must take our relations as they come to us, flaws and all. I believe you told me that once."

Patrick flicked an annoyed glance at that corner of the room and growled again.

Colm tried to crane his head to see who was speaking, but his attention was brought back to his American relative, who'd grabbed a chair and sat down next to the bed.

"Look here," Patrick said, then stopped.

"I'm looking," Colm said. "What's to see?"

Patrick leaned close. "When my mother arrived in America, the aunt and uncle she'd been sent to refused to take her in. She was all alone. She made me swear not to treat any blood of ours as badly as she'd been treated. Family is sacred, she told me. That's what she thinks."

Colm, who'd been surrounded by relations all his life, had never considered the ties of kin anything worth mentioning. "You don't owe me a thing."

He'd had little enough time to plan after fleeing Ireland. He'd worried about his horse—would they return her to the barracks? He said, "I'll write to the RIC and see what can be done. They might find another place for me. I don't think the people who…the villagers…I don't think they will protest." Oh, that was a joke, and he knew it. Someone would tell about his moral turpitude or some such fine phrase. He'd never work as a guard again.

His cousin said, "Tell me what happened. Did you get a girl pregnant? Did you bugger a sheep?"

Something about the word bugger must have made him flinch, because Patrick Kelly suddenly leaned forward, interested. "Not a sheep, then."

"Shove off, Cousin Patrick. If you hand over my clothes and my belongings, I'll be on my way and thanks to you for your aid."

"You had nothing. Someone must have stolen your bag when you were passed out on the train. Like I said, you only had that paper."

He closed his eyes and cursed under his breath.

"You're trapped here with us for the time being."

"Who's us?"

"I live here with my pal, Mr. Sloan."

Something in the way he said the odd word pal seemed to imply something. Was it about Colm himself or those two together?

"I got to know," his cousin said. "All these injuries. You a combative sort of guy?"

He leered at Colm, who froze, covers most of the way down his thighs, then he pushed himself up into a sitting position. "No, I'm not. I might be battered, but I think I can take you on if you try anything. You and your friend together."

Patrick snorted. "You flatter yourself. So far, you've called me names and insinuated that we're going to do unholy things to your person. And instead of tossing you out on your rear, I'm going to help you. You worked for the Royal Irish Constabulary, you said? That should be easy enough to find out."

That sounded like a threat to Colm, but apparently not to the Englishman in the room, who spoke up again. "Your mother would be proud of you, Patrick. I'll have to make sure she finds out you're lending a hand to a relation."

Colm said, "I apologize if I mistook your intent. But I don't think my plans need—"

His cousin interrupted. "Colm Kelly, unless you have a better invitation, you should probably stay with us, and once you're healed, we'll find work for you. Care to go into service?"

"Be a house servant? Never."

"Yes, I'm guessing you'd rather be a ditch digger. You have the build for it."

Colm suspected it was supposed to be an insult, but he immediately answered, "All right."

"Hold up. Tell me, when you were a constable, did you do anything like an investigation while you wore the uniform?"

"Nothing more than finding lost sheep." Of course he'd had to track some sheep hidden in a cave once, but that would take too much explanation.

"I hear you guys couldn't serve in your home counties."

"True enough. I managed to be near, though." Due to some coaxing and a small bribe, Colm had been placed in Wicklow, barely ten miles from the cottage where he was born, so he could ride over to see his family. He already missed the wild beauty of the Kilmichael dunes.

"You had no desire to rise in the ranks."

Colm pulled the covers to his chin, relaxing again. He was tired, and the question didn't seem to be a challenge. He had nothing better to do than talk to his up-and-down, moody cousin. "I was a sergeant, and, yes, with no desire to rise above the rank of an ordinary guard. I didn't want to live in the barracks. I liked the cottages well enough, and even the low pay wasn't bad, you know, since the residents gave me eggs and milk and fish."

He swallowed hard to stop the latest wave of regret at being banished from that world. Where else could he ever fit a life as easily?

When he'd caught the sheep rustlers single-handedly, he was a hero. And then when he managed the delicate balance of keeping peace between the travelers and the locals, everyone at the inn bought him a round of ale.

Liam had said he was proud to know him, and that had been the moment he'd begun to hope. Christ, losing Liam's regard was the worst of all. Trying to pervert their natural, friendly affection into something unholy, Liam had said. And Colm hadn't even gotten so much as a kiss, just a lot of insults, then a beating.

That night he'd drunk too much for the first time in years was the night he got into trouble. But he didn't want to think about that.

His cousin asked, "You can read and write?"

He grunted assent.

"You obviously speak English well enough to be understood."

"Same to you."

"Very funny. Can you keep your mouth shut? Your proclivities hidden?"

"My what? Whatever you're talking about, I won't flash it around in public."

"Your tastes."

He swallowed another curse. "I can keep plenty hidden," he said.

"If you're not lying, then maybe I have a job for you once you recover, assuming you can get past that dislike of acting as a servant."

The relief was enormous. He'd been holding back the fear, telling himself he'd find a way to survive—an able and strong fellow like himself. Never mind that he'd heard stories about the sort of jobs available to Irishmen in England.

He looked around the room, which was bigger, cleaner, and more magnificent than anything he'd seen in his life. He closed his eyes. "Thank you."

"I'm going to make sure you're not lying, Colm Kelly. I have ways of checking up on the truth."

He only nodded, suddenly exhausted beyond anything he'd experienced. Too much new to take in, and all he could do was fall asleep in the palace, he mused drowsily.

"You've still got a fever. Some sort of infection." His cousin's voice came from far away.

"No doubt," Colm said.

His cousin and the gentleman with him walked out.

Something creaked and clunked, then made a moaning, roaring sound. Colm started up and looked around, but he was alone in an empty room. "I've fallen into a den of dragons." He went to sleep anyway.

When the clink of china woke him, he felt nearly human again. A servant arranged a tray on a table next to the bed. "Tea, sir," the servant said.

Colm pulled himself up and regarded the delicate porcelain plate with matching cup and a funny triple tray of food. "I fell into a fine situation, didn't I?"

The man gave him a narrow-eyed, suspicious look, but then rearranged a cloth on the tray. "You'll see that Mr. Sloan and Mr. Kelly are good employers. Slightly eccentric."

"How's that?" He wasn't sure he wanted to know, especially after the man hesitated.

"You're in a guest room, not the servants' quarters."

Nothing about the strange tension he'd felt humming between the two men, Sloan and Kelly. Maybe Colm had been imagining it—or the servants were discreet.

"I'm a relation of Mr. Kelly," he said. "My name is Kelly too."

"Oh, I beg your pardon, sir." The servant might have sounded sarcastic, but that wasn't Colm's problem.

"No, no," he said. "I know I look the part of a stablehand. Don't hang about for my sake, laddie. I'm well enough to feed myself."

It bothered him to be among superior folk, all these jammy people. In his village, he'd been something of a big noise, and here, he was a nobody who knew nothing and looked like it too.

Within a few days, his headache had vanished and all the swelling had gone down. He asked for paper, and with his bandaged hand, he wrote a letter to Aileen, reassuring her and telling her about their cousin's generosity.

He awkwardly dressed himself with two fingers still in splints, then went downstairs in search of his host.

A servant—how many prowled the place?—found him and ushered him along corridors to meet with Patrick Kelly. He was led to a big room that looked something like a grand office and a huge library. Colm took in the details, all the carved and complicated dark paneling, the thick rug under his feet, a huge fireplace, and then noticed his cousin had started talking to him about taking on work. Good.

"Whatever you want, I'll do it," Colm said.

"We've had another man on the job, but he claims he can't do it any longer."

"Claims, eh? You don't believe him?"

"Let's just say that our subject, Mr. Marrill, didn't make his life easy. At the moment, we have someone watching from the outside."

"Will I need to keep hidden from the subject?" He'd done a bit of that when tracking the sheep rustlers.

"Not at all. That's why the replacement I wanted is no good. He refuses to move into the apartment. You'll be a servant, but I'm fairly certain the man you'll be watching already knows you're more than that."

A servant? "Begging your pardon, I'll take a ditch-digging job, if you please. I'm a *culchie* at heart."

A pale face appeared at the corner of a bookshelf. The room was so complicated, Colm hadn't seen him standing and reading near the big, looming case of books. He strolled out, his well-cut gray suit and even-better-cut hair in perfect order, not a wrinkle or smudge on him. Mr. Sloan, the owner of this huge, fine house, fit its polished perfection.

Colm thought his cousin was dressed as beautifully as a gentleman could be, but compared to Mr. Sloan, Patrick was a peasant. Sloan was a good-looking bloke, as well, with features as pretty and neat as any of the statues about the place and dark hair without a strand out of place.

Sloan gave him a nod of greeting. "Indeed, you're from the country, though your accent isn't atrocious."

"Thank you," Colm said. "If that's a compliment."

"And you've apparently gained a bit of polish. From your training with the constabulary, I expect." The Englishman stopped and examined him. "Tell me, is there a reason other than some strange stubbornness that makes you say no to acting as a servant? You'd be doing more than fetching tea or brushing coats, you know."

This man might be trying to push him into impatience, but Colm wasn't going to let that happen. "I know how to 'keep a suspect under observation,' as they call it, but not the other, acting as a slavvy. London ways are beyond my ken. The only wealthy man in my part of the world was a stingy devil who hired in girls from the village and then chased them around the kitchen."

"Then you must be taught." The Englishman rang a bell to summon a servant.

"Ach, no." Colm held up a hand to halt this ridiculous idea. "You know what they say about a sow's ear, Mr. Sloan."

"You want the work, and I want to hire you." Patrick perched on the edge of his desk. He waved a hand to Sloan. "If you'll take on my cousin and turn him into that silk purse, I'll be grateful." He sounded far too amused.

"Of course." Sloan's answering smile was genuine and happy as he gazed at Patrick in another one of those private moments Colm could read far too easily.

Colm snorted in an imitation of a pig.

"That," Sloan said, still not looking at him, "will be the first thing to be eliminated."

Soon after, Patrick left for some sort of meeting. Colm's education began, and less than an hour after that, he understood he'd never fit the disguise of valet. Unfortunately, Mr. Sloan showed no interest in giving up.

At least Colm had come to appreciate Mr. Sloan, once the gentleman had stopped being an arse and thrown himself into the job of teacher. His patience didn't run thin even after Colm put down a tray on the library table too hard, knocking over a teapot and slopping lukewarm tea on his host.

Colm handed Sloan a napkin and sat down next to him. "Please, sir. This is a waste of time."

"No," Sloan said, dabbing at his waistcoat. "We shall make a success of this assignment."

"If that's the goal, it wouldn't hurt me to know why I'm watching this man so close."

"Ah, yes." Sloan summoned a servant. He told the man, a very quiet and efficient sort of servant, what he wanted, and the footman whisked away the sopping-wet tea tray and returned with a dispatch case of papers.

Sloan handed it to Colm. "Read these and do not hesitate to ask Patrick any questions. I won't be able to answer them, because I know no details of the case."

"You must know something."

"I help Patrick's business when I can, but I'm busy with charity work." He hesitated. "That sounds far too frivolous to a man like you, I expect?"

"Nil, then, *An tUasal* Sloan." Colm adopted the thickest of country accents. "Praythee, but frivolous isn't a word I'd use 'bout you, and not only because a man like me can't be sure what it means."

"Did you just insult me with that Irish?"

"No such thing. I called you sir. The rest of it, yes, perhaps it was a bit of a dig at you."

Sloan laughed. "You're a rogue, Kelly."

"And you're a snob, Sloan," he said, grinning. "No wonder we get along so grand."

Sloan left him to read through the folder, wondering at the ill luck of the Marrill family. Even after he read, he wasn't sure if he'd be set to watch a man who was a murderer or a murderer's next victim. Patrick had scribbled a note that he suspected the father was "barking up the wrong tree" to think Q.M. was a killer. In the notes from the interview with the father, there was mention of Quade Marrill's disposition being deviant.

Now what could that mean? He looked up the word and discovered it only meant nonstandard. Although with a name as odd as Quade, no wonder he turned up peculiar. As Colm read the papers a few times, a prickle of excitement about his assignment ran through him—the first he'd felt since the night he'd been beaten.

CHAPTER THREE

Quade dropped the papers he held as someone noisily climbed the stairs; the confident, quick steps seemed to announce an authority, and by the thump of boots, it would seem to be a bobby. Even as he rose to answer, Quade gave a quick prayer it wasn't more bad news. But the man who knocked at his door didn't wear a uniform. He opened it to find an ill-dressed man who seemed tall, but perhaps that had to do with the proportions of his body. He was about the same height as Quade's own five feet eleven inches and clutched a shapeless brown holdall.

Of course. His new minder had arrived. After Whitmore departed, Quade had thought perhaps his father had given up on the idea. Not that his father communicated with him about anything.

"You're my new valet, I expect?"

The man gave him a long look. "I'll be more than that, you know?"

Quade knew, of course, but he was sliding into a bad mood. He disliked insinuations, perhaps because he missed them far too often, and at any rate, he had to finish the index for a book going to press in less than a fortnight. He was tired of interruptions. He was tired of fear, but he opened the door wider. "You'd best come in. No need to stand in the corridor." He stepped aside to allow the man to enter the antechamber.

"Surely you know I've been sent along as a guard?" the new man said.

The man's open admission reminded Quade of all the nightmarish possibilities he'd been trying to forget—at least for a few hours so he could get some work done. He scowled at his new valet. "It's rather surprising you'd come right out and speak of your position."

"And why is that?" His accent was Irish.

"The last one acted as if he were nothing more than a very persistent, clinging servant."

"Huh." The man with the gray-green eyes, curling auburn hair, a slightly curled lip, and a direct, pugnacious stare hardly seemed servile. Quade wished he hadn't noticed the color of those eyes. He looked away.

The faux servant said, "You'd figure it out too soon. I expect I'm not good at the job of valet." He seemed thoroughly unworried about his incompetence.

Quade shrugged. He should be glad his current watchdog would drop the pretense. The proprietress of his rooms employed maids and other day labor, and Quade didn't need any sort of personal servant.

"I expected someone bigger," the Irishman said as if Quade had disappointed him.

"I expected someone more polite."

A brief grin flashed over his face, lighting the gray-green eyes. "Whoops. Like I said, not such a good servant." His soft brogue was rather intriguing.

"Come along." Quade led him into the only sitting area, which was cluttered with books and papers. He turned to face this new version of a human sticking plaster. "Your name?"

"Ah. Colm. Colm Kelly." He dropped his grip and seemed about to put out a hand, then apparently understood that wasn't appropriate. He still wore his hat, a gray bowler. Both hat and bag looked new. Kelly turned in a slow circle, examining the rooms, and Quade saw that he had the very last signs of yellow and green bruising around his eye and a bandage on his hand. A fighter? That might be good, as long as he didn't make a practice of losing.

"I'll show you to your room." Quade walked down the corridor, his latest watchdog on his heels. His back prickled with awareness of the man. When he'd taken these rooms, he'd had no need of an overnight servant and used the two smaller rooms set aside for servants as a storage area for the projects awaiting him. They entered the room, and Quade said, "It's not exactly the Albany, but the landlady is pleasant enough and—"

"And would you look at all these books!" Kelly exclaimed. "I've beheld more books in the last two days than I have my entire life before now. And they're all thick as doorstops." He hummed as he looked around himself.

Quade had grown used to the peace of living alone, and now he'd been landed with a babbler. He'd resented the last man, Whitmore, who'd insisted on pretending to be a valet. His hovering presence had been a true nuisance, so ridiculous remarks about books might be better than a man who stayed too close. Whitmore had messed around with his clothing and brought him cups of tea in the morning when he preferred coffee. And the man went through Quade's possessions. When Quade found him opening drawers in his office, Whitmore had only shrugged. "Just doing my job, sir."

Quade suspected that job was to find evidence that Quade was a killer. He'd written a letter to his father asking him the question point blank. *It is past time to have the matter out*, he'd written. I *am not a killer. Do you think I am? Is that why you hired this man?*

The next letter he'd received from his family had been impersonal and made no mention of death or murder.

He'd stared down at his father's uninformative note about crops—a non-answer to his last note pleading to share information—and understood it was as good as admitting his father thought him guilty. And now he'd sent this hulking Irishman, who already took too much interest in Quade's belongings.

"Are you the Kelly who spoke to my father? The man he hired?"

"No, sir." Kelly tilted his head to look at the titles of the books.

After his odd introduction, Kelly had become more closemouthed about himself, just like Whitmore. Had these guards been instructed to withhold information from Quade? He could use some damned help, but not from the men who worked for his father.

Quade shoved his hands into his pockets. Dismay was useless. He should be glad someone was actually taking the search for a possible killer seriously. Yet he couldn't help resenting the men set to watch him, and not only because it seemed a sign of his father's distrust. Why waste time and money on him when a possible real killer roamed free?

He had another reason for his confusion—although really, he should have been pleased with the news. Hemner had written back saying that Jack's last cigar contained only tobacco.

A lack of poison ought to have been a relief, but Quade didn't feel as reassured as he should have.

He still jotted lists of dates and questions into a notebook. Even picking up that notebook made him queasy, as if the inquires he considered might do more than reveal something evil, but actually conjure it.

Kelly reached toward a book at the top of two-food high stack, and Quade spoke up. "Even though this is where you'll sleep, you're going to have to leave those piles of books be."

Kelly straightened and examined him with friendly eyes, more gray than green, the corners creased with the hint of a smile. "Beg pardon?"

"I have these organized for my work. I will endeavor to finish the project as soon as possible, but in the meantime, you will have to avoid moving any of these stacks. It would take me some time to hunt down what I need if you move anything. I don't want anyone to disturb anything—those books or my routine. I have neither the time nor interest in reorganizing my life or work."

It would take him perhaps ten minutes to put the books back in order, and he knew he behaved in a petty manner. But if these men refused to help him discover the truth, then he'd be damned if he'd help them try to find evidence against him.

"You're a scholar, then?" Kelly asked. "You earn your bread thus?"

"Don't you know who and what I am?" Quade asked. "Aren't you aware of why you're here?"

Kelly examined him head to toe now as if making some sort of evaluation. And then, startlingly, he gave an actual response. "I am near sure I am to protect you from a murderer."

The direct answer astonished Quade, but he couldn't help adding, "That's a strange way to put it. You're not entirely certain?"

Kelly ducked his head and tugged his forelock.

"And you're not here to stop me murdering people?"

The man dropped the momentary servile air as he waved a hand, indicating the apartment, and Quade. "Now that I see what's what, I doubt you're the one."

The dismissal of his father's suspicions gave Quade a moment of warmth, until he recalled Kelly had no reason to think him innocent beyond his slender build.

Without thinking, he said, "I might be thin, but I am strong."

Kelly laughed. "You telling me I'm wrong? You are a killer? Very well, I'll shove furniture in front of my door at night and be sure to prepare all my own meals so you don't poison me."

Quade's face went hot. This valet was going to be even worse than the last, who at least hadn't joked about what was hardly a humorous situation.

Kelly picked his way around a pile of notebooks and put his bag on the floor next to the armoire. "Nice room," he said. "Very pleasant."

It was a dark, cramped space, badly in need of a whitewash, but Kelly was either a very good actor or he had low standards. Irish probably meant poor.

Kelly tossed his hat onto a stack of books. He ran his fingers through the rough half curls of his bright hair. It made him look as if he'd run through a windstorm, but when he checked himself in the small mirror over the bureau, he seemed satisfied. He turned back to Quade. "All right, then, tell me what sort of rules do you have for me?"

He didn't have a list, but it was easy enough to come up with one on the spot. "Allow me to do my work and stay out of my way. Don't entertain your lady friends here, or bring any sort of guest here, for that matter."

"I don't know anyone in this city anyway."

"If I should have guests, do not disturb us." He tried not to look away or blush and felt he succeeded in appearing cool. "Since you admit you're not good at playing the role of servant, don't attempt it unless I require it of you. If you must spy for some reason, be discreet. If you follow me when I leave the house—"

"I'll follow whenever you leave," the man corrected. He gave a wince of a smile, either a dislike of the chore or an attempt to show sympathy.

Quade ignored it; he had no need to be any intrusive devil's friend. "No matter where I go, you must stay outside if it's possible."

"Of course, if I can," Kelly said. "You have a kitchen I might use?"

"There is a small stove and pantry. I usually purchase my meals from my club or restaurants. Mrs. Eldred has occasionally made me a meal." Her food was overcooked and bland, but he often resorted to asking her for a meal when he'd forgotten to leave the house.

"No one in the home? I'm a fair cook, and I can help. You need one to put some meat on your bones."

"My meat is not your business." Good Christ, would everything that came out of his mouth today be mortifying?

Kelly's attempt to hide a smile at Quade's comment didn't improve Quade's mood. He turned and stalked out. Kelly trailed after him.

The Irishman made Quade self-conscious, and the one thing he treasured about his narrow existence was the way he could go days without encountering other people. He had never been good at casual conversation.

"What do you require?" Quade sat behind his desk and refused to look up.

"You'll give me warning at least ten minutes before you go out," Kelly said. He added, "If you please, sir."

"If I can," Quade grumbled. He unstoppered the ink and prepared to make more notes.

"That's fine, that's fine," Kelly said. His accent made the "th" into "d" but otherwise, he was easy to understand. "That's all I need."

He rocked back on his heels and beamed at Quade, who nodded in the manner one did to dismiss servants.

Kelly continued to study him and didn't move. "Do you mind if I read some of the books, then?"

"If you can read."

The Irishman made a snorting sound.

Quade felt his face grow hot. "No, I beg your pardon. I don't mean to insult you."

"You'd have to do more than that to manage the job, sir." Kelly's smile held no malice.

"Still, it was wrong of me to assume. I'd best go back to work now. Do whatever you wish as long as you don't disturb me or my possessions."

Thoroughly nettled, Quade waited for Kelly to go or to say more.

"Remember to give me notice before you leave here," the Irishman said as he walked to the door. No "please," no "sir." That lack of deference was all right, Quade decided. Better than pretending Kelly was here to oblige him.

Alone again, it took several minutes before he could settle himself back to his work.

After a time, he forgot the presence of his constant companion. He was swallowed by his task.

He made endless lists of names. Who could he approach for help on the matter of his family's losses? He'd already spoken to a barrister he respected who'd thought Quade's theory a bunch of rot.

"Bad things happen in this world," he'd told Quade. "We can only carry on the best we might."

"My father apparently agrees with me. He's hired some sort of guard for me."

"Vivid imaginations run in families. You'd do well to get back into your routine as soon as you can."

So Quade did accept work, but he also made his lists. His barrister friend was correct, though. It was a relief that after all the days of fidgeting and the inability to concentrate that followed Jack's death, he could allow himself to be dragged in by the words in the manuscript he studied. He worked on the glossary at the same time he did the index.

This "valet" hired by his father seemed more promising than the last as a source of any information. He'd allow Kelly to stay on, though he wondered how long it would take to grow accustomed to sharing his space with another man. A servant, he reminded himself. He'd grown up with servants, and they'd been a part of the house and scenery. This Kelly, though... Never mind the engaging smile and the interesting way his trousers fit. Quade had dispelled such nuisance awareness in the past and would do so again.

He managed to avoid his unwelcome minder, seeing him only in passing, until the next night, when his door slammed open and a shape filled his bedroom doorway. The manservant barged in, demanding, "What the hell is that?"

Quade had been lying awake and fretting about Jack and the others, and had picked up a law book, hoping to bore himself to sleep. Startled, he nearly dropped the heavy tome on his lap. “Knock, if you please.”

“If I think there’s a threat, I act without asking for permission from you, sir. I cannot wait to explain.”

Quade glanced at the open bedroom door. “What can you mean there’s a threat? We’re alone.” Alone and in his bedroom—and he wore only a thin vest and pair of drawers under his covers. He refused to pull the blankets up to his chin, however. This was his room.

The Irishman was pacing back and forth. “Then what is that noise? It’s in here too!” He cursed in Gaelic.

Quade wondered how that phrase could be spelled. “What bloody noise are you talking about?”

Colm Kelly moved to the edge of the bed, glaring over his shoulder. “I wasn’t imagining things at Patrick’s place. But here again is the thumping like a mad thing, far louder. That’s hissing.”

Quade listened for a moment before he at last understood what he meant. “The radiator.” He pointed at the large cast-iron object under the window.

Kelly walked over to it and squatted. He put his hand on the side and then drew it away with another, longer exclamation. “Well, damn me for a fool. It’s even hot.” He rose to his feet. “I’ve seen ’em, of course but we had nothing like that at home. I had no notion they were that loud. Pardon the interruption, Mr. Marrill.”

Quade choked down laughter. Even he understood that would be rude. “What did you think it was?”

The manservant rubbed the hand that had touched the iron and looked sheepish. “I’d heard one at my cousin’s house. I was sick, you see. I thought it was just the fever.” He began to chuckle. “A dragon or monster of some sort.”

This proved too much, and Quade found himself breaking into laughter that expanded almost out of his control. Kelly wore a grin, so he couldn’t have been too insulted by Quade’s enormous amusement at his expense.

“A dragon.” Quade gasped when he could speak again. His middle ached a bit from the unfamiliar exercise of laughing.

“Ah well. This time I wondered if someone were using peculiar tools to break through the walls. Nearly as absurd as a dragon, eh? I suspect I'll make even more absurd mistakes before I leave here," Kelly said without a trace of embarrassment or resentment.

He looked around again, his gaze landed on Quade, and he seemed to notice his state of undress at last. His eyes widened, and his mirth died away. He actually bowed, then backed out of the room, saying, "Good night, sir. I am sorry to have disturbed you. Um. Good night."

The absurd man acted like a commanding officer one minute and an almost reasonable facsimile of a servant the next. And really, a dragon?

Quade pushed the book from his lap onto the table by his bed. He lay down to listen to the hiss and gurgle of the radiator. What would it be like to live in a world that had no radiators? The Irishman must have come from a nearly primitive land of peat fires and open hearths, a place where monsters weren't impossible. That was intriguing. The house's steam pipes hissed a new language as Quade classified the various dragons he knew from literature.

Except when Kelly brought food, Quade didn't speak with the Irishman again for two full days and nights, yet he felt his presence in the house far more than he had any other servant. Their rooms were close together. That must be it.

He found himself listening for evidence of Kelly. At night, there might be a rustling of bedclothes, a soft mutter of Irish.

During the day, Quade could hear him since Kelly hummed and sang. The soft sound didn't bother him. The uncomfortable mindfulness of him did, awakening an itchy awareness of bodies and breathing and skin Quade really had no use for. And so soon after poor Jack's death, he scolded himself.

He was deep in thought of something other than Kelly, bent over a book about tort reform. The man in hobnail boots moved quietly. Quade became aware he wasn't alone only when Kelly stood just behind him and spoke his name. Quade started, dropping a blob of ink on the page.

"What do you want?" Quade snapped.

"As far as I can tell, you haven't eaten anything today, and the jam and bread in the larder are gone. I ate the last of the porridge. You need food."

Quade's mouth dropped open. The last time he'd been scolded by a servant, he'd been six years old and his nanny didn't want him to bring a snake into the house. He closed his mouth, swallowed, and decided he must nip this sort of thing in the bud. "Didn't I make it clear that my habits are not your concern?"

"I can't help noticing that you're not eating, sir."

"Unless I'm murdering someone, what I do is none of your business."

Kelly didn't look annoyed or abashed. He just nodded a few times as if considering an intriguing argument before he said, "Thing is, my employer wants me to eat on occasion, and everything is gone. I found not so much as a handful of groats. It's bare enough, a mouse would starve."

Quade rubbed his eyes. "You're saying that *you* are hungry."

"So are you."

Actually, he felt nauseated, unsure if either hunger or Kelly's presence caused the sensation.

"All right. Please fetch food." He reached into his pocket and pulled out some coins. "Will this do?"

"I can't leave you, sir."

"The last minder left all the time." He'd been glad of the man's absences. He'd even managed to walk over to his brother's widow's house, but she'd been "away from home." Mary Marrill had hidden away from him and didn't answer his notes.

"Oh, did he, then? But my instructions were to guard you at home or out."

"And I'm telling you that it's unnecessary." He exhaled with a grunt of frustration. If his guess was correct and Kelly's agents had been hired to spy on him and report back to his father, he didn't want his father to know what he was doing and saying. Not when he couldn't trust him.

Kelly was more honest than the last guard, but still, he was pretending to only be a guard and not on the lookout for evidence. Quade had grown impatient waiting for the truth to come out. "I'm tired of lies. You might as well tell me why you're really here."

"God's honest truth, I am here to watch over you." Kelly's face at rest wore an expression of puckishness, as if he were about to break into some sort of song with lewd lyrics or he'd just thought of a terrible pun. At the moment, he managed to school his features into a more solemn appearance. "I am sorry, sir. I expect my trailing along after you doesn't fit with what you want, but you're not the man who employs me."

Quade almost wanted to laugh at Kelly's attempt at a doleful expression. "Don't pretend you're not relieved by that," he said dryly.

Kelly cocked his head like a puzzled dog. "So you're saying I should be glad you're not my employer? Only because you wouldn't have hired me in the first place? As to that, you and I are in about the same position, neither one in charge. Although," he added thoughtfully, "you sound unhappy, and I am pleased as can be. This is the easiest work I've ever signed on for." He had a coat slung over his shoulder, and now he pulled it off and held it up. Quade recognized it as his own.

For a long moment, he considered what to do. Accept Kelly giving him orders? No. He might not be Kelly's employer, but he sure as hell wasn't at the man's beck and call.

Except he'd have to figure out an answer later, because a wave of hunger hit him about then. He figured out a way to make sure Kelly wouldn't win this round. Some of the names of people who might help him were members of his club. None were suspects—he was sadly short of those.

"We'll go to my club," he said. "They'll feed you sandwiches, I believe." He had no notion. He'd never employed a servant who required care. The last one had left the apartment for his meals.

Kelly fetched his own coat, a dark blue wool thing dotted with moth holes.

"A pity you're not my size. I have several coats I rarely wear. The shoulders would be too small," Quade said. Broad shoulders were not considered attractive, but he couldn't help thinking they suited Kelly.

"Aw, that's generous of you."

He suddenly understood that this man's smile was dangerous. He glared back. "It could be that I don't wish to be seen in the company of a beggar."

"Could be," Kelly agreed affably.

Out on the street, Kelly trailed after Quade at some distance.

Quade grew exasperated at the way Kelly hung behind several lengths. He felt guilty about his beggar remark. When he looked back, he saw that Kelly's head moved up and down and side to side as if he were trying to see everything at once. Quade stopped in the middle of the pavement and called to him. "If you want to play tourist in London, do it on your own time."

Kelly hesitated, then trotted up to him. "Indeed, yes, I should like that. So far I've seen the inside of my cousin's house and yours and not a deal more'n that. On my day off, I'll see some sights. Because the truth is, being a tourist isn't my job, which I'm doing at the moment."

"I beg your pardon?" Quade wondered what that jumble of words meant.

"I was looking around every which way because I have no notion where the threats to you might lie." He sounded as cheerful and earnest as ever. "I look in windows, along the streets into alleys. Checking them each, if you understand."

"Yes. I do." Quade considered apologizing, but instead asked, "Have you learned there might be an actual be a threat? To me?"

Kelly clapped him on the shoulder. "I don't know of anything, and to be sure, it's fine with me if you don't believe there's a threat or if you forget such a thing might exist. As long as I don't forget." He narrowed his eyes. "But see here, if aught should happen, you must listen to me and listen well. If something bad occurs, then you will take orders from me." He suddenly sounded like a different man—all traces of the jolly clown had vanished.

Quade stared into his eyes. This man honestly believed he was supposed to protect Quade. "All right," he answered. He suddenly grinned. "Like two nights ago when you heard a dragon?"

Kelly blushed but didn't take offense. He didn't seem stupid; he must have either a remarkably thick hide or no pride. "Exactly like that." He smiled and held up a hand in the simulation of a claw.

He was proving too entertaining to Quade, who sped up to get to his club quickly. "You can wait in the foyer," he told Colm. "Although the last man didn't bother to wait about the place."

"No, I expect he didn't," Colm said.

The porter opened the door as Quade strode toward it.

Quade returned from his visit to the cloakroom to find several members gawking and pointing. He ventured closer to see what drew their interest. The porter was attempting, unsuccessfully, to eject Kelly.

Quade called out, "He's with me."

Kelly pushed past the porter, then turned back to address him. "No need for me to go into the dining room with Mr. Marrill. Although might you bring me something from the kitchen?"

The porter eyed Kelly with disfavor. "We're not equipped for such a request."

"All right. I'll wait to eat, but I must remain inside," Kelly said genially. "I'll need to stay in sight of the dining room since I expect you got more than one door to this place?"

"You can't hang about inside or out," the porter snapped. "We don't allow beggars near the property."

Kelly raised his eyebrows but otherwise seemed unperturbed.

"I *said* he's with me." Quade might be willing to speak to Kelly rudely, but he found he didn't want anyone else to.

The manager approached and spoke quietly to the porter. The two of them finished their little chat, then presented a united front, gently guiding Quade and Kelly toward a dark corner in the passage outside the smoking room. "We can't have him lurking in the passages or bothering the members. I'm sure you understand, sir," the manager said. With some doubt, he said, "Perhaps he could be your guest and enter the public dining area—if he were properly attired. His tie…" He trailed off. "I suppose we might find a jacket that would fit him."

"Give me a moment," Quade said.

The two of them nodded and backed away to the entrance.

"Couldn't you simply dine at the pub on the corner?" Quade tried not to sound as if he were begging.

"Certainly, if you came too."

In fact, that sounded appealing, but Quade didn't want to give in yet. "No. This is my club. I'm comfortable. No one would attack me here. You go along to the publican."

If Kelly left, Quade would be free to ask an acquaintance, Billbrook, to look up information for him. Until he was certain that Kelly was not a spy against him, he had no desire to allow him to listen in on his conversations.

"It will be fine if you ate elsewhere," he said, more impatient now.

Kelly frowned at him for a long moment, his lips pressed into a flat line. "Look here, you write, don't you? Or put books together. Didn't you say something about…about making a part of a book? You make the lists of words in the back."

Had he said anything about what he did? "I edit and sometimes I compose glossaries and indices," Quade said patiently. "An index is the list at the back of a book. But I don't recall telling you anything about what I do."

"Maybe I noticed because of what I see around the apartment. The books and papers and whatnot."

"Are you looking at the manuscripts?"

"Don't fear, sir," he said earnestly. "I put everything back in the proper piles."

At least he admitted he was poking about Quade's possessions. Perhaps he'd reveal if he'd discovered anything incriminating. But that was an argument for later. At the moment, he had to wrest back control of the current situation. "What does any of this have to do with you popping off to the pub for an hour? Just go along."

Kelly gave him a nod as if in agreement. "As I was saying about you and your work. I imagine you have a way of doing your job? Your lists. What if some oaf, someone like me, say, told you not to bother with doing the letters D"—he hesitated and looked up, clearly silently chanting the alphabet— "the letters D through G. You'd say the job wasn't done properly, yes?"

"But a list isn't—"

"You wouldn't stop doing the job the way you know to be best just because someone who didn't know the work gave you permission, would you?"

"Oh, for pity's sake," Quade muttered. "Come along, we'll go to the pub."

"It's not necessary, sir," the club manager said. "We've found a suitable jacket for your, er, guest." He glanced over his shoulder at the entrance to the dining room, and Quade understood that poor Peller had been egged on by some other members who stood watching the drama with considerable interest.

"Is Billbrook here today?"

"No, sir, he's in Europe"

"That's right," Kelly said. "T'was in his condolence card. One of the great many piled in the parlor."

"You read my correspondence?" For a moment, Quade's outrage at Kelly overshadowed his discomfort created by the gaping club members.

"Yes, sir." Kelly's shrug might have been apologetic. "I decided since I got not much else to do, I'd figure out what was going on that has people in a pother."

Quade stared.

"And could be I'd notice a threat that you might miss. Sometimes when a person is smack in the middle of a situation, he might not see possible menaces."

Was the man mocking him? But Kelly only gave him a beatific smile, then looked around the club dining room with eager interest.

A creeping hope came to Quade. Perhaps he might find an ally in this peculiar valet after all.

"Marrill? Come on, man!" Westchester, near the dining room, beamed and beckoned to Quade. "Bring in this 'gentleman' and introduce him. Irish, is he?" He turned to an older man. "Grace, you were right about the fuss. Can't have that. We don't generally allow such…unusual guests, but we'll make an exception in this case."

Quade cursed under his breath.

"I am sorry, sir," said Kelly. For the first time, one of his apologies sounded real. "I truly have no wish to cause trouble."

"Ah, they would have found some other soul to torture. It must be dull here if they're going to goad us for entertainment."

"And do I understand you to mean that this is where you come for peace and quiet?" Kelly had lost that brief moment of true contrition and had returned to his usual lighthearted self.

"I come for the food," Quade said. He was going to add *and for the company*, but it was more accurate to say he'd simply come to be around other living creatures. He didn't have close friends here, not even Billbrook. He'd grown uninterested in the condolences that were thinly disguised attempts to get the salacious facts about the Marrill family. And now all the interest directed at Kelly seemed ominous. The gentlemen of the club would get up to larks, as the manager liked to put it.

He stopped and turned to the man who acted as his sticking plaster. "You seem fairly even tempered, Kelly. Don't let these buffoons get to you, eh?"

Kelly regarded him with raised eyebrows. "I'm not easily scundered, sir, and I shan't embarrass you."

"What does scundered mean?"

"Mortified."

"Good, good." He waved a hand impatiently. "For myself, I don't care about that. I dislike attention, but I will survive."

He stood in the door and looked about the dining room, finally spotting his sister-in-law's brother, Alfred Hoyt, sitting at a table now joined by that older gentleman. When he nodded at him, Hoyt glared in return, then very deliberately turned his back on Quade. "What the devil?" He glanced at his keeper. "I need to go speak to someone I know."

Kelly gave a brisk nod as if granting permission, but Quade was too baffled by Mary's brother's response to grow offended by Kelly's effrontery.

CHAPTER FOUR

Colm followed his odd charge, still unsure what he thought of the man. All contemplation of Marrill's behavior vanished as they entered the huge, paneled dining room, and Colm paused for a moment to examine the space. Such a vast, open room. He'd expected rows of bare wooden tables like the club he knew in Ireland, but this place contained round little tables, set close together, and each with snowy linen and polished silverware. Not as staggering as Mr. Sloan's place, but a near second.

Mr. Marrill headed toward a round-faced man sitting at a table far away.

"Hoyt," Marrill said as they approached. "I am glad you're here. Perhaps you know and might tell me why your sister isn't home to me? And I've had no replies to my letters."

"You need to ask?" The man's face went red, reminding Colm of a sunset. The name was familiar, and he recalled the file about the Marrill family.

"Is that Mrs. Mary Marrill's brother?" he whispered to Marrill. Poor lady to be stuck with such a name. Perhaps Jack should have changed his name to hers.

Marrill flicked a look of annoyance at him before turning his attention back to Hoyt. "I shouldn't have taken such an offensive tone just now. I'm merely worried about my sister-in-law."

Hoyt rose to his feet and threw his napkin down on the table. "You have gall, I'll grant you that," he said and gave a bow to the older man at the table. "Thank you for the invitation, but I'm afraid I cannot remain."

Marrill couldn't have looked more startled than if he'd been attacked by a pack of dogs that had wandered into this dining room. "What on earth was that about?" he muttered. But just then, the man in charge, the manager, stepped between Marrill and the table, one hand outstretched in silent invitation to move along. Colm recognized it from all the occasions when he'd had to escort rambunctious drunkards from inns.

"The far corner, if you please," he told the manager and Marrill. "Against the wall—under the picture of the man in robes."

He did another slow circle, turning to see everything and everyone. The lunching gents all stared back as they forked up their food. Colm hurried after Marrill.

The attention didn't go away even as he took a seat that looked out over the room. It wouldn't be easy to move quickly in the coat he'd been given—it was tight at the shoulders and loose across the middle. He shifted his arms in a small circle.

"Not a good fit, eh?" said a gentleman with a clipped, tiny mustache who sat next to their table.

"I expect the previous owner might have been an egg," Colm said. Should he have kept his mouth shut or muttered a polite *yes, sir*?

But he wasn't playing the part of servant at the moment, was he? More like a performing ape.

Colm was well aware that the English considered the Irish an inferior species. It drove his brothers and cousins mad with rage. He'd never much bothered to worry about what a bunch of strangers he'd never met thought of him. But here he was, meeting them and on their patch of land, not his.

They had the advantage of money, education, wealth, and knowledge of which spoon and glass to use when. He had the advantage of ten years dealing with a rough crowd and a firm philosophy about avoiding ridiculous pride. Marrill, seated across from him, also watched him warily.

Kelly said, "I'm sorry Mr. Hoyt was unfriendly. Has he been so before?"

"He's not a friend. But I hadn't thought him an enemy."

"Why do you suppose he's angry?"

Marrill scrubbed at his eyes with the palms of his hands. "I suspect that he feels I'm somehow to blame for my brother's death. I can't think what else would have sent him into such a fit." He slumped back in his seat. "Perhaps coming here is a mistake."

"Should we leave?"

Marrill shook his head. "No, no. Just don't you make anything worse."

"What do you mean?" Colm asked in a low voice.

Marrill whispered, "If anyone provokes you, allow me or the manager to deal with the matter. I don't want to have to fetch you from a police station."

Despite his carefully cultivated lack of vanity, Colm felt a surge of annoyance. The other men here might have the idiot notion that he was a drunken monkey, but he'd thought better of Marrill. He said, "I'm not a brawler."

Marrill's eyes narrowed. "When you came to my door, you presented the very picture of a fighter. Do you think I'll believe your black eye and other injuries came from a fall?"

Colm relaxed. "Oh, indeed, I can see why you jumped to that conclusion. But I assure you, I've coaxed many a drunken man out of a fury and broken up fights before they've gotten serious."

"Indeed? How did you manage all that?"

"I was a constable, sir. Back home." Colm couldn't hold back a sigh. His old life had been such an easy one. Dull on occasion, but he missed even the boring evenings of watching the rain alone.

"Why did you leave the position?"

A waiter placed a glass of whisky in front of Colm.

"That's for our honored guest, from me!" A man at the far end of the room waved a hand and bellowed loud enough to heard over conversation and clinks of silver against china. "Drink up!"

"Thank you, sir!" Colm raised the glass and touched it to his lips but returned it to the table without swallowing a drop. Pity, because this meal would go down easier with something to blunt the coming storm of mockery. "Would you care for it?" he whispered to Marrill.

Marrill said, "It's for you."

"Not while I'm at work."

"It's a gift for you."

Could the man be so naïve? And Marrill, a person who'd read and taken notes on the most inhuman events documented in law. In a low voice, Colm said, "Aw, come now, sir, you and I both know alcohol for the likes of me is meant as an insult."

Marrill looked startled. He puffed out his breath and glanced at the man who'd ordered the drink. "By Jove, I expect you're right."

"You'd be doing me a favor if you'd take care of it."

When no one else was watching, Marrill picked up the glass and gulped down the contents. He let out a gasp. "That's better," he said. "I was going to order a drink but would much rather get Piney to pay for it."

A man in a starched shirtfront stopped next to them. Colm waited for him to pull out a chair and sit, but he only stood and watched them.

"What do you want to eat?" Marrill asked Colm.

Oh, the overdressed fellow was a waiter, of course. "Would you mind ordering for me?" Colm said.

"I forgot you might want a menu," Marrill said.

"Does our new friend know how to read?" a pudgy bloke one table over asked, then let out a bray of laughter.

With an effort, Colm joined in the laughter, because that was what one did in situations like this. Marrill did not so much as smile. He glowered at the neighboring table and was about to speak until Colm touched his arm. "Mr. Marrill, remember what you said about the manager. Don't engage in any battles."

"And you might remind me that I said much the same thing when we met." Marrill shifted his glare at him and then moved his chair in order to look around the room. In a loud, carrying voice, he called out, "I simply believe that it's neither right nor proper to disparage guests to our club."

"Hear, hear! We've insulted our honored guest! Do bring him another glass of whisky," a thin man called out, the older one at the back that had been sitting with Hoyt.

The waiter vanished at once and reappeared with another drink on a silver platter. He placed it in front of Colm. The waiter and the three gentlemen seated near them watched Marrill reach over, grab the glass, and empty it in one swift swallow.

"Food, if you please. We have empty stomachs," Colm reminded Marrill. "Order anything at all, sir. But order it quick."

Thank goodness, the man had sense enough to ask for a raft of food, soup, fish, meat, cheese.

The waiter vanished again, moving as quickly and silently as James O'Malley, a bounder and thief, back home.

"That order is more than a man can eat in a day," Colm said.

"Do not look so astounded, if you please. It's regular fare here," Marrill said.

Colm laid a hand on his arm and squeezed lightly. "Remember you said you didn't care if I acted like a…a rustic? I imagine that's what I've done. Ha, that's two rules you gave me for this meal, and both are good ones. One is don't mind what the others here in your club say, and the second is don't mind what I say."

Marrill leaned back in his chair and shut his eyes. "You're right. I must say, Mr. Colm."

"Kelly," Colm reminded him. "Colm is my given name."

"I must say, Colm Kelly, you're a levelheaded chap."

"Thank you, sir." He felt a warmth that was outsized for the remark. He'd read enough of Quade's work and acid notes to authors to know that he'd been given a huge compliment.

The soup was put in front of them. It was a thin sort of broth, hardly enough to keep a man fed. No wonder Marrill was all skin and bones. Colm watched him pick up a spoon. It would have been easier to pick up the bowl and drink it straight off, but he imitated his host. He did well enough that no scornful remarks came from the riffraff around them.

"Well done," one of their neighbors said as the waiter took away the bowls and replaced them with a fish covered in green sauce. "Allow me to congratulate you, Mr. Irishman, with another drink."

"For what are you congratulating him?" Marrill leaned toward that neighbor, going so low forward, the lapel of his jacket briefly grazed the sauce. His hands gripped the edge of the table tightly enough that his knuckles went white.

Colm nudged him. "Remember."

Marrill straightened, picked up his fork, and glared around.

"I shall write to my sister about all the types of food we've ordered," Colm said quietly, hoping to distract his host. "More dishes in one meal than we had on all of Christmas day."

The waiter delivered another drink. Colm moved it away from Marrill's hand.

"Aren't you thirsty?" the man with the skinny mustache called over to Colm. "I understood your sort has a powerful thirst."

"Not at all sir," he said cheerfully. "Would you care to have a taste of it?"

"Thank you, no, I have my own," said the neighbor. "How long are you visiting London? And where are you staying? Somewhere near the harbor, I imagine?"

Even Colm, with his small knowledge of the world, knew that was every city's traditional location for whores and cheap alcohol. But he wasn't about to announce the truth about his job with Mr. Marrill. He smiled broadly. "I've been staying with my friend Mr. Sloan. Do you know the gentleman? He lives over near that Hyde Park."

"Mr. Sloan? Mr. Edmund Sloan?" the neighbor said.

"Yes, that's him. Ned is good friend." He hoped he'd correctly recalled what his cousin Patrick Kelly had called Sloan.

"I should venture to say he's quite well-known," another man said uncertainly. "And you're saying he's a friend? Of yours?"

"Yes, indeed," Colm said. This might prove the ticket to get out of their ridiculous attempts at shaming. He really didn't want to cope with any more glasses of liquor—or, more to the point, he didn't want his charge to drink any more.

The three men at the table fell into quieter conversation, something about cricket, which Colm had no use for. Marrill reached across Colm, grabbed the whisky, and swallowed it down. Again.

They managed to get through the fish and then some sort of bird course, all delicious food, though rather too oddly spiced in some ways.

He pushed around some greenish vegetable he didn't recognize as he kept an ear and eye open for more trouble, but he must have provided no entertainment, because the tables' attention had turned from him, or so he believed.

Just as he was tucking into the best beef rib he'd even tasted, someone put another glass in front of him.

Marrill rose unsteadily to his feet. "You are all disgusting. You call yourselves gentlemen and you treat a guest to your club like this?"

"We're standing him drinks," another man called back. "What can be wrong with that?"

"You make me sick," Marrill snapped. "A decent man, trying to do his job and you—"

"What sort of job is that? Is he your molly-poppet? Your mary-ann?" the thin mustache man asked.

With a deep roar, Marrill went after the man. Colm managed to grab him in a good hold before Marrill flung the whisky he held in the man's face. The other gentleman had gotten to his feet, ready to fight.

"Alcohol," Colm said with disgust. He shoved Marrill behind him and grabbed the mustached gent's hand as he struck out and twisted it around the way the sergeant in the barracks taught the recruits.

Colm pushed the man back to his seat speaking soothing phrases like, "Just a big misunderstanding" and "Beg pardon, sir, that must hurt, but understand—not going to allow you to punch me," and "Thank you for the drink. It was delicious," and when the fool got up again and lunged at Marrill again, Colm wrestled him back to his table and into his seat with a "Beg pardon, your foot must have slipped."

The mustached man sprawled in a chair and gulped at Colm like a carp. Had he hit him too hard in the belly with an elbow? The fight was over at last.

The gentlemen who'd risen to watch the brawl strolled back to their chairs as if just returning from an outside visit to the privy—although, of course, a place like this would be like Marrill's house and have plumbing. All of London seemed to have water closets. But perhaps the veneer of civilization was thin, because no one seemed as shocked by a fight breaking out as Colm would have expected.

Marrill still stood, staring around himself as if he had no idea how he'd landed in such a place. The manager approached. "I'm afraid I have to ask you gentlemen to leave."

"Sure," Colm said and wrapped his left hand around Marrill's arm. He kept his right free in case he should need it for some latecomers. "Let's take our leave, Mr. Marrill." He paused and turned to the manager. "And you'll wrap up the rest of the meal?"

The manager looked offended. "That is not our usual practice sir."

"Today, you will do this, if you please." Colm took a step toward him. The manager squeaked and hurried off.

As a waiter returned with a parcel, another approached with a drink. "It's our best brandy," he said, stopping a good distance off, smart lad. "A member says you deserve it and don't let Mr. Marrill take this one."

"What fellow sent this?"

The waiter nodded to the older gentleman in the corner, the one who'd sat with Hoyt, and who raised a glass to them. Everyone watched. Hoping this would buy Mr. Marrill some sort of peace, Colm lifted the glass and drank a mouthful of the hottest, smoothest alcohol it had ever been his pleasure to consume. Marrill glared at the glass and then at the man who'd sent it over.

With a lurch, he made his way to the corner and—damnation. Colm put down the glass and took off, but not quickly enough.

The older gentleman had said something that outraged Marrill, and he took a swing at the seated man and actually connected with his face. They both gave yells of surprise. The attack ended with that single blow.

The older gentleman shook off the waiters' hands and assured them all he was fine, even as he stanched a trickle of blood. Other men in the room leaned close and muttered to each other. This wasn't good for Mr. Marrill's reputation. Colm should have done more to stop it. A sour thought.

"He has a temper like his brothers, or so I've heard," the man said, holding a napkin to his nose. He looked at Marrill with bright eyes and some sort of interest that Colm had to wonder at. Had he heard the comment about the molly-poppet, and was he wondering about their relationship?

"I—I am appalled. I shouldn't have done that." Marrill rubbed at a scrape on his knuckles that oozed blood His eyes, which had grown hazy with drink, seemed to sharpen when he shifted his gaze to the man—as if he'd suddenly understood what he'd done. "I beg pardon, have we even met?" The poor fellow sounded appalled that he'd struck a stranger.

"No, no. I'm John Grace." The man lowered the napkin and looked at the smear of blood on it. It seemed to amuse him.

Marrill must have noticed the blood too, because he made another apology.

"No need to worry over a little tap like that. I've suffered far worse in my day. Far worse." Grace waved a hand. "My own club is closed for cleaning and renovation, and some of us were offered a chance to use other facilities in the meantime. I must say this club is a deal more exciting than my own stodgy place."

Grace was older than nearly everyone in the room, almost gaunt, and he had lines at his eyes that spoke of pain, perhaps some illness. He didn't look nearly as well-dressed as the other gents, and he didn't sound like them either. Though Colm didn't recognize the accent, he could tell Grace wasn't from London or America.

By the time they'd gotten out of the dining room, Marrill had apologized to Colm and, of course, Grace—but refused to speak to anyone else. Colm made apologies to anyone who looked in their direction. He fully understood how self-importance worked and the strength it held in most men's hearts. He had no particular interest in maintaining such a delicate, worthless flower in his own.

All his groveling made no difference. The porter and manager handed them their coats and sadly informed Mr. Marrill that he had been banned from the club, at least until the next election, when it would be decided whether or not he would be allowed to return.

One of the friendlier club members approached Colm in the corridor as he waited for Marrill, who continued to argue his case with a group of members and the manager. The member, who wore a plaid waistcoat and his hair slicked back from his temples, looked like a friendly version of Wagner the Wehr Wolf, an old Penny Dreadful villain. The gentleman tottered a little closer, and the scent of whisky washed over Colm as he whispered, "Marrill's temper shows the rumors could be true."

"Rumors?"

Whisky-breath ignored him and bent close to Colm again. "You surely have heard the stories? It's hinted that Mr. Marrill has done away with his relations in a truly infamous and treacherous manner."

Such fancy language—apparently Colm wasn't the only one who read Penny Dreadfuls. He asked, "What else have you heard?"

"Insanity. He don't take money from his father. He cut himself off from most of society. Why is he entirely secre-secrat…?" He hiccupped and managed to finish at last. "Secretive?"

Colm was torn. On the one hand, he wanted as much information as he could get. On the other, the rumors were nonsense. Seemed best to go with his instinct to defend Quade Marrill.

"Mr. Marrill won't take money from his father, and he is uninterested in gain. You're speaking of greed? Isn't in that picture you paint, is it?" Colm spoke loudly enough for the other gents to hear. He hoped they didn't notice that his simple explanation didn't mention the possibility of a grudge.

Colm had already begun his inquiry, partly out of boredom but mostly because the situation deserved some looking into, even if it wasn't his job. In his part of the world, the policeman and the detective were the same man. He'd protect the peace even while he'd look into what disturbed it.

He'd been poking around in Marrill's bills, all tidy and paid. The man had no extravagances.

The clubman scratched his head. "You could have something there," he said. "At any rate, never mind Marrill. I came over to say that if you have time and inclination, we have a boxing concern, and I would stand for you any day. If you are in need of making a few extra quid, contact me." He pulled out a card and thrust it into Colm's hand.

"Thank you." Colm shoved the note into his waistcoat pocket and wondered if it would ever come to that. He had no desire to use his fists to earn his living, but perhaps he wouldn't be given a choice should this assignment for his cousin become a disaster. Correction, should it become a *worse* disaster.

Mr. Marrill had slipped out of the group, and Colm watched him. His careful footsteps spoke of a man pretending to be sober. The way he seemed ready to stare down anyone glancing in his direction more than amused Colm and touched him in a way other drunkards' behavior didn't.

The manager appeared and handed Colm several paper-wrapped packages.

Colm handed Marrill the warm packages that contained their dinner. "Carry this, please, sir," he ordered. "I need my hands free."

Marrill wrinkled his nose. He handed the brown-wrapped objects back to the manager as if they all played a game of Pass the Parcel.

"I think it best if these were delivered to my rooms." He sounded perfectly reasonable, not a word slurred. He even dug a few coins from his waistcoat and handed them over. "And I apologize for any inconvenience to you and your staff."

One of the gentlemen in the corridor spoke up, a large man with small eyes that darted in Colm's direction. "You really did step over the line with today's activity. We are a tolerant bunch, naturally, but—"

"Do be quiet before you insult my guest even more than you already have," Marrill said, still sounding reasonable. But when Marrill walked toward the door, he lurched a bit. The whisky had hit.

The pleasant gentleman who'd been smashed in the nose by Marrill stood near them. "I hope Mr. Marrill will be all right," Mr. Grace said to Colm. "I hear he has had a rough patch of late." He shook his head mournfully, but his eyes danced with humor as if he thought the whole thing was a lark. And perhaps it was.

Colm hoped he wouldn't have to haul his charge onto his back to carry him home.

When they emerged into a soft mizzle of rain, it seemed to wake Marrill. He stopped under a streetlamp and wiped at his face with a hand. "Didn't bring an umbrella, did we?"

"It's not so terrible at the moment." Colm had liked the fog that came to his little village now and again, but this seemed dirtier. "We'll go back to your rooms, light a good fire, and warm up immediately. What did that gentleman, Mr. Grace, say to you that made you take a swing at him?"

***

Quade considered the question Kelly had asked. What *had* that stranger said? Quade's head swam. It had been something about the way young gentlemen handled fights. *"I wondered if you'd be like the others and not play fair."* Had it been a jest? Yes, of course. Was he speaking of the other men at lunch who'd sent the whisky? Was that what he'd meant? The heat of Quade's anger seemed entirely unnecessary now. Oh, but the unfairness that had been directed at

Kelly… They judged when they were hardly worthy—and he was angry because before he'd talked to Kelly, he'd judged too.

He should have asked the scarecrow of an old man why Hoyt was so angry instead of growing ridiculously upset himself.

Quade trudged ahead of his watchdog for a few steps before whirling around to confront the Irishman. Moving quickly proved a mistake, for his head tried to disengage from his neck and float off. "Why aren't you more upset? The way they treated you. The things they said. I think I feel sick with rage."

"More like you're sick with liquor."

Quade straightened his back, or attempted to, and looked over at Kelly, who gave a friendly wave to him.

"That might be true. I don't drink often." He stumbled over a tree root pushing up the pavement. Kelly caught him.

"You are very strong," Quade said. A moment passed. Did that comment hold the note of admiration he felt for strong men? He asked, almost fearful, "Was that an inappropriate remark?"

"No, you don't weigh enough."

"That answers the first part of my comment, about your strength, that is to say…" He temporarily lost track of the conversation as Kelly gently gave him a push at the small of the back to keep walking. "That's the first part of what I said, but not the second. Is it inappropriate to remark on your strength?"

Kelly chuckled. "If you're wondering about good manners, you're asking the wrong man. But see here. My cousin gave me a book of what the proper gent should and shouldn't do or write in business or social situations, and I can lend it to you." He was probably only trying to be funny, but Quade was caught by the idea of such a strange book. He loved peculiar volumes of nonfiction.

"Who is the author?"

"No notion. I didn't read much at all, just the section about the duties of a coroner—how to write the proper letter to announce the cause of death as murder." He stopped and suddenly grew serious. "I beg your pardon about that, Mr. Marrill. I shouldn't jest about such a thing with a man who's had to deal with it in his own life."

Quade waved a hand, inviting more. At last someone spoke to him honestly. "You mean about death? Or even murder? But yes! Yes! One prefers to have it right out in the open, what's been said, I mean. Better than pretending."

Kelly's face was creased in either worry or puzzlement, so Quade clarified, "I'd rather hear that sort of remark than cope with the whispers and stares."

"Ah, but even a man like myself can see it's rude to speak of such things lightly when the loss of so many of your kin must weigh on you." He dropped back a few steps and began peering around the place again.

It would never have occurred to Quade that Kelly meant sorrow over the deaths in his family and not the suspicious muttering that he was a murderer.

He honestly thought Quade needed protection. He gave sincere condolences on his loss of kin. Bereavement. Perhaps he even believed Quade innocent. That was enough to push Quade over the edge.

Quade blurted, "It is all such a stupid waste, and I do miss my brothers." His nose and eyes prickled. No, he mustn't. Tears accomplished nothing.

He stopped and pinched the bridge of his nose. "Such a stupid waste," he muttered. "They're gone, gone. Phillip, Jack, Mark, Joseph. Those're my brothers, did you know? And silly Cyril, my cousin, and even my bloody uncle, lost and gone. Joseph drowned years back and I have nothing…nothing to remember. But the rest went not long ago. I thought I heard Cyril's stupid laugh at the club. He brayed like a donkey."

Suddenly, someone in an ill-fitting suit was pulling on him and grabbing at him for some reason. In his astonishment, he forgot to struggle—and then he understood. This was an embrace of some sort, even though he wasn't falling. Kelly drew him into his strong arms, let a heartbeat pass, and another, then, quick as that, released him.

Quade stumbled, then began to walk, and Kelly fell in behind again as if nothing had happened. But something had shifted for Quade, an understanding that had very little to do with Colm Kelly and everything to do with the Irishman's action. That awkward and peculiar hug was the first Quade had received as a gesture of sympathy. Quade had given his mother one, but she'd stood straight and perfectly still as he'd wrapped his arms around her—just as he'd just stood and waited a moment ago.

The embrace from a stranger—one that smelled of camphor and, oddly, the ocean—had been more powerful than he would have guessed. It seemed to open and slightly ease a tight bitterness in his chest.

Could his mother have also felt the same flow of warmth from his embrace and had her spirit been too pulled in tight to show a response? A tear trickled down his cheek. He wiped it away furtively.

Their footsteps seemed muffled by the thickening fog. Something pattered—water dripping from a tree, not footsteps. They seemed alone in the busy street.

Behind him, Kelly cleared his throat and said, "Here now, Mr. Marrill. You see how absurd it is that you asked me of all people how to behave correctly? I'm sure that grabbing another man and hauling him close for a hug isn't the proper way to go on."

Quade remained too overcome to speak. His voice might crack. He coughed and tried, "Yes, it isn't the way of gentlemen. Of course, drinking too much and engaging in fisticuffs in one's club is hardly what one would call genteel."

"Next time, we'll find a pub where that'll be more standard behavior. A city this size must have such establishments, eh? Down by the docks is where I'd look, and so your club friends advised me."

A wheezing sound escaped Quade. A laugh. "I have just this moment made a promise to myself that I shan't drink more than a single whisky in an evening," he announced.

"Bah," Kelly said. "That is just the sort of promise that gets broken at once."

"No," Quade said. "I never go back on that sort of resolution."

"You are stronger than most men."

"I'd say I am more stubborn, and more easily made drunk," Quade said. "I wish I'd been drunk enough to ask Hoyt why he suddenly hates me," he added in a mournful tone. "His sister must as well. Poor Mary."

"What did Mrs. Marrill say to you after your brother's death?"

"Nothing. I saw her only briefly and she was speaking to no one. She wept continuously."

They reached Quade's house, and he reached into his jacket pocket and withdrew his keys. Kelly pushed in front of him and took the latchkey from his hand. "I go first."

Not a single *if you please* or *excuse me, sir*. Obviously, Mr. Kelly should read that guide to etiquette he'd mentioned; then again, the keys and lock did seem to swim and sway.

Quade leaned against the low wrought iron rail and watched Kelly deftly open the door and make a quick examination before beckoning him in.

Quade pushed past him. "You are absurd. Did you expect to find a monster? A burglar? A murderer? I've been waiting. No one has come after me so far. I bloody well wish they would, do you know? I want this done with."

Kelly smiled at him. The bloody Irishman was apparently entertained by the situation.

Quade glared at Kelly, then stumbled a bit as they walked into the sitting room. "I fail to see what is so amusing. I was not put on this earth to be an organ grinder's monkey or a clown for your amusement."

"No, no. O' course not."

"And don't talk to me as if I am a child."

The smile didn't diminish in strength. "Weren't you satisfied with the fight in your club, sir? Is that why you're trying to get a rise from me? You want more—what was it that man called it—more of an argle bargle?"

Yes. That precisely described what he wanted. To flail at Kelly, smash into him and pummel him and shove him down and land on top of him and rip into his clothing until… Desire sent him reeling; it could have been a punch. Another few heartbeats, and, despite the drink, he'd gone totally erect. His breath came fast and ragged. Kelly watched, his dark brows raised. His gaze seemed to be caught by Quade's midsection.

"You've had too much to drink," he said, sounding uncertain.

"Yes, that's what I thought. Not enough, apparently," Quade muttered. "I want, I want…" He trailed off, because what he wanted had to be clear to a blind man.

"Ah. Now. You can get in deep trouble with some desires, Mr. Marrill. Believe me, I know." Kelly seemed sad suddenly, the amused smile completely wiped from his face.

What did that mean? Before the tipsy, outspoken part of Quade's brain could demand what he meant, Kelly had returned to the front door, closed and locked it, then he was suddenly back at Quade's side. Time must have passed. Quade wondered why the seconds had gotten slippery. Whisky, he reminded himself. And that blasted door to hunger had swung wide. Because of the large hand holding on to his arm, warm strong fingers.

Let go, he wanted to yell. *Go away. Come here. Take off your clothes. Let my skin and yours touch every possible inch…*and need, and all those muscles; that hair would be coarse, but not as rough as the hard, thrusting heat and—

"Here now, don't go even more wobbly. Shall I help you to your room?"

Quade rubbed his eyes.

Hadn't Kelly said he knew about that sort of trouble? He understood. That must mean he had seen what Quade wanted from him.

Quade, who had kept a firm grip on all such nonsense—and that was not a grip on his organ—felt his will sliding. He'd thought of a door. No. His self-control was something stronger. It could be seen as a huge iron gate blocking desires, and now it wasn't merely cracking open. It was dissolving into mist. This wasn't fair.

"You know what I want. You said you know." He panted a little at his own audacity and because the whisky and desire made him forget how to breathe properly.

"Yes." Kelly pointed to the yellowing skin near his own eye. What did that mean?

That's right, he'd engaged in battle before he'd come into Quade's life, in that murky past before Colm Kelly had come clomping into Quade's rooms and disturbed an already troubled existence.

"Someone attacked you because…because…" He wasn't sure he knew how to ask. "It wasn't because you were a constable. Tell me what happened," Quade ordered.

Colm shook his head in answer.

"Oh. I suppose you don't have to tell me." Quade heaved a sigh, then made his way past a pile of books to his favorite chair. He attempted to twist in the large chair so he could rest his legs over the arm, but the room spun the moment his feet left the floor. He gave up and slumped nearly flat, heels firmly on the rug. "It's not fighting. That is, I don't really want to get into a fistfight. It's just… It's just one is so full." He thumped his hand down flat on the top of his head. "No, not one. *Me.* My head. I'm up to here with anger. From my toes to here. Oh, and self-pity. Lord knows we don't want to forget that particular unappetizing feature of my current condition." He wanted to hold his tongue but didn't seem able. "One doesn't understand why now? Why? A lack of control hasn't been among my failings before now. All this, and an inability to hold my drink. Though that is hardly news." He closed his eyes. "Good. The storm is passing. This episode of the megrims must be done by now. I can ignore the—the whispers of whatever the hell it is that makes me want to know more about you. Kelly. You. Yes, and I don't require help to my room. I'm fine."

Kelly spoke up. "I got battered after stating my interest in…in unnatural behavior."

Quade opened his eyes, startled. "Pardon?"

"You asked what happened. The eye." He pointed at it again. "Why I know about…deep trouble." He shrugged after the last word.

Quade suddenly recalled that Kelly was, and yet was not, a servant. He should respect the distance he'd just tried to cross. Intimacy was off-limits for servants. One must not cross lines to misuse one's power.

Curiosity won. Quade licked his dry lips. "You were beaten by a man who didn't welcome your attentions?"

Was that too forthright? He couldn't recall speaking so frankly with anyone else about such matters. He'd had several episodes in the past, and there'd been Bentham, but there hadn't been much conversation before, during, or after.

"I made the mistake of confessing interest, the sort that gets a man in trouble with the law. I told someone I thought was a friend." For the first time since they'd met, Kelly sounded brooding and angry.

He stopped talking. Quade waited, but when the silence remained, thick and unpleasant, he volunteered the only phrase that came to mind. "I'm so very sorry."

The smile flashed on Kelly's face again, lifting the darkness. "Well, perhaps it was time for me to be brought down a peg. I was too full of confidence and happy with my life."

Quade nearly asked what that life had been like, but another wave of dizziness made him close his eyes. A very bad idea, as it turned out, because it only served to make the giddiness turn into something more like illness.

"I'm very drunk," he announced, and the words seemed to come from some other corner of the room, not his own mouth.

"Yes, you are thoroughly *stocious*." And now his bodyguard and companion seemed back to his normal annoying, cheerful self.

"You are annoyingly cheerful," Quade said without opening his eyes.

"Ah, and you're a charming *omadhaun*," the bodyguard responded, but charming couldn't be right. Although Kelly had admitted he knew about desiring men, hadn't he.

"What's oh-mad-what?"

"A bit of a fool. Let's get you to your room."

That would be wonderful. Suddenly, Quade's flagging desire perked again. "You and I?" he asked. "In my room?"

He must have been mumbling, or the valet/bodyguard ignored him. No, he had actually vanished, gone into another room. Was Quade supposed to follow? The thought more than intrigued him and gave him purpose. He rose to his feet and managed to make his way from the sitting room to his bedroom.

His bed was empty, and that was a pity. "Where are you?" he called.

Kelly appeared at his side. Lord above, he moved quietly. "Here I am. Sit down here." He put a tin pot on the floor.

"What's that?"

"In the event you puke."

"I'm never sick," Quade said, yet even as he said the words, his body seemed to consider that notion and decide to make him a liar. Nausea filled him, a head-to-toe vileness. "Perhaps something like a purging would help this dizziness," he said with as much dignity as he could muster. "But I will not require the pan." In the past, he wouldn't have rejected the use of a chamber pot. He would've allowed a servant to assist him—after all, that was why one *hired* help—but Kelly wasn't truly part of his domestic staff. Quade said, "I don't need a pan, and I don't need a servant."

He rose to his feet and lurched off toward the water closet.

"Would you want a friend?" Kelly called after him.

Quade went into the room, slammed the door, did what his body demanded—and vowed never to drink again. Not so much as a swallow, and certainly never Irish whisky.

He lay down on the floor and decided the cool tiles were just what he required. Kelly had asked him something about friends. What was that Kelly had said? Did he need a friend?

In normal times, one didn't require close friends if one had other resources. Work. Interesting places to visit. To feel a part of mankind, one could count on friendly acquaintances, such as the sort one met in one's club—

"Oh, damnation." Quade groaned.

"Need help now?" The voice came from just on the other side of the door.

"I can't go return to my club. How shall I take my meals?" Egad, best not to think of food at the moment.

"Aw, we'll find a way to get around that one, Mr. Marrill. Not today, though."

"Not today," he agreed. He sat up. His head still spun, but the rest of his body seemed less hideously angry with him. He ran the cold tap and slurped some from his cupped hand, spitting out several mouthfuls before drinking down several more.

"Shall I help you to bed now?" Kelly called.

"I don't require any help," he said. Yet moving out of the bathroom seemed too much work. He lay back down on the floor and curled into a ball.

He woke to find himself in being dragged up into strong arms. "Yes," he murmured. "That is precisely what I want."

"Can you walk?"

"Of course I can."

He must have, though he didn't recall how he got into the bed. Someone touched his forehead brushing aside damp, sweaty hair, and that cool stroke felt perfect. He opened his eyes and smiled. "Kelly. Colm Kelly."

"Yes, indeed."

He closed his eyes against the distraction of Kelly's looming presence. Quade must speak the proper words for a situation he'd never encountered, a man in his apartment, a thoroughly appealing person who seemed to be aroused by men. Pity Quade was crapulous.

You would never think like this if you weren't drunk, he pointed out to himself. *Now concentrate.*

He must say something seductive that promised nothing. He had nothing, only a pittance he could share with his mind, but he'd be delighted to share all the physical pleasure he had ever imagined. *Embrace Pleasure Phallus Pulchritude Ecstasy Touch Stroke Lick Climax.*

He wanted Colm Kelly. A list of words gathered in his mind, and he automatically arranged them in alphabetical order. He said, "I don't have any page numbers associated with the words I can offer, but they're all yours. An entire index of whatever you want. What I want too. What we want."

"Madman." The voice came from far away.

"Lie down with me," Quade ordered.

"Water on the table next to the bed. And despite your protest, the pot is on the floor. I'll check on you soon, Mr. Marrill."

***

Colm closed the door and went to his room. He lay on his back and stared up at the plaster decoration that rippled along where the ceiling and walls met.

He thought about Jack Marrill's brother-in-law. Quade Marrill had sounded so forlorn when speaking of the man who'd apparently been a friend before. Why would Hoyt turn against Marrill? If there had been foul play, might it have been Mary Marrill—poor dear, such a name—who killed her husband? But why would she try to lay the blame on Quade when the death was ruled of natural causes?

Colm tried to remember the details of Jack's death and the list of people who'd been in the house when he died, a list he'd glanced at while thumbing through Patrick's files. He didn't think she'd been there, but wasn't sure.

He wasn't going to find answers inside his head. He sat up and looked around the room. Décor and books all over the bloody place. Mr. Marrill probably cared nothing for the first—only books held his interest.

But that wasn't true, was it? There'd been a begging light in his eyes, a sort of hunger that had been difficult to resist. Could that be why Hoyt was so angry? Marrill had given some indication of interest? Foolish Hoyt, if that were so. Colm snorted at himself.

He'd managed to walk away only by reflecting that Marrill, sober, would wake in horror at what he'd done. There was also the fact that Colm's job depended on keeping his distance. Getting this new life of his in London settled and smooth should matter most.

And with the money he'd make from working for his cousin, he'd be able to send home a sum every month. Perhaps he'd go from disgraced son to returning hero.

No. He would neither go home nor think of the family he loved and longed to see. His own brothers, who'd stood in the crowd as he'd been beaten and didn't lift a hand to stop… The horror filled him again, as always. Far better to turn his thoughts to the present, such as contemplating the habits of the strange man he watched day and night. And, as always when he thought of Marrill, he felt a warmth and wanted to chuckle. Colm had sensed a fierceness in Marrill from the day they'd met, but it took drink to bring out the warrior.

For a man who'd seen more than his share of idiot warriors emerge from the bottom of a bottle, Colm shouldn't have found Marrill's blustering endearing or funny. Perhaps because the combativeness had been on Colm's behalf? Mr. Marrill the gentleman, taking up for an Irishman's right to visit a gent's boring club.

Oh, damn. Marrill hadn't just peacefully fallen asleep. He was singing. He had a good voice, and he sang in a language Colm didn't recognize. Colm pushed up on one elbow. The hour had grown late enough he should go stop the drunkard from disturbing their neighbors.

Even in this well-made, sturdy building, his voice would carry.

He walked into the other man's room. "What are you caterwauling about?"

"It's a funeral dirge," he said. "For my brothers. My brothers. *Est quaedam flere voluptas.* There is some pleasure in weeping. Ovid."

That reply dissolved Colm's annoyance at once. He sat on the edge of the bed. "Best sing more quietly, Mr. Marrill."

Marrill turned his back, then muttered something.

Colm leaned over him, and the unexpected waft of fresh sheets and a well-washed body seemed to beckon him closer. Bad idea, and he breathed deeper, half hoping he'd catch the smell of puke, which would surely act as a deterrent.

Nothing but Marrill, a light yet potent draft of man.

"'Tis the indoor plumbing," he told Marrill. "You must bathe more than anyone I've known." He tentatively put his hand on Marrill's shoulder, just at the skin at the back of his neck, which was warm, slightly damp with perspiration. The light tickle of hair over his hand brushed his knuckles, and he didn't move, only let his fingers mold into the perfect shape.

A quiet snore rose from the bed. Colm carefully, slowly removed his hand and rose to his feet.

"Stay," Marrill said, as clearly as if he wasn't drunk or asleep.

"We need our sleep, Mr. Marrill."

"Lie down, then. Right here."

"Here, now, didn't I just say? We need our sleep." He walked to the door. "You are the very devil," he added in Irish. He went to his room and lay down on his back, unwilling to risk having his erect organ pressing against the bed. The friction would be more than he could bear.

As it was, pulling the covers up meant the slightest brush moved over him, and he arched up. Moving without thought already—he was already too close. If he drifted off to sleep, he'd have one of those charged dreams and make a mess of the bed. If he were home, he might go splash in the lake.

He took himself in hand and stroked, up and down, his mind filled with the slender form and eager mouth of Mr. Marrill, just as he'd been, only sober as an excited judge, one with a glorious rear, calling him home. Pressing himself against that arse.

He climaxed at just the thought of pushing against a naked arse, Marrill's round, hard rear.

He fell asleep at once and, despite his efforts, dreamed of Marrill, kissing him, lying down next to him.

And when Marrill turned to him holding a knife in the dream, he wasn't surprised. *"You knew I was a murderer, didn't you?"*

"You're not, you're not, you're not," Colm yelled over and over in the dream, the rhythm of the knife going into his own belly.

When he woke before dawn, Colm was cross with himself and the world. He climbed out of bed to do the exercises his cousin had shown him.

In the middle of one particularly awkward motion with his arms flailing and his feet kicking, he noticed he had an audience.

Marrill leaned against the door of his room. Some of his hair was matted and some stood on end, and his eyes had that heavy and weary look of a man nursing a hangover. But the crease in the center of his forehead showed puzzled interest, not annoyance.

He was as lovely a sight as Colm had ever seen.

At that moment, Colm knew he was in trouble. Serious, deep-down trouble he hadn't experienced before because he'd never lived in such close quarters with Liam, the only other object of his interest. And worse, if he did the proper, intelligent thing and walked out the door, he'd leave behind the only possible living he had in this strange city. But his Mr. Marrill could request a new guard, couldn't he? And if Colm could contrive that sort of situation, his cousin wouldn't give up on him as a coward who couldn't hold a job.

"Good morning to you, sir. I hope you're well," he said, determined to be as full of sunshine as possible. If he drove the man crazy with cheerfulness, perhaps Marrill would demand that Colm be removed from the job and they'd both be safe.

No such luck, because instead of a scowl, a brief, tentative smile touched Marrill's face. "I assume you're not having fits?" he asked.

Colm scratched his head. "Sir?"

"You were jumping about and grunting."

"Oh yes. Exercise for proper posture and strengthening," he said. "Now that I don't do proper work or ride about the countryside, I must keep myself fit."

"Ah." Marrill glanced down at his own feet, then across the room at the wall, then back down at his feet. He didn't look at Colm. The poor blighter was so uncomfortable, he must have had something to say. Hard to imagine the self-confident, slightly boorish gentleman at such a loss on how to speak to a mere servant.

Colm knew better than to interrupt someone gathering courage to say something awkward.

A long silence passed. Outside, a costermonger bellowed about his superior po-tatties, potattie-ohs.

Marrill spoke in a rush, "I apologize. I must. For the distress."

"Eh?"

"I beg your pardon for my behavior yesterday. I am a little unclear on the details, but I know that I am…that I was more than a little worse for drink yesterday. I behaved badly."

"Not to me."

The crease between his brows appeared again. His chin went up in that familiar manner. Could that slightly sour look of superiority come from a need for spectacles? Marrill's dignified air remained steady despite the red eyes and the silly hair. No. Colm refused to be charmed.

Marrill said, "I can't recall every detail about last night."

Colm said in too loud a voice, "And you probably feel like death warmed over by hellfire."

"A bit, perhaps."

"You go and sit, and I'll make tea or, no, now I recall you would rather have coffee."

The tightness promptly vanished from his manner, and Quade was back to his tetchy self. "You're not actually my servant. Didn't we make that clear at the start?"

Some devil prompted him to ask, "Tell me, Mr. Marrill, if I'm not your servant, am I a friend come to stay?"

The horror that came into Marrill's eyes might have insulted some people.

Marrill wiped his hand over his mouth. "Last night… Did I? Did we? Was I? Were you?" The unfinished questions stuttered out of him.

Colm felt his face grow hot. If Marrill was uncomfortable, Colm was utterly mortified. "No, no, and no. You were sick, and I put you to bed. You sang a little."

Marrill closed his eyes for a long moment. “Yes, I rather recall that part. And I became dreadfully maudlin.”

“I think you can be forgiven. And no need to worry about my tender nature. Men getting drunk and singing sad songs about the dear departed is hardly new in my experience.”

“Now you’re laughing along with the idiots at the club who mocked you for being Irish. Doesn’t that seem wrong to you?”

“I’m the one mocking myself, and I’d say I’m speaking more of my old profession. Thank you again for taking up against the disrespect they directed at me.” He pulled his shirt on over his vest and brushed his hands against his sides. “Best get to cracking on a hot drink. I could use some tea myself.”

Mr. Marrill didn’t answer. He looked a little slack-jawed and glassy-eyed. “Are you certain nothing happened?” he asked again and gave a flip of his hand, indicating first Colm, then himself. “Because I recall some…things.”

“Your vivid imagination.”

“God,” he muttered.

He turned and stumbled away from the door.

This idea of driving Marrill to beg for another keeper might do the job and probably wouldn’t take long. Through no real fault of his actual work, Colm would get out of the sticky situation and stay in Patrick’s good graces. He’d been told if he left this task, he wouldn’t be offered another. But if he were booted, that wouldn’t be true. He’d be free to take another, less fraught job for his cousin. Leaving this house would be a relief and it would be torture.

Worse pain to stay, likely.

In all his years, Colm had encountered only one other man he knew desired other men, and Barnaby was hardly the attractive sort. They’d done well enough, the two of them in neighboring villages. And it hadn’t been as lonesome knowing another was nearby and available when the nights seemed too long.

He’d never felt heart-thumping, breathless yearning when he thought of Barnaby.

Hours alone in these rooms with Marrill, who had such expressive eyes and that occasional half smile that made him want to kiss the corners of his mouth where the small lines formed—Colm felt constantly swollen and on edge.

He contemplated those dimples. No, not dimples, not precisely. Oh heaven, to let his tongue trace the line, and, then slide back to that full mouth, pursed in some sort of disapproving sneer, of course. Hiding the sensual curves of lips and…

And there it was again, inside craving that stirred to life, stretched and yawned. Outside, it rose and brushed the fabric of his drawers.

Should he have let himself go, lying on the bed next to him last night? If, for once in his life, he felt the touch of someone he desired this much, perhaps he'd get his fill of whatever kisses or fondling…

Shit. The dream came back to him. Murder haunted Marrill. Colm couldn't leave this man with his sorrow and fear. He must not think of abandoning Marrill.

"Tea," he said out loud. Not enough distraction, so he pushed his palm against himself, which, of course, didn't help restrain his organ.

"Coffee, if you please," Mr. Marrill said from across the hall. Thank Christ he wasn't hanging about in the doorway.

Colm went to the small, nearly empty but very tidy kitchen. There was barely enough coffee to make a pale brown brew for one cup. He'd have to go buy food, or hire a lad to fetch some. How did such things work in the big city?

If he locked the doors behind himself and told Marrill to stay put, he expected the illness from excessive drink the day before would keep him in place. But did he trust the man not to allow anyone in? Had the landlady been told about keeping visitors at bay? He didn't know if one slender old lady and her two maids could fend off murderers. That odd question brought back his impatience to discover what might be responsible for the fear haunting the Marrill family. Was it rumor or reality? If only Mr. Marrill would pay some visits so Colm might get a chance to listen or even ask a few questions—the hostile Mr. Hoyt for instance.

In the meantime, he'd do his job and stay close. Which meant that he couldn't leave Marrill alone with just Mrs. Eldred, but she might know how to hire someone to fetch food.

He made the coffee and tea, then went downstairs to discuss the topic with Mrs. Eldred, the landlady.

"I hadn't known Mr. Marrill had hired a new…man." The tone in her voice dripped with scorn and the silent "Irish" she didn't say aloud could have been a curse. Her unspoken dislike was almost amusingly obvious.

Colm smiled and nodded and explained that he was only there temporarily. By the time she promised to send around a boy to take an order for the grocers, she'd grown less hostile, though she'd never be one of Colm's closest friends.

Scraping and bowing again, Kelly, he thought with a trace of disgust. *You have no pride nor dignity.* Still, it didn't hurt him to make one old hag worry less about being murdered in her bed by the uncouth Irish.

As he climbed the stairs, he thought again of the best way to remove himself from the danger of Marrill's seduction—by removing the danger to Marrill.

Finding and removing the threat wasn't the task Colm had been assigned, but as long as that side job didn't interfere with protecting Marrill, he'd keep right on looking for answers.

He had an opportunity that very day when the skinny and chatty delivery boy appeared at the door. "Sorry I'm late. I went to the wrong Marrill's house to take the order. Them that just got back from the country, the widow lady, 'bout a whole mile off."

Colm supposed there were plenty of people with the name, but just in case, he'd ask a few questions. He led the boy into the kitchen and offered him the very last bit of bread with jam.

"Are you speaking of the older couple or a widow with a recent bereavement?" he asked as the boy crammed the bread into his mouth. The boy drank down the cup of water.

When he could speak again, he said, "Second one. Her husband died from a bite from a bug. The maid says the family got death haunting them. She wants another job but needs references and is scared to ask in case she gets in trouble like the other servants did."

"She told you that?"

"Well. I listen."

And better still, he talked, Colm thought with approval. He drew out a ha'penny and handed it over.

"I h'aint brought back your order yet," the boy said, but he pocketed the coin.

"That's for telling me about the other Marrills. I'm supposed to learn what I can," he lied.

The boy's eyes, already a bit protuberant, widened comically. Colm hastily added, "To help them out, you understand. It is my job to help the family."

The boy nodded and seemed to believe him.

Colm said, "If you bring me more information, I'll pay you more money." He handed over the grocery list and his firm new friend, the delivery boy name Teddy, trotted off down the stairs, whistling.

Colm and Marrill returned to existing side by side. When he wasn't far too aware of simmering attraction, Colm would have called it a comfortable existence.

Over the next two days, Colm brought every meal to Marrill, who'd thank him but usually add another statement to remind him he wasn't in service.

"It's appreciated, though one grows tired of reminding you that you're not a servant," Marrill told him without looking up from his writing.

"Of course not," Colm said. "Just bringing you the extra from what I cooked." He added, "Isn't that the normal and friendly way of two men living together?"

Marrill did look up then. "I don't know. Is that what we are? As simple as that? Except that you follow me about like a guard dog."

Colm put down the tray with a clink of crockery. "That is the most important part. You're correct to remind me."

Marrill's brow furrowed with concern "No, no, I beg of you, I'm not trying to put you in your place—"

"No, Mr. Marrill." Colm straightened and couldn't help laughing. "I wasn't solemn because I took offense. I meant that keeping you safe is truly what matters."

Marrill jerked and dropped his pencil. "Then you think something is happening? I asked you before, and you said you didn't know."

Colm wasn't certain about anything, not even Marrill's own innocence. Though he *felt* sure of it, he knew better than to believe anything without more proof. But he wanted to keep them both on the alert. "I don't know, but I suspect. And we'll find answers too, Mr. Marrill."

With finding answers in mind, he placed a group portrait on the tray that held Marrill's coffee, then put the tray on the desk between two stacks of books. When Marrill leaned toward the coffee, Colm picked up the cup and saucer and stepped back. "I shan't serve you until you tell me about these people."

Marrill put down the sheaf of papers he held. He cradled the silver-framed photo in both hands and stared down at it. "Where'd you find this?"

"In a drawer when I was tidying my room."

"Yes, of course." Marrill's voice was drenched in sarcasm. He clearly thought Colm was there to find evidence—or do worse?

In a soft voice, he said, "I'm on your side, Mr. Marrill."

Marrill licked his lips. A few seconds later, he pointed at one of the boys who sat on a studio sofa. The boy, about ten, had long limbs and gazed solemnly into the camera, a small furrow on his brow as if he were trying to see through the lens. "That's me."

His mouth tightened, and he blinked hard.

Oh, sweet Lord, Colm realized all the other lads in the picture were his brothers, and so were likely dead.

Marrill's hand and voice steadied at once, though. "That's Phillip, the oldest." He pointed at a stocky, angry-looking man who seemed to resent taking time for the portrait. He stood behind the others, his hand resting over the back of the sofa, as if he carefully showed off several heavy rings he wore.

Still calm, Marill pointed at a smiling fellow who leaned against the arm of the sofa. "Jack, the next in line. He, ah, died very recently. But you know about that story."

Colm knew. The most obviously attractive person in the picture, Jack looked like a self-confident golden lad, a demigod with straight white teeth and the upright, strutting posture of a randy satyr.

Another boy, this one probably about to start university, sat next to Quade. He wore a dark suit and a flower in his buttoner. "Mark was rather a prig and hated to get dirt on his clothes. Hmm. What else do I recall?" His voice went low very suddenly. "That's my strongest memory of him, though I was fourteen when he died."

The last of the group sat on the floor in the front, a skinny boy of about six.

"Joseph." Marrill lightly touched the glass. "He had a bit of a stutter. I barely recall him, though we were closest in age." He carefully placed the photo facedown on the tray. "Now I want my coffee."

Colm handed it over without comment. And at that moment, he knew he trusted Mr. Marrill. He had no notion if there had been any foul play at work. Three brothers, the uncle, a cousin, all dead —and though the police didn't seem to be hunting for a connection between the deaths, it was hard not to wonder. Colm only knew that if there was foul play, this man wasn't the culprit and might well be a target. Evidence, his smarter cop-self reminded. There was no proof of anything.

The sorrow in those eyes might be guilt. *Shut it*, he told that smarter thought that crept in.

"There's no reason for you to hang about," Marrill said. "Thank you for the hot drink."

"I'm sorry to bring up some painful memories, Mr. Marrill."

"If it's something else for you to tell your employer, that's a good thing."

"I don't tell them anything," he said gently.

"Oh, indeed? You don't?" He sounded disbelieving, and Colm almost lost his temper, but that wouldn't help either of them.

He asked, "Where shall I put the photograph?"

"Back in a drawer, I should think," Marrill said. "My office."

"Thank you for telling me who they were." He'd known the names, of course, but he had to say something, anything to make Marrill's tight mouth relax.

Marrill looked up from the papers again. His eyes were dry and steady. "How peculiar that I couldn't tell you much about them though they were my brothers."

Colm lifted the tray. "If you do remember more and want to talk, I'll listen."

"No need for any of that. Unless it helps solve a problem, I have neither the time nor interest to explore the past."

Colm was glad he held the tray, or he'd have put his arms about the poor man who'd lost so much and refused to allow himself to grieve. That impulse hit Colm far too often. He left without another word. When he looked back from the door, Marrill had picked up the papers again but seemed to be staring up at the ceiling.

When Colm came to take away the dishes, Marrill said, "Sally will tidy up."

"You have a great many servants," Colm said, because he enjoyed the way Marrill grew indignant at the mention of wealth.

"I'm a simple man who leads a simple life," Marrill said indignantly. "And they're not my servants. The landlady pays them."

Colm thought of the neatly folded clean shirts and ties that smelled faintly of starch and lavender, clothing that appeared once a week, and of Mrs. Eldred's maid Sally and the other maids, who collected and took away the dirty clothes to be laundered by a professional; then there were the boots and shoes that were magically cleaned when left on the mat in the hall. Colm had only caught sight of the bootboy once."We're off to the Lincoln's Inn again. Gray's Inn doesn't have what I want," Marrill announced. He grabbed his hat, a satchel of papers, and waited for Colm to lead the way out the door.

On the pavement, Colm stepped aside and let Marrill go ahead, falling back in his usual spot where he could look for trouble. At the moment, all potential trouble consisted of a governess and her two charges.

Marrill looked over his shoulder and met his gaze. "I shall go out into the air as often as possible to attract the villains who might attack me."

Colm felt an uncustomary surge of irritation. He walked faster and caught up with his charge. "That's a poor plan, Mr. Marrill. You're not to make yourself bait."

Marrill's steps slowed. "Oh. Ah. I beg your pardon. That was a joke."

Colm nearly fell over in a faint. Marrill? Joking? A ham-handed effort, but still, a sign of humanity Colm should nurture, tend as if it were a crop, a fresh patch of good humor. "Then I must beg your pardon, sir. And I'm glad we're out in the fresh air for a change."

Laura, Mrs. Eldred's parlor maid, passed them and tipped Colm a wink. He gave a solemn nod but no other greeting.

"You were almost curt with her," Marrill said. "Nothing like your usual manner."

What sort of worm had lodged itself in his brain this morning? Colm glanced over his shoulder and saw no sign of Laura before saying, "I think she's interested in me, and I don't want to raise her hopes."

"Why not?"

Was the man that dense? He repeated the words Marrill had used with him more than once. "I have neither the time nor the interest."

Marrill laughed. "That was a terrible imitation of an English accent."

"'Tis far better than your attempt at my accent."

"Nay, laddie, you're wrong." And then Marrill said something that sounded like, *Dia dhuit ar maidin,* good morning.

"Are you speaking Irish?"

"I was trying to."

Colm's heart seemed to swell with pleasure, as if he'd been paid a compliment. "Well, isn't that fine, Mr. Marrill."

Marrill's expression was half-annoyed and half-pleased. "How many times must I tell you there is no need to treat me like a child with water on the brain."

"I must get my amusement where I might," Colm said.

Marrill's startled smile made him laugh.

They made their way through a narrow corridor built hundreds of years earlier for shorter, smaller men, but Marrill didn't head to the library.

Colm followed him down another rabbit warren. "What are you looking for today?"

"I want to speak to a clerk. No need for you to come into the office."

"Not a history question, then? Something to do with modern law? Hunting for answers to your own situation?"

"If I were and I found anything, I'll be sure to tell you," he said. "I'll visit the clerk first and then head to the library to check some facts for my work."

Colm wondered if he was telling the truth about sharing what he'd learned from the lawyer. Marrill tended to hide his notes when Colm walked into a room. Colm would let him keep any secrets for now. Eventually, though, Colm would grow too impatient waiting for him to speak. He'd discover what Marrill was hiding.

As they left the library, Marrill seemed almost light-hearted for the first time since Colm had met him.

"Have you learned anything interesting, sir?" Colm asked.

He glanced at Colm behind him. "I've gotten an answer to a question about medieval investitures."

"Nothing about your own family?"

"Perhaps. But don't bother to look in there, Detective Sneak." He tapped the satchel he carried. "I took no notes."

"Would you tell me?"

"Perhaps later."

"Don't you trust me?"

He paused in their walk toward the gate to look back. "It is more a matter of how useful the information is to anyone."

"I notice you didn't answer the question, sir. Do you trust me?"

"As much as I do anyone, I suppose. But you're smiling, Kelly. It's your turn to be quizzed. Why are you happy?"

Colm reflected that Marrill wasn't far wrong. When they were not in that apartment, stewing in the frustration of unsated lust, he enjoyed Marrill's company. "If you trust me, then this is a grand life," Colm said. "I shouldn't mind following you around forever."

"Except for the threats and possibilities of intimidation and so on," Marrill said dryly, but he didn't seem upset.

"What do you mean?"

At last Marrill would spill his secrets. No, because his only answer was, "You've been hired to guard me, after all."

Colm should have been paying better attention to their surroundings, because he was startled when someone called Marrill's name.

The gaunt figure of the older man from the club stood next to the Lincoln's Inn gate. He raised his hat at them and said, "Good morning, gentlemen."

Colm recalled his name, Mr. Grace, and that he'd seemed pleasant. He still did—the way he said *gentlemen* without the hint of a smirk.

"Oh, ah. Good day," Marrill said.

"How do you do, Mr. Grace?" Colm said, mostly to remind Marrill of the name.

The man gave a little bow to each of them. "You're looking better than the last time we met," he said to Marrill. "And you too, Mr. Kelly. How are you?" He really did treat Colm as if they were mates together, without a hint of disgust or arrogance.

"Good to see you again, sir. I hope your nose has recovered after its accidental run-in with Mr. Marrill?"

"What could you mean?" Marrill looked alarmed. "When was this?"

"It was at your club." Mr. Grace said. "That last eventful visit of yours."

"Good Lord." Marrill seemed to shuffle on the spot. He pressed his lips tight. "I'm very sorry—I recall now that I struck you. That's dreadful. Did I also call you names?"

"Not at all," Mr. Grace reassured him. "And you had been sorely tried that day. May I walk with you gentlemen? Are you up for a spot of tea or even a luncheon? There's a coffee stall on the street nearby, but I can do better than that."

He escorted them to a tearoom on a side street, a dark room that smelled of perfume, stewed tea, and dust. "Just as if we were proper sorts of matrons," Mr. Grace said with a smile. "Will that suit you? Tea and a selection of cakes?"

"If it is all the same, I'd prefer coffee," Marrill said to the stiff-backed lady who didn't seem to want gentlemen in her shop, though it didn't have a sign indicating it was a ladies-only establishment.

"You prefer coffee to tea?" Mr. Grace asked Marrill.

"Always."

Grace looked at Colm. "And you, Mr. Kelly?"

Colm made a face. "Can't abide coffee." He perched on an uncomfortable and too-small wrought iron chair, but managed to relax for the first time in hours. The large room at the library with the hidden dark shelves had been a nerve-racking place to watch for dangers. This tea shop was far smaller and nearly empty. In the opposite corner, a bored woman in black played a harp.

The lady returned, pushing a rattling cart with plates, cups, and a ruffled display of tiny cakes.

Why would Grace bring them to a place like this? Although perhaps Grace enjoyed the shop—he certainly seemed happy to be surrounded by lace curtains and endless garlands and vases of silk flowers. Was he something of a Miss Molly? He didn't have the outward signs.

Grace was chatty and pleasant as he served out the cakes, and seemed to be trying to understand Colm and Marrill's relationship. He was almost as pushy as a cop with his interest and managed to uncover the fact that they lived together, were not servant and master, not really, and that the apartment was spacious enough for each to have his own room.

Marrill didn't volunteer the fact that Colm was a paid guard, which pleased Colm.

Mr. Grace's questions were mostly directed to Marrill, and he watched him closely, wearing a wide smile of interest. Was that a look of passionate awareness?

Between sips of tea, Mr. Grace twisted a gold band on his finger, a wedding ring. But of course, men who liked men stayed hidden and married women.

Colm pointed to the ring. "You're married?"

"I was, yes. I am a widower now."

"I am very sorry to hear of your loss. Do you have any children?"

A smile lit the older man's face, and his eyes went rather bright. It reminded Colm of that look he'd worn in the club. But Colm suddenly realized the brightness was due to tears, and the smile was a rictus of pain.

"I had a daughter, a beautiful girl. My good girl is in heaven now. I do believe that with all my heart."

"Of course," said Colm soothingly. "I'm very sorry, sir."

The defensive way Mr. Grace spoke of his daughter meant something about her death—or perhaps about his religion.

"My wife died soon after my daughter. It was a very difficult time." He looked at Marrill for a long moment, then spoke softly. "Forgive my impertinence, but members of the club mentioned your own story, of your family."

"They are a gossipy bunch." Marrill shifted in his chair. He wouldn't be much of an actor, for he showed his awkwardness about certain subjects too well.

Grace's smile reappeared. "I've heard you're going through a terrible time too?"

"My family, yes." He waved a hand a strange move-along gesture.

Colm had seen that before—Marrill acted as if he were an imposter should he show sorrow over his brothers' deaths. Others mourned, but he didn't have the right.

It might be a sign he felt no sorrow, or it could be a signal of guilt, Patrick would warn. Colm wouldn't say any such thing. Not after witnessing Quade's face as he'd gazed down at the photographs of his brothers.

"My condolences," said Mr. Grace, and he leaned across the small table and put his bony hand on Marrill's shoulder for a moment that stretched too long.

Colm wanted to bat it away, to shove him back. Perhaps some sort of guard's instinct or, far more likely, jealousy.

"Thank you." Marrill cleared his throat and resumed fidgeting with his cup and saucer, rearranging the spoon. "I think I recall you said something to me at the club."

Grace's smile was wide and real. "Yes, a clumsy comment, and I do apologize for it."

"I don't recall what it was."

Grace winced, his thin lips puckered. "Best if you don't. I was only repeating what my new friend had said."

"Hoyt," Marrill said slowly. "You sat with Hoyt."

"Yes, and I'm afraid he really is rather a gossip."

"That is not my memory of him," Marrill said.

"Ah. Well, he was mightily stirred. Apparently, his sister is not well, and he suspects the problems not naturally based."

"Mrs. Marrill is ill?" Colm said.

Grace bowed his head. “So I am given to understand. And Mr. Hoyt is suspicious, as I said.”

“My family,” Marrill said slowly. “He thinks it is to do with us.”

Mr. Grace shrugged. He seemed ill at ease and almost as fidgety as Marrill himself. “Perhaps. But I beg your pardon, gentlemen, it is wrong of me to ask you out to tea and speak of such unhappy matters.”

“I’d better return to work anyway. Thank you for a pleasant interlude.” Marrill stood and pulled out his purse.

“Please, allow me to pay. I invited you,” Mr. Grace said.

“Oh no, please allow me to assuage my guilt over that stupid day when I drank too much.” Marrill pulled out some coins. “Next time, perhaps, eh?”

Grace, who hadn’t touched his cake, rose and walked with them to the door of the shop. “I hope to see you again, soon. At the club, do you think?”

“I doubt it,” Marrill said. “But thank you.”

Marrill grew quiet as they walked home. Colm followed behind, his gaze straying to Marrill often—a foolish action since he was supposed to be keeping his eyes on the rest of the world. Marrill’s hair had grown too long, and the strands that showed under his well-made hat caught what little sunlight there and had a touch of red. Like the man, that hair looked ordinary enough, but something hot lay beneath the surface.

Colm gazed at a large Alsatian dog that trotted loose down the street in their direction. No, it was busy about its own dog business and wouldn’t attack his charge. His job of protecting Marrill struck him as silly—he had found nothing so far that showed a campaign to go after the man.

Colm could only hope that was the truth.

As they climbed the steps to the apartment, Marrill said, “Hoyt must truly be upset to gossip with near-strangers. I wrote to him and asked him why he was offended, and he’s sent no reply.”

“Like your father.”

Marrill shot him a suspicious glance. "Did I tell you that my father is uncommunicative, or did you read the letters from him?"

Both, Colm supposed. He pulled off his hat and tucked it under his arm. "Don't forget that I hope to help you, Mr. Marrill."

"So you tell me." But Marrill gave one of his rare smiles, his lips tucked in as if he had forgotten how to express humor. "Sneaking around is a funny way of helping."

"Funny? Perfect, for I aim to amuse as well as serve," he told Marrill, who actually laughed.

CHAPTER FIVE

For supper, Colm made some sandwiches. Marrill put down the book he held and looked up at him. "You really are quite remarkable."

"Thank you, though the food isn't worth that much praise."

"Not the sandwiches, numbskull. You."

Colm waited, half hoping and mostly dreading he might say more, but apparently, the subject was finished. Marrill settled into a chair and picked up the book with one hand and the sandwich with the other.

Colm asked, "Will you tell me what you discovered today in the library?"

"I needed to know who precisely gets what in my family."

"Inheritance?"

"Yes." He took a bite before answering. "I have written to Mary and to Billbrook and, as you know, to my father and Hoyt. I think it's clear they've heard or invented news about me, something false, and I should like to know what it is."

False news, or was their dislike and avoidance based on the fact that Marrill was a sodomite? Colm didn't think he should mention that. He said, "Good plan, sir." He wondered if they might actually pay some visits to those people, but Mr. Marrill preferred writing to face-to-face contact.

Colm didn't have the possibility of making visits and decided to draw an example from Mr. Marrill. "Might I use some of your ink and paper? I'll buy some on my day off," he added apologetically. He was past due for that day off. He'd been working for a fortnight already.

"Naturally. And no need to worry about replacing a few measly sheets of stationery. I go through cartloads of the stuff." Marrill didn't look up from the book open in the middle of his lap. He gestured toward a carved and elaborate thing, a sideboard, perhaps. Colm had seen one like it at his cousin's house but that one held drinks, glasses, and other objects designed to hold food and drink. This was filled with stacks of paper, bottles of ink, small pile of pens, and ledgers. Everything inside lay neat and well-organized.

He might leave papers and open books all about the place, and he seemed to always forget to cut his hair, but Marrill was at heart an organized man.

Colm wrote a note to his cousin to remind him he was due a day off, and another to his sister. As he waited for the ink to dry on the note to Aileen, he imagined her standing in front of her cottage reading his words, perhaps reading some of them to their mother, who'd lean close to hear and scold Aileen for her soft voice—the daft woman refused to admit she was going deaf.

A longing for home hit Colm. He resolved to write at least once a week. That seemed to be what people did who left their village voluntarily in search of adventure and good fortune. He'd pretend that he was just such another of those emigrants. And perhaps someday he'd send a casual greeting to his other siblings. After that, if he should send along money, that would certainly open the door for his return.

Perhaps she and her mother might visit London some day, and he'd take them to that tea shop Mr. Grace had shown him.

Aileen would know how to gently introduce the subject of the black sheep. Maybe eventually, years from now, he could go home as a success. It was an innocent, pleasant dream, he argued with himself.

When his day off came at long last, Colm had to wait until another bodyguard showed up. Someone came thumping up the stairs before eight a.m. When he opened the door, expecting to see his replacement, there was Teddy the delivery boy. "I got news," Teddy said, out of breath. "Of those other Marrills."

"Let's go down the stairs," Colm said. "Himself needs to sleep, and I could do with some fresh air."

They stepped out of the house into the cool morning breeze, laden with mist that promised to become rain. Colm pulled out a tuppence. He was low on money, so this would have to do.

Teddy seemed pleased enough. He drew in a long breath, then spoke so quickly, Colm had trouble catching the words. "There was a great to-do over there this morning. A dead bird and a note. And the bird lived in this big round thing behind the house. It belonged to the mistress. A great hullabaloo." He waggled his eyebrows up and down.

"What did the note say?"

"Oh. Dunno. But it was bloody, even. And stuck to the pigeon. The cook's girl was in hysterics. She dropped the sack of potatoes I delivered."

Colm thanked him and, before the boy ran off, asked, "Where do these Marrills live?"

Teddy was young enough to just blurt out the address without asking why he wanted to know or demanding more pay.

Soon after Teddy left, a round-faced, taciturn German appeared and said he'd been sent by Mr. Kelly. Colm considered saying goodbye to Marrill, but the man had nearly finished the index he was working on and disliked interruptions.

And Colm had the unnatural desire to talk to him about the dead bird—not a good idea until he had some facts.

The mist had dried up, and the day had turned warm and pleasant for a change. Colm had found a map of London and walked to Widow Marrill's house.

The constable still stood in front of the house, leaning against a pillar but, unlike Teddy, didn't seem the sort interested in chatting with curious strangers. He gave Colm a cold look that clearly said move along.

Colm walked past quickly and wished he'd brought along a package or some such to look like a man with a delivery to make.

He walked back around the corner and, a street away, saw a flower seller with a shallow basket slung from her shoulders. With the last of his funds, he bought several bouquets from the delighted woman.

He hoped the cop didn't remember him, though they'd looked at each other's eyes. He was in luck—as he approached the house, a maid came out from the back carrying a mug of something hot to the constable, who only had eyes for her.

Colm scuttled toward the side of the building and the elaborately shaped wrought iron fence with the word "servants" engraved on a small plaque. He held the damp bunch of white and red blossoms up high near his face in case the constable happened to look away from his maid and tea.

The dusty passageway beyond the wrought iron fence opened to a garden. At the back of the narrow path stood a centuries-old round brick building—a dovecote. Sure enough, several pigeons perched on the roof.

The kitchen stood open, and just inside the passage to a scullery was a small puddle of red on the slate flagstones.

"Here now, watch out," a woman called from behind him. "They're just giving us leave to clean, and we don't need you to track the blood."

He stepped away from the small patch, his shock genuine. "What? That's blood?"

The woman, a large person in mobcap and apron, with a pale face and wisps of pale hair peeking out from her cap, wasn't dressed like a maid. The cook, he guessed. She held an enamel bowl filled with fragrant green leaves. Yes, she must have been out picking herbs for her work.

She frowned at him, but her eyes looked bright. "Don't tell me you don't know all about it."

"Not so much. Tell me, missus. Sounds as if something dreadful took place," Colm coaxed.

"Hours ago, they came and looked about the place. And I just now got leave to clean." She clearly thought he meant that he was interested in her travails.

"They? D'you mean the police?" He tried to make his accent more like Mr. Marrill's. "Was it a body?"

"Only a bird," she said and might have sounded disappointed. She walked past him into the kitchen, avoiding the puddle.

He trailed after her as if he'd been invited. "Why summon the police for such a thing?"

"It was killed on purpose. And when Tansy, the scullery, started screaming her fool head off, they must come running, mustn't they. Such a fuss about a pigeon." She shook her head. "We thought the door was locked, but it weren't after all, and someone put the bird just inside the door." She pointed at the puddle and gave an disapproving sniff. "It was there, just there, with a knife and note."

"Awful," he said. "What did the note say?"

She put the bowl on a big table that was already cluttered with eggs and flour. "Rubbishy nonsense. Here now, give me the flowers, why don't you? Who sent them?"

He handed her the flowers and wiped his hands on the sides of his trousers. “Some man said to deliver them.”

Her invisible eyebrows rose. “Now isn’t that most peculiar. Best you tell that fact to the constable. We’ve had enough of the strange things, notes and so on.”

“More’n one note? They come by post?”

She bent her head to sniff the flowers. “No. As for the other from a while back, it was to the police. We know about that one, don’t we.”

No, we bloody well don’t. That thought came to him in Marrill’s most acid tone. “Is it a great mystery who sent the notes?” he asked.

“Hardly a mystery with this one, is it? We all know who it is. The brother of our late master. He’s a madman who don’t like that there’ll be another member of his family.” She fetched a jug hanging from the ceiling. “That’s what the letter said.”

“Another in his family?” Colm prompted. A threat to Marrill. A threat that was supposed to come from the man. That was absurd.

She ignored his question. “And the madman lives less’n two miles away from here. Shudder to think of what he could do. The mistress with a baby on the way has too much to worry over as it is.”

A baby on the way. Jack had left his widow with a baby. Perhaps that explained why she had felt poorly. The note Mrs. Marrill just received might signal a new threat, but the fact that her illness was based on a natural event removed another.

Colm asked, “The note threatened the baby?”

“It was only the one line, ‘another in the family dies’ or some such. Here now, are you the police?”

“Me? Not at all.” He laughed, then said, “I suppose the note wasn’t well written? Block letters, maybe?”

“How would I know such a thing?” She sounded prickly enough that he realized she might not be literate.

“Yes, silly question.” He improvised, “I just expected a madman to have a scrawling sort of handwriting.”

She wrinkled her nose. “Don’t know about that. You’d best be getting along. Go talk to the bobby out front.”

He agreed, but then paused a moment. "Is there a person hired to watch Mrs. Marrill? By way of a guard?"

"What? That's nonsense."

"No new footmen or servants?"

Colm supposed he could ask his cousin, but there was a chance Mr. Arthur Marrill had employed another agency for his son's widow.

"No such thing," she said. "I have work to do, and I'd thank you to move along and speak to the constable immediately."

He agreed to, wondering if perhaps that cook herself worked for Patrick.

Once he slipped away from Mrs. Jack Marrill's house—avoiding the constable—he unfolded his map to look for the place his cousin Patrick lived with Sloan. He didn't have enough money for a hack and didn't know how to use an omnibus properly, so he consulted his map and set off walking again, quickly now.

The cook thought it was Quade Marrill who'd sent the note, but maybe she was the only one. Maybe no one else suspected Quade. That seemed wishful thinking.

When he'd taken on the assignment for Patrick, he'd glanced through the pages of the file about the Marrill family to find out what he'd needed to know for the bodyguard duty. Now he could see those files again, he wanted to dig out as many details as he could.

Mr. Sloan's butler met Colm at the door, led him into the drawing room, and left him to wait.

Colm walked around the room, all shining marble and mahogany, and cluttered with sculptures and giant paintings with elaborately carved frames.

The butler returned soon after to tell him he could find Mr. Kelly in the room that he used as an office. He politely inquired if Colm needed direction.

"No, I can find my way around, thanks." Not like that first morning after his illness when he'd stumbled about the place.

As he walked into the library, he caught sight of Patrick and Mr. Sloan standing next to a desk. They moved apart quickly, jolting away from each other in an obviously guilty manner. How strange to learn all the hints they'd given about their relationship were true. And what a thought, to live with a person you wanted. He'd watched his family and friends marry and then get that flushed look of amazed satisfaction.

But two men, and from such different worlds, living together seemed extraordinary, almost as shocking as seeing them near embrace.

"You oughtn't jump," he told them.

"I beg your pardon?" Sloan could put on the entitled gentleman act better than anyone Colm had met—even better than the fools in Marrill's club.

Colm fluttered his hands, imitating a shy maiden surprised in the bath. "Should you need to move away from one another, do it slow. Deliberate-like. You look more innocent, then."

"What are you doing here?" Patrick asked, walking toward him and obviously drawing attention away from the flustered and worried Sloan.

"It's my day off. You sent round some German." A jolt of sudden fear tore through him, worse than the night the mob came to his door. The threat of the dead dove, of murder, and Mr. Marrill at home with a stranger. "Holy mother. Didn't you send someone, Patrick?"

The moment of horror lasted until Patrick gave a nod. "Right, I thought that was tomorrow. Dorman is the man I hired for the job."

"Oh, heavens. Thank heavens, but I shouldn't have assumed." Without invitation, Colm sat heavily in a wooden library chair next to a desk that was all dark wood curves and curlicues. "I was careless."

Sloan vanished. Patrick, who'd been discreetly smoothing his hair and adjusting his waistcoat, sat across from Colm. "No need to beat yourself up. You did fine. I guess I got my answer about whether or not you'd take the work seriously." He tilted his head to the side. "I'm still not convinced you're the right man for the job. I heard a story about a brawl in a gentleman's club. Does that sound familiar?"

"And how did that come to your ears?"

"London's a small town, as it turns out."

"Hardly as tiny as a village." Colm tried to sound unconcerned when his heart was lodged in his throat.

All that planning and scheming to leave the position at Marrill's apartment had become unimportant now that Colm suspected a real threat to his Mr. Marrill. Worse than that, he'd botched his good chance to work for his cousin after that damned bout of fisticuffs.

He would have to find another job. He rubbed his face as cold dismay filled him. And what would his Mr. Marrill do to the next minder who stepped up? Would Colm's replacement treat the threat seriously?

That dead bird—did the police even now visit Marrill to interview him?

His thoughts skittered about in utterly useless panic.

He reminded himself that once they caught the villain, his charge would be safe. After that, well…if he couldn't be with Marrill, he might leave London. He might escape back to green fields, fresh wind, and the sea. That had to be some consolation for the loss of the newly interesting companionship of Mr. Marrill.

Patrick was still babbling about the club. "The story I heard was you did a good job of keeping your temper in check."

At that, Colm let himself lean against the back of chair, dismay replaced with relief. After the scene at Mrs. Jack Marrill's house and now this, he'd grown jumpy as a marsh hare. "You wanted to frighten me, didn't you, Patrick."

His cousin raised his eyebrows. "I'm glad to know I can put the fear of God in you."

"If that helps me stay on in your employ, then yes, I admit you can." Colm's heart slowed, and he took in a long breath. "That damned fight at the club shouldn't have occurred. It was absurd."

He told Patrick about the incident and was taken aback when the American began to laugh.

"You did as well as you could, I suppose. Now, why are you here? What can I do for you?"

"I need to see the Marrill file again."

"Oh? Don't you recognize your charge by now? Your job is quite simple, you know. Watch that one man."

"Yes, Mr. Kelly, sir, I looked at the file, but want to look harder. I should study where possible threats might arise, don't you think?"

"You believe there is a true threat?"

Colm tilted his head to see if his cousin was jesting again. No, Patrick seemed serious. "My work is to keep him safe," Colm said. "But finding the cause of danger? Aren't you working on that end?"

Patrick shook his head. "No, the father who hired us said he only wanted us to make sure the boy himself didn't get into trouble. He was particularly vague about what he meant by trouble, as if he thought it could be his son who posed the danger. I don't believe it. I think the hints of threats and innuendo were created to scare the family for some reason. Some cruel person noticed the deaths and used them to make trouble."

"Do you know which cruel person?"

He shrugged and gazed at Colm too steadily without answering. He obviously had ideas and no intention of sharing them.

Colm said, "Scare the family? Wouldn't whoever it is go further with violent action, perhaps?"

"To be honest, I don't know. That's why I wanted men who could protect themselves for that job."

"So you have others protecting more than Quade? Do you have someone working for Mrs. Jack Marrill?"

"There's no reason for you to know the details of who I've assigned where."

"Here's something I do know. Mr. Marrill, I mean Mr. Quade Marrill, is not a murderer," Colm said with too much emphasis.

"Why are you so certain?" Patrick examined him, those very expressive eyebrows raised. After a long moment, he said, "Mind you, you're probably right. Someone is trying to make trouble."

Colm wanted to shake him. *Names, you pain-in-the-arse. Give me names and places.* "You sound so decisive, Cousin Patrick. Can you tell me what you mean?"

"Fine." Patrick sighed. The leather of his padded chair squeaked as he shifted and crossed his arms. "I did a bit of poking around and learned the police got a note from a crackpot a while back. Not really relevant to your charge, and the authorities are fairly certain they know who sent it. As the investigator in charge said, no one's more malicious than a servant who's been shown the door."

"Tell me about the letter." The cook's comment about the *other note from a while back* came to him. This must be what she meant.

Patrick wrinkled his nose. "Say, I'm not sure it's your concern, Colm. It's not directly related to the work you were hired to do." He sniffed—even he seemed doubtful about this sad argument of his.

Colm was careful not to sound eager when he prompted, "If it's to do with Quade Marrill's family, I should know, shouldn't I?"

"I oughtn't have mentioned it. The inspector held back its existence from the public, and I think even most Marrill family members don't know about the letter."

"Ha, maybe. But I'll wager the police didn't hide anything from the servants of Jack Marrill's household."

"What do you mean?" Patrick demanded. "How would you know? You said you haven't had any experience in service."

Colm laughed. "You tell me what you mean, and then I'll tell you. Now that you've begun, you must tell me the rest. And it's not gossip if you're filling in details for an employee working on a case."

"An employee I knew I could trust, sure."

"Yes, yes. Do you require me to take an oath, sir?"

"There's no need to be disrespectful, Colm." He pulled open a drawer and fiddled with some papers, then drew out a stack and began leafing through them. "At any rate, the letter the police got was a few months ago. I didn't get a chance to examine it closely, but I can tell you that it was delivered soon *before* he died and was all about Mr. Jack Marrill."

"His death got the Marrills to act at last? To hire you, though they don't want you to do anything useful?"

"Hmm," agreed Patrick. "Though I couldn't do a thing about Jack Marrill's death. It was a bug that killed him."

Colm thought of bug-bitten Jack, the cock of the walk in the photograph. The man whose widow had gotten a nasty message this morning. "I'm serious, Patrick. Talk to me about that letter sent to the police, and I'll tell you about the one Mrs. Jack Marrill got this morning."

"Indeed? And how do you know about her correspondence?"

"I'll tell you. But you first."

He thought his cousin would balk, and he had the right since he was the boss, but Patrick just tapped his fingers on his desk for a moment, then flipped through the pages he'd pulled out. "The letter sent to the police was long, had a great many details, and the basic claim was that Jack had killed off his brothers and uncle and cousin. It listed his dislike for his family and that he was greedily attempting to gather in as much money as he could. The police held on to it even after Jack's death."

"I should think so." He shook his head with disbelief. "You didn't tell me there were actual accusations. Don't you think that puts a whole new light on the matter?"

"Could be. But accusations are easy to make."

Colm didn't want to argue. He needed to get to the bottom of this new twist. "Did they discover who wrote the letter? You said they had a suspect, a servant who had been dismissed by Jack?"

"They're fairly sure it was a valet, but from what I've heard, the police didn't interview the man for more than a few minutes." Patrick glanced down at a note. "He wasn't in town when Quade Marrill's cousin, Cyril, died."

"That's the one who was bludgeoned?"

"Yes. I guess that's why they didn't push the valet harder. A verified attack, and he wasn't in the area."

A former servant might still have keys to get into the house, which meant Jack's ex-valet could have left the dove. But why would he bother throwing accusations at another Marrill brother if he'd been angry at Jack? Why hold a grudge after Jack's death?

Patrick had no way to know that. Colm asked questions he might be able to answer. "Did the police interview Jack about the letter?"

"I don't think so, and there was no point in talking to his family or the valet because, soon after the police received the letter, Jack Marrill died."

"Do you believe he died because of a bug?"

"Why not? More to the point, the police think it's true. They decided the valet was an ex-employee with a grudge who was nowhere near the spot when Jack died. And why would they bother to investigate that letter about Jack further? The gentleman died of natural causes. They are convinced his cousin was killed in a robbery gone too far. Bad luck and nothing more." He frowned.

Colm thought the displeasure was directed at him, but Patrick said, "By golly, I hadn't thought of it before, but I imagine the reason the police trying to the inquiries about the latest Marrill incident secret is they don't want to make a big fuss. It would be best for them to have the Marrill deaths be seen as nothing more than a bunch of coincidences. Less work, less outcry. No stirring up the hornets' nests when the bugs have gone to bed—that seems to be the way the cops think. They don't like the press getting hold of sensational stories."

Colm snorted. "Hornets are ill to mention, considering how Jack Marrill died." *Allegedly*. "Sakes, I wish I could see that letter the cops got. It's an actual accounting of the crimes?"

"Err, could be."

"What? Don't you remember details?"

"Not many." Something about the way he snapped the words and the reluctance to share the letter made Colm put the pieces together.

"No need to be prickly with me, Patrick. You don't strike me as a man who'd forget anything you managed to get into your hands. But you didn't, did you? Get your actual hands on it, I mean. You didn't read the whole thing."

"Yes, all right. I noticed the note when I visited a detective's office. I sure couldn't push the matter or discover more than the name of the subject and some history. Or even admit I'd taken a good long look at the note." Patrick's half grin, half scowl made him looked precisely like one of Colm's brothers. "They don't like it when I ask too many questions. Information is a one-way street for some of those policemen. I give, but they don't. Now you tell me about this other letter."

Colm described his informant the delivery boy, the discovery of the dead bird, and his visit to Mrs. Jack Marrill's household.

Patrick's thick brows shot up. "Holy Jumping Jehoshaphat, why didn't you tell me that before? There's a madman out there, but I guess the police are on it—as much as they are on anything."

"Or madwoman," Colm added. "And it's not my Mr. Marrill who left that note last night. I've been watching him this entire month and more."

Patrick rubbed his chin. "Mebbe. But that does point out another thing I've done wrong. Not given you a day off. I had no notion you'd take the job so seriously, you wouldn't leave his side for as much as a minute to send word. I should have sent help over before. You should have sent along your grocery-boy informant."

He rose to his feet. “Speaking of which, investigating was not what you were hired to do. Come to me first before you start skulking around.” Patrick shook his head slowly. “I suppose I have my answer about whether or not you’re a thickheaded fool.”

“A Kelly trait,” Colm shot back.

Patrick laughed. “All right, all right. You can look at everything I have about the Marrills, and I expect you to write up that information about the pigeon and its gruesome note. But it will have to all be done here. The information and the folders do not leave my office, understand?”

Colm wanted to mock him for treating the notes as important state secrets, but he really didn’t know his cousin well enough yet. “I understand. Thank you.”

Soon after he sat down to read the papers, all notes in Patrick’s hand, a servant arrived with a tray of food, which Colm accepted eagerly. He wasn’t a terrible cook, but he was more than tired of eating the meals he’d prepared. Though if cooking meant he could stay with Marrill, he would prepare three meals a day—and this wasn’t the time to daydream about an impossible future. He bent his head to read his cousin’s notes again.

By the time he was done reading, he had few new facts. It seemed his own Mr. Marrill—his? Yes. Definitely—Mr. Quade Marrill was not party to the conversations that took place between any authorities and his father and late uncle. There’d been a few after the cousin’s murder. When Quade said he had no idea of what was going on, he likely wasn’t lying.

Quade wouldn’t know the details of the deaths in his family unless his father or the authorities chose to tell him.

After the cousin had been killed, and soon after the uncle, Jeremiah Marrill, died, Quade had been interviewed more thoroughly. Colm grinned as he deciphered the notes scribbled in Patrick’s hand—likely lifted from a police detective’s notes about the interview. Through the scrawling handwriting and odd abbreviations, he made out Marrill’s distinctive voice from the interview with him.

No, Mr. Q. Marrill reported he had no notion at all what was going on with his family because he had been busy with his own work.

And then he told the befuddled officer what he did and went off on a tirade about how the history of law was the backbone of law itself and without good record keeping, they were all bound to make the same mistakes, and by not understanding the world in which the laws were crafted, they didn't understand themselves, then they made the mistake of never moving forward…

He suddenly wished he could hear those words in Mr. Marrill's actual voice instead of just reading them. Lounging around the apartment all day and night, Colm had read plenty of Marrill's writing, but none of it echoed the way he spoke. The professional dry speech in all the papers and notebooks Colm had read wasn't the passionate dry speech of the man.

He read through the notes one more time, and, then another, absently flipping back to check the date of the cousin Cyril's death and Quade's statement of his activities at the time.

Patrick came into the room. "When you're done, you'd best go buy yourself some clothes. You shouldn't look shabby while you travel about town with Marrill."

Colm stretched and eyed his cousin. "I think that after today and that pigeon's death, my job is more than just being a watchdog."

"That can be discussed at a later date."

Colm shook his head. "Not too much later, cousin. Not if there's a real threat out there that must be taken care of."

"I'll take action, believe me. I'll contact my employer today."

"Arthur Marrill is a stubborn man. He won't answer Quade's questions. There are plenty of questions to be asked as well. Who would have it in for the Marrills is the big one."

Patrick held up an envelope. "Look, I've brought your pay packet."

"Yet another man who refuses to address the topic at hand," Colm muttered.

Patrick thumped the envelope onto the desk and pointed to it. "Go now. Use some to buy a better jacket and trousers. And new boots."

"They're fine." Colm stretched out a leg to show off his footwear. "I've got plenty of dubbin on my boots, and the water don't come into them."

"I don't care how waxed up they are, they're clomping and scratching up the floors. That won't do for places that actually care about their polished parquet. Come on, you know that incident at the club shows that you're not fine enough for the city, despite the extra clothes we gave you."

Colm tapped the papers he'd been reading and rose to his feet. He pocketed the pay envelope. "All right. Where should I go?"

"You could go to Whiteleys in Bayswater, or if you don't want to spend as much, I suppose Lumber Court might be what you want. I'd offer to go with you, but you need to learn to fend for yourself." Patrick added, "Besides, I loathe shopping."

He scowled at Colm. "Do not let the salesmen of Lumber Court get their hands on you. You'll end up with suits and hats you don't need and maybe a ladies' sunbonnet as well—they are that persuasive."

"I am not interested in hours of shopping." He wanted to get back to Mr. Marrill.

"Nevertheless, make a list. One suit for day wear, one for evening should you have to change for dinner. I'd say at least two more hats, and make one a top hat."

Sloan must have been walking past or lurking nearby. He came to the desk where Colm had been sitting and rested a well-groomed hand on the chair, a frown creasing his forehead. "One would say that he required a better overcoat as well."

Patrick nodded. "You're right. Damnation, I should have thought of this before sending him out to watch a gentleman."

Colm folded his arms. "Marrill barely leaves his house. The men in the law libraries and British Library or the British Museum don't care how I'm dressed. And I don't expect we'll be visiting that club of his anytime soon."

The other two didn't pay Colm any heed.

Sloan examined him up and down. "Spats would be too much for a man in your position, but at least two pairs of shoes, one black, one brown." He glanced at Patrick over his shoulder. "I say, has he enough of the ready to purchase what is required?"

"I don't need all this," Colm said, impatient to be off now. He wanted to make sure the police or worse hadn't disturbed his Mr. Marrill. Someone evil was lurking at the edges of his life, and Colm didn't trust that German Dorman to keep him safe. He didn't trust anyone else.

Mr. Sloan frowned at him. "You should be able to follow your charge anywhere he might go, Mr. Kelly."

Sloan turned his entire attention to Patrick, even his body leaned in his direction, and his expression softened in a wholehearted smile. "How peculiar to call someone else by that name." A smile passed between them, their gazes held—nothing so very much. They didn't touch or move closer, but the obvious warmth told Colm what they meant to each other.

More peculiar that another man like Colm would be in his family—an invert was the more polite name he'd heard for men who liked men. And did these two know how obvious they were? And how much danger that could bring them? Money might protect them, but the hate would be there.

"I gave Colm plenty of money. He'll be fine." Patrick still gazed at Sloan.

"I'll be going, then," Colm said.

"Goodbye," Patrick said, his attention still fixed on Sloan.

As the door closed behind him, Colm wondered at their interesting relationship. He had never seen anything like it before, other than two women in his village who shared a house and seemed closer than most married couples.

Two women who laughed together and squabbled, as close as sisters, everyone said. And yet… His steps slowed. Did ladies ever have the same interest in other ladies? He knew women could be ardent, perhaps too passionate.

As a nearly grown man, he'd thought he could force himself to appreciate women. He'd held a woman and kissed her. He'd enjoyed the touch of soft lips and the pressure of a warm body against his.

Then Aislinn had pushed for more, and tried to meet him in a private corner, and he'd panicked. So he'd kissed Sorcha in front of her. He was young, and that action had seemed a way to show her he wasn't looking for anything—a heartless but effective way to destroy her interest in him.

That had only given him the reputation as a man who toyed with female affection, which turned him into something of a target for some women.

When he became a constable, he'd explained to any interested women, and their relieved mothers, that he'd taken a sort of vow of chastity. He told them that the force discouraged married constables and he wouldn't be a rake. The truth was he couldn't promise himself to a woman, not when his most ardent encounters with females didn't awaken his body even as much as thinking of kissing a man.

Liam. And now Colm was glad to be all those miles away from his old friend.

He turned the corner onto a busy street, walking faster to get away from the memory of Liam. He knew better than to allow that thought to enter his brain. He broke into a trot, the hobnails in his boots occasionally causing him to slip a bit on cobblestones. They were designed for striding through his old life in the country. Hell, *he* was designed for that lost world.

He felt that urgent tug to hurry back to Marrill's place—that dour German might be the sort of man who'd leave Quade alone in the apartment. But Patrick and Sloan were right: if Colm was to keep following Quade, he'd best buy the clothes he'd need.

He wanted to get it done quickly but soon discovered shopping in London was a much different proposition than it had been back home. Every day seemed to be market day here, filled with noisy and unpleasant people too. When he'd smile and nod, many passersby would give him a frosty glare or pretend they didn't see him.

He quickly made his way from cart to cart in the open air, and when they proved useless, tried the basement shops filled with used clothing. The chattering salesclerks and piles of clothing didn't penetrate the fog of his thoughts.

He wished he could have read the letter the police got about Jack Marrill. Had the valet really written it? Why? It seemed as if evidence had been invented to make Jack look guilty of killing his family members…but was it part of a greater plan or just some whim of an ex-servant?

"Sir? This would look best with your bright sort of hair."

"No, thank you kindly," he said to the wheedling and coaxing merchant. How could anyone stand this much attention?

In a shop full of just gentlemen's hats, he found a black homburg. No more flat caps for him, he thought, but never the straw boater with the red ribbon. No need to look like a dandified fool.

Back on the sidewalk, he thought about going back to Mrs. Jack Marrill's house and finding a servant other than the cook to speak to. Never mind what Patrick said, Colm needed to dig deeper.

Who would have it in for all those Marrills—and now the coming baby as well?

The notes he'd read at Patrick's house had shown that, before the series of tragedies, the Marrills had been a family filled with men who enjoyed their power. Quade's father and uncle had seemed close. He'd gotten that impression from a transcript taken from an interview with the uncle, Jeremiah Marrill, which had been included in the folder when the police interviewed him after his son Cyril's murder.

"We might squabble, yet when it comes to trouble, the family draws together," Jeremiah Marrill was quoted as saying.

The interviews also revealed that the two sets of cousins, all boys, had a few troublemakers. Was it normal for university students to be sent down from Oxford? There were many details in the files of what the boys had done, and the crimes seemed related to too much drink and free time, not to mention too high an opinion of their own worth.

Jack had seemed the worst culprit. He'd been dismissed permanently from university before he earned his degree, but there was no description of that final reason he had to leave. Something had happened, and the family lawyers had managed to stop the talk.

Whatever he'd done, his activity had to be something worse than breaking the windows of a tavern, which he'd accomplished during his first term.

Losing a chance at education wasn't worth any sort of fun Colm knew of, but he was a stodgy constable at heart. The Marrill boys and their cousins, except for Quade, acted like farmhands at the end of a long harvest season. The only difference was that a Marrill's revelry lasted for months at a time, not a single day every few seasons. Just as the markets in London were always open and crammed with goods, the gentlemen were always ready to act like fools.

That gentleman's club, for instance. Colm still felt amazed when he thought of the idiots who hung about that place. Only the older gent, Mr. Grace, had seemed a civil sort, and he wasn't truly a member.

After only a half hour's shopping, Colm bought two suits and some formal evening garb. He went to the fancy tailor only two streets away from Mr. Marrill's apartment, which was a mistake. The skinny tailor with the gold-rimmed spectacles made it clear he didn't like working on a lesser being's wardrobe.

Colm's sister had measured and sewn his clothes before he'd joined the constables, so he was used to standing still and being pricked by needles. But those sessions had been accompanied by laughter and cups of tea and teasing. This tailor didn't turn down his business, though apparently he didn't like Irishmen or the ready-made clothing that had obviously been purchased used, or borrowed from a long-legged giant.

Colm soon gave up trying to engage the man in conversation. He stood on the chintz-covered platform and was measured in silence. At least the man was swift about it.

Colm bought some more handkerchiefs and made his way back to the apartment carrying a few wrapped parcels, with his old boots in a burlap sack. He wore new brogues. His boots might not be right for city wear, but lighter shoes felt too flimsy for his feet. The rest of his purchases would be delivered, of course. No one seemed to buy and carry anything in the city.

London still struck him as too crowded, too exotic, as well as too poor and too rich at the same time. He wondered if he'd get entirely at ease with the noise and hurry of the place and didn't think such a thing was possible.

When he got back to the apartment, he had to pull out his keys and was glad to note both locks had been engaged. Upstairs, the skinny German with the oddly round face was alone in the parlor.

"Anything to report? Did the police come by?"

Dorman rose to his feet and gave Colm a pitying look. "No to both your questions. Except to that first, I might say Marrill is a disagreeable hermit. I pity you having to live with him."

Colm laughed and walked with the man to the front door. "Leave him to his work and he's fine."

"Yes, but he hunted for you and was not best pleased that I had no notion where you were gone to. He demanded very rudely to know when you'd be back. I said in this day and age, we have no owners and any man might go where he wished and not answer to anyone."

"You're a socialist?" Colm asked with interest. Following Mr. Marrill one day, he'd seen one of those standing on a box, bellowing about workers' rights, in Hyde Park.

"Indeed. It will be the working man's world someday. No more of the insolent aristocrats telling us what to do."

"You'd hardly call Mr. Marrill high and mighty aristocracy."

The German grunted. "I would. That unpleasant, insolent man."

Colm felt a flash of temper. He actually had to pause a moment before he could speak to the German in a normal voice. "I'll see you in a fortnight, then?"

The German grabbed his overcoat and shoved his arms into it. "Yes, I shall return. Perhaps by then, they'll have sorted out the threat to the man."

"What do you know of a threat?" He tried to sound interested not eager or suspicious.

"As much as you, I'd suppose."

Colm said, "Do you think anyone is sorting it out?"

"The police, yes? Others, perhaps? But I would think Marrill's father would wish to know as well."

Dorman knew more details than he'd get from Marrill. Colm guessed, "You went to the office and read the papers about the case?"

The German hesitated, then nodded. "Yes, yes, I read."

Colm liked the man better for taking the time to find out about the man he'd been sent to guard even if only on rare occasions.

"There are some odd facts, hey? And I ask you, do you suppose our own Mr. Patrick Kelly is looking into it?" Dorman demanded.

Well, now, Colm wondered if perhaps his replacement's curiosity was a bit too strong. Was this intrusive manner what made Marrill grow sullen?

Colm said, "I don't know. Why are you interested in the case?"

"Ach, why not? I don't know why I ask you about what is happening. Mr. Patrick Kelly wouldn't tell you or me if he were doing that." He snatched up his hat and regarded Colm a moment. "Though you are a relation? Kelly, also?"

"I only recently met him."

"You should know that American tries to be a mystery or worse."

"Really?" Colm hazarded a guess about Dorman's cryptic warning. "Do you think Patrick Kelly might lie to us?"

"I cannot answer to what he does, because I work alone. Most of my work is following so-called ladies and gentlemen who are fornicating with anyone they're not married to. Despicable fools."

"I'm guessing you grew to dislike the rich because of their infidelities?"

"There are many reasons. I'm going now." He left the apartment without saying goodbye. Another bad-tempered, abrupt man—perhaps it was an effect of London. Too many people living too close together, although Colm knew, despite all those anti-London thoughts, he was more comfortable in the city than he had been at first.

He went to his room and placed all the purchases in a line on the bed to gloat a little. He was glad to have the presentable clothes so he might not look shabby as he went out with Mr. Marrill. Because after what he learned today, he would be damned if he'd leave the man alone for a second.

An irritated voice broke in on his thoughts. "Where the hell have you been?"

Perhaps this was why the German described Marrill as an ill-tempered idiot. Colm felt like laughing. And would his employer be insulted if he chucked him under the chin the way one might attempt to cajole a snarling child?

He settled for an exaggerated tip of his hat. "Even Irish lackies get a day off now and then."

"Oh. Oh, ah. Yes. Of course you must have time for yourself." Marrill stood in the doorway and stared at him for a long minute. "My apologies." He nodded and clumped off, carefully closing the door to Colm's room behind him.

Such a strange man. Seeing him again brought back the bottomless lust. Colm wanted to chase after him.

Colm could only imagine what would happen if he touched Marrill at long last. Even the thought of murder and mayhem and the threat from some letter writer wasn't enough to dispel Colm's haze of desire.

Only a few minutes back in the apartment and he felt scalded to the bone with pure lust. His blood pumped harder just thinking of following him down the hall into his bedroom and…

Colm groaned. He pushed the brown-paper-wrapped purchases off the bed and lay down, willing himself into some sort of calm. It didn't work. Restless as he'd ever been on a spring day, he heaved himself up to go to the kitchen in search of food.

Until he found the valet or the truth or both, he and Mr. Marrill would be like the Siamese twins who'd been such a sensation in America. The thought of being so close to Quade that they'd be joined together was comical, intriguing, and unsettling.

***

Quade had come out to forage for food at about ten a.m. and had discovered that Kelly was not in the flat. But where had he gone? And forever? Perhaps he'd left the position without notice, as servants often had in his family's home. The German replacement guard apparently didn't know or care, though he ventured to say that perhaps Kelly had been recalled to the office to work on another project. He implied that any other assignment would be an improvement.

Quade, trying not to plead, had asked Dorman, "Surely you saw him leave?"

The German had just shrugged and eyed him with dislike. Quade had considered going to Kelly's room to see if his things had been taken but didn't want to discover an abandoned bed, the few items gone.

And then Kelly had reappeared in his apartment as cool as you please. And why not? He'd only taken the day off. People did that all the time. Not every person who went out alone was found later smashed over the head or dead in the woods.

Once he'd calmed down, Marrill went straight back to work, to the books he'd been unable to concentrate on for the entire day. Work, yes. These words. He'd have to go to the Lincoln's Inn library later, perhaps tomorrow, to make sure the author hadn't made a mistake in his citations.

And he'd waited for results long enough, and it had been more than long enough since he'd last gotten a straight answer from his father.

He listened to the sounds of Kelly moving around the kitchen, singing under his breath. Lately Marrill had been teaching himself Irish Gaelic, and the song seemed to be about a girl who'd lost two lovers at sea.

Now that Kelly was back, he felt like a fool. A relieved and happy idiot who should know better. He would root out this bizarre interest in Kelly. After all, he'd done something similar in the past: he'd developed feelings, then soon understood that it would be bad to continue to act on them. Because of his unrequited attachment to Bentham, Quade had left his work at Cambridge, and after a brief period of discomfort, life had returned to normal. He could tame himself again.

Bad enough that he should grow to care for another man—at least Bentham had been of background similar to his own. This person was basically a badly educated member of the servant class. So terribly inappropriate to cultivate a friendship with such a person, he could imagine his father and older brothers saying. And as for anything more than friendship, that wouldn't bear discussion or thought.

Although, no, Jack would laugh and say something about seizing whatever opportunity offers.

Jack wouldn't have cared a fig for what the world thought. He was what they called a lusty lad and had gotten into more than one scrape. There was one incident that had been so serious, Quade heard vague rumors at school, though what had occurred never became clear. It had involved a girl, one of Quade's classmates told him. Hardly surprising, since nearly every rumor at school about every man, young or old, involved a girl.

His own family hadn't spoken of the peccadillos of the Marrill boys, but there had been an indulgent understanding, which annoyed Quade.

Quade once met his uncle Jeremiah in a bookstore near the Strand. His uncle had said something sneering about a dull scholar's life, calling him a monk.

He told his uncle that no matter what the older man thought of Quade's attempt to enter a profession the family considered dull or ungentlemanly, at least he didn't behave like an overbearing idiot with women.

Even today, recalling Jeremiah's response could make him cringe.

Quade should have been working on gathering his notes for the next day's visit to the library, but instead he was holding a silent argument with his dead uncle, reliving an ancient fight that had lasted two minutes.

He and his uncle had bumped into each other near the entrance to the bookshop and only moved as far as the philosophy section for their brief, whispered conversation—and even at the time, that had struck Quade as quite appropriate that they'd hissed at each other in front of Epicurious's works.

When Quade pointed out that his cousins' and brothers' antics should carry some sort of consequences, Jeremiah had called him a faint-hearted poltroon.

"Every lad should sow oats. I don't trust the mind of a man who doesn't." His uncle had obviously aimed that barb at bookish Quade.

Quade had retorted that acting like an overheated idiot was hardly the sign of a sound mind. Within a few minutes, his uncle raged in that shouting whisper that carried so well and Quade had only listened. Puritanical souls shriveled, his uncle said, and only cared to pursue ridiculous causes against their more lively citizens.

Soon after that, Jeremiah had stormed out of the shop. That was the last time Quade had spoken to his uncle, who died only a few days later.

Too much emotion, too much oat sowing, and a man could keel over, Quade pointed out to the imaginary version of his dead relation.

And what was Quade doing instead? Staring unseeing down at a book about torts and holding a silent argument with his dead uncle. Perhaps his mind wasn't so settled. Time to work or go for an invigorating walk. He smiled as he thought of his keeper, Colm Kelly, stalking along behind if he went to Hyde Park.

Instead, he closed his door to finish writing the notes and gathering questions to ask about his own family. He would ignore the whole of his silliness—the attraction to an unsuitable person. He'd done it before and could again. Still, he found he listened for the creak of floorboards, and his heart lightened when the sound of Kelly's singing reached him.

CHAPTER SIX

The next morning, Quade was up early, even before his so-called valet. He managed to scrape together his own toast and cheese for breakfast. He paused as he loaded a tray. Should he prepare food for Kelly? Even the thought seemed odd. Work beckoned, and he was glad to answer.

He carried his food into the study and settled into the chair behind the battered desk. Yes, life was easier when one worked. The suspicious deaths, the threats, they lingered, and he would return to pursuing them. God knew a little normalcy, that is, using the part of the mind that only concentrated on thought without careening fear or other animal emotions, was such a relief.

He finished his notes on a chapter and rubbed his eyes.

A moment later, the air around him changed. Was it a shadow or a footstep? He could sense when Kelly came into the room now. Perhaps he was attuned to some faint scent he didn't consciously recognize, a scent that made him far too eager to smile and relax.

Quade didn't look up from the book.

"Did you have a good day out?" he asked and turned the page.

"Sure." Kelly moved closer.

Quade's shoulders itched, and his skin seemed too sensitive. What if Kelly moved just a bit closer? If he laid a hand on his shoulder. The servant stood, the master sat as it always was, but Quade wasn't the superior to the man looming over him. And what sort of silliness was this? Again, so much awareness and the hunger for touch that he could ignore until he came near Colm Kelly.

Perhaps he could dismiss him or beg for whoever had hired him to let him go. Alternatively, he considered twisting in his chair, beckoning him close for a kiss. Neither seemed to be a reasonable man's solution to a problem that wasn't a true problem. Of course not. This attraction could be ignored. A sensible man would go back to work instead of inventing complications to his life.

Instead, he raised his eyes and saw Colm Kelly, dressed in new clothes that fit him. His hair had been brushed. He'd gotten a shave and looked neat, respectable, and more appealing than any man Quade had ever seen in his life. When he smiled at Quade, showing that slightly crooked crease in his cheek and the white of that bottom tooth… When had Quade memorized each detail and grown so aware of them all? He didn't want this. He couldn't seem to stop.

"What do you want?" he snapped.

"Ha. I heard you were in a bad mood. Turns out to be true."

Quade gave up the pretense of reading and placed the book on the stack by his chair. He reflected that even as the unwelcome tension grew, something inside eased now that Kelly was back in the apartment. When one part of him relaxed and another woke up, he'd do best to ignore the second.

He said, "If you got your information from your replacement, the pumpkinheaded Herr Dorman, he was hardly in a pleasant mood himself. He stomped around muttering about *verdampt* gentlemen who took time from more interesting work."

"He said this in front of you?"

"Quietly and in German, but I speak the language."

"Do you now. That's grand!"

"Oh come, no need to pretend amazement. You speak English and Irish after all. I speak English and German."

"And Latin and French, as I happen to know."

Quade looked Kelly up and down, pretending not to be searching out and memorizing more of those details: the way his unruly hair curled at his collar, and the upturned corners of his mouth.

"You look pleased with yourself. Did something interesting happen?" Quade waved at the tall-backed chair next to him. "Go ahead and sit. I'm getting a crick in my neck staring up at you."

Kelly didn't protest. He moved the books onto the floor, then slumped down onto the seat in a most informal posture. "So you couldn't recall where I'd gone? Ach, Mr. Marrill, I told you day before yesterday I was taking a day off."

"Did you?" Quade shifted uncomfortably. That all his worry might have been created by his own inability to function whilst reading—that felt uncomfortably possible. "By any chance, when you spoke to me, was I working? I tend to focus closely when I work."

Kelly laughed. "You're admitting fault? And here I thought that you ignored me on purpose. Your brain is so caught in words, you can't even hear ones spoken outside your head?"

Caught in words. He liked that description. “Yes, it’s true. I don’t always listen, when my brain is engaged elsewhere,” he admitted.

“If I have something important to say, I’ll make sure you actually hear it.” Kelly looked and sounded solemn now, as if making an oath. “I wouldn’t leave you, not even for a day or an hour, without saying anything.”

Quade wanted to retort, *What does it matter to me if you go?* But he did care, and too much. He sat forward, resting his elbows on his knees. So much for ignoring that tense, overly alert part of himself. His mind and body were not going to allow that. It annoyed him so much, he decided to be reckless. “The other night. When I drank too much. I have a memory of trying to seduce you.”

Kelly’s back went straight, and he made a gurgling sound that might have been denial. His face flushed a startlingly deep red that was almost purple.

“Come now, even I must understand that look on your face. I shan’t badger you again,” Quade said quickly. “I only wish to say that I am sorry if I offended you.”

“Oh, not at all. I mean it was all right. I don’t mind,” Kelly said, with a kind of heartiness that Quade suspected was to cover embarrassment. Scundered—that had been the word. Kelly went on without looking at him. “That is to say, I’m not offended. I can’t say yes, of course, to anything because of what that… That sort of thing. That is I can’t, not really. Not in my future, you see.”

Fascinating to realize Kelly was at a loss for what to say. And he turned into a gushing broken waterspout of chatter. Quade raised his brows and waited for the flow to peter out. How interesting it was that Kelly was the awkward one for a change. Quade rather liked it.

When Kelly fell silent, he prodded, “You can’t do what, precisely?”

Kelly shook his head as if he were trying to drive off an annoying insect.

Quade waited for a time before repeating, “What is it that you can’t do?”

Kelly drew in a long, audible breath and released it before he spoke again. “I was that close to losing everything, even my life, and I hadn’t even done anything. And I am hoping to leave it behind, if you understand. *It*’s not what I want for myself.”

There was an *It* in the room with them, taking up space that Quade needed to think and breathe properly.

It was attraction, desire, hunger, yearning.

Quade snorted. "I understand, yes. One wishes one could shut off such nonsense entirely."

Even as he spoke, he wondered if he lied to them both. He'd so rarely experienced passion, it intrigued him to feel it quickening in his body and mind.

He'd never spoken of this with anyone, and it should have been dismaying to reveal so much of himself, but when he looked at Kelly, he felt almost compelled to explain himself, a compulsion almost as strong as the primitive urge to touch him.

He examined the blunt fingers of Kelly's hands, his knuckles, which showed signs of past fights. His skin carried small white scars that Quade wanted to caress, kiss, and even bite. Kelly's hands rested on his trousers, and that meant Quade's gaze moved in an unfortunate direction.

He forced himself to look into Kelly's face as he spoke. "I had left desire. I had shut down all that sort of thought of it, except now and again, when part of me went out of my control, if you understand…"

Kelly must have understood, because his blush deepened. His ears were positively scarlet.

Quade said, "There are the standard dreary episodes in my sleep. Otherwise, I have been content."

"Oh." Kelly's face remained blank with astonishment. Or perhaps he registered dismay and nothing more.

Quade barged ahead anyway, straight into unknown territory. He and Bentham had never spoken of what they did together. In the past, Quade had even tried not to think of it. But something had changed in him lately. Perhaps he'd learned that death hits so easily — his uncle, his cousins, his brothers dead and gone—avoiding risks such as this seemed silly. He was more afraid of death and less afraid of life, and some of that had to do with Kelly's appearance. Granted, much of the change came from all those men and boys in his family keeling over.

It made him try to listen to their lost voices more closely. And hadn't Quade asked for his dead brother's advice on the day of the funeral? He knew what Jack would say: carpe diem. Jack would seize whatever he could, after all.

Quade said, "When you came into my pleasant existence, you woke me up as surely as if you'd reached over and shaken me in the middle of the night. Now I'm unsettled and have trouble concentrating."

"Oh," Kelly said again. He cleared his throat. "And why is that?"

"I want you."

Kelly's eyes widened, and he jerked, thumping the back of the chair in evident alarm.

"Oh, pray be still. I won't do anything to you. We shall stay away from anything that could be construed as physical affection. No touching."

Kelly nodded vigorously. "No touching. No."

Quade wasn't sure if he wanted to laugh or snarl at the man's response. "You needn't be so obvious about your revulsion. What I'm saying is hardly a surprise to you. And do recall your own words to me about what happened to you in your village because of your own…because you have had the same sort of urges. Otherwise, I would most definitely have held my peace." He hesitated. Could he have misunderstood Kelly's story? "At any rate, I can see by your reaction that the topic is closed."

A surge of panic hit Quade. His eagerness to share suddenly seemed stupid. "But allow me to make it very clear that should you feel the need to tell the world about me, I—"

"See here, I would never do such a thing."

Quade raised a hand. "I'm sorry. I know that you are discreet and professional in your duties. I am sure you'd never repeat any of the private matters you encounter."

But Kelly, the mildest of men, had barged up from his chair and began pacing. His shoes, not boots, thumped hard on bare wood.

"You and I." He stopped and glared at Quade, the fire in those eyes rather startling. He might not often show temper but that didn't mean he didn't feel it.

"Calm yourself, I know. There is no you and me," Quade said. "I understand perfectly."

"You are just so right. I am a not going to allow private matters that concern no one ruin my life again. I am not going to give in. D'ye hear me?"

Before Quade could decide if he should apologize or make some sort of humorous response, Kelly stormed from the room—an astonishing change from his usual manner. Quade recalled what a friend once said: a mild man with a long fuse exploded harder than most.

Prodding at a man's weakness shamed Quade a little. And yet there was a piece of himself that fumed because he'd been rejected.

Quade picked up the book, then put it down again abruptly when he understood. Kelly wasn't merely upset with him and Quade's unnatural lust. Kelly's own desire angered him. Quade wanted to crow. Kelly admitted attraction. Kelly wanted him so much that his astoundingly strong calm had cracked. But what would he do? Quade wouldn't blame him if he left.

He understood something new about himself as well. He'd rather have Colm angry and untouchable in his apartment than no Colm at all. He'd always craved solitude; now it seemed the height of dreariness.

An hour passed, during which Quade tried to work but couldn't concentrate. He started and dropped his pen when Kelly appeared in the doorway with tea.

"Oh, good." Quade heaved a loud sigh of relief, and Kelly's mouth twitched. A suppressed smile would be excellent.

"You don't have to feed or water me." Quade repeated his rote response to the offering. He had never been one to be uplifted by formal ritual, but he liked this pattern very much.

But Kelly didn't stick to the catechism, only mumbling, "Hmm."

Quade reached for the tea, and Kelly moved to the door.

"I beg your pardon for causing you discomfort earlier," Quade said in a rush. He wasn't used to apologizing but discovered it was far easier than admitting out loud that he wanted to fuck a man.

Colm clomped back and sat in the chair near him. "You don't owe me an apology."

"Very well, I regret your discomfort. Will that do? One can see that you're unhappy. Your usual manner is far less volatile."

"Don't I know it." He sighed and scrubbed at his face, leaving it pink.

"I do wish you'd tell me why you're upset."

"There is not much to say. Changes have caught up with me."

"Oh?" Would the man require a prompting every few seconds? Quade supposed he must learn patience. "What do you mean?"

"I have always known who I was and my place in the world. I'm Mr. and Mrs. Kelly's son, brother to five, a good lawn bowler, and the local guard. Though it was the only life I knew, I understood I'd been blessed. And then I put my own foot in it by telling someone those secrets that are best kept…secret. That life I loved is gone for me." He got up and began pacing again. "Truly, you do not mind if I speak of this?"

"Damnation, Kelly. Didn't I say as much? I've practically begged you to tell me."

Kelly smiled. "Thank you."

God, that smile seemed made of something powerful. With each passing minute, Quade, who'd never cared for emotion, grew direly interested in this man's feelings.

"The person I thought was my best friend is my worst enemy. The family I love…" His thick voice trailed off. "I have no notion where I belong."

Quade spoke around the lump in his own throat. "Tell me more."

Kelly shook his head. "No, thank you, but I'd rather have a kick up the arse than speak of this, Mr. Marrill." A ghost of the old jaunty smile appeared. "I'd have thought you'd be just the gent to do the job. The kicking, I mean."

"One hears that it is best to talk about what—"

"I don't care to indulge in a fit of the sulks, Mr. Marrill. No need to let all these—these doldrums rule my life."

How odd to hear that when, for the first time he could recall, Quade allowed emotion to be his guiding force. When Colm had brought the photograph of his brothers and had tried to coax him to speak of them, Quade had had nothing to say. He certainly had no right to force anyone else to choke out words.

Quade rose from his chair.

"What are you doing?" Kelly sounded wary. He rose to his feet, hands loose at his sides as if ready to respond to whatever Quade had in mind.

Quade should have said the truth, that if the conversation was done, he wanted to get ready for his walk to the library. Instead, he tilted his head to the side and narrowed his eyes. "Can't a man get up in his own house and not face questioning?"

Kelly's face relaxed into a smile. "Now you sound more yourself."

"An ill-tempered, oblivious fool," Quade said.

"No, sir! Not at all." Kelly rocked on his heels.

Quade walked to the door, tired of passion already. So much for that attempt…and then suddenly, hands were on his shoulders, gripping him, turning him around.

They stared at each other for a long moment, those eyes more green than gray now, and filled with perplexed hunger. Quade forgot to breathe. Kelly stepped close slowly and kissed him.

The shocking and fierce heat of Kelly's mouth on his, the strong arms around his middle—his body immediately understood what he must do. His body issued urgent instructions: put arms around Kelly, pull him closer, part his lips and he could taste the kiss with all of his mouth, then twist his neck so the kiss might go deeper still. Kelly's lips were full and soft on his even as their exploration grew more intense.

Kelly's moan was muffled into his mouth and could have been a complaint, but no, because Kelly pushed him. His back thumped against the door. They breathed hard and fast until they came together for a kiss, no fumbling but perfect and deep immediately.

Quade reached up and shoved his fingers through Kelly's hair, something he'd longed to do for days. The curls felt softer than he'd guessed. He closed his eyes as they sank into another long kiss, and refused to allow regret to cloud the best physical experience of his life.

CHAPTER SEVEN

Colm didn't want this. Why the hell had he gone after Marrill? The tension had curled so tight in him, it had gone off like a spring inside an exploding mechanism.

Now he had wrapped himself up in Marrill. He must let go. This was a terrible idea.

But the smell he'd memorized drenched him now, and he needed to get closer and soak up all the heat and taste of the man he could. *A dhia*, this was better than anything he'd imagined, and when it came to matters of touching Quade Marrill, he had a rich imagination.

Just one more kiss. Just the chance to run his hands over the skin under the fine wool jacket and silk-backed waistcoat. Oh, his Mr. Marrill was thin but warm, and sleeker than the silk. Colm wanted to melt into him, wax to the fire in that fierce, slender body. He pressed closer, his erection pushing against Marrill's because they were such a perfect height for each other to touch and enjoy. Just what he'd needed for all the long nights and days waiting for this moment.

But nothing more than this. Just once. Only this next kiss and then he'd stop. Colm startled and huffed a groan when the hands exploring his back slipped down under his trousers and smalls to grab his rear, hold him tight. Now they truly couldn't get closer to each other. Hard cock to hard cock. No air between them, only layers of useless cloth. Why did they need to wear all the layers of clothes in these private rooms?

The confusion of thoughts circled around to a rebuke: *Stop. All right, just this. One more kiss, then I'll stop.* He had trouble drawing breath and couldn't stop panting. Much more of this touch and he'd go too far. He'd lose his mind.

And then he did lose it entirely, because Marrill moved to the side and thrust his hand down the front of Colm's trousers.

His clever fingers immediately found their goal, tightening around Colm's cock, squeezing and sliding, clutching the part of him that begged for touch. He cried out and shoved up into the fist that held him with such assurance and power and moved as if he could read what Colm needed, just harder. The rough cotton of his own drawers scraped the end of his penis while Marrill worked him up and down.

He probably should return the favor, but he couldn't do more than wiggle in the man's firm, hot grip.

He pressed his mouth to the fine weave of Marrill's jacket so his scream emerged as a hoarse growl as the man's touch brought him to the edge and then over.

Colm trembled. Thank goodness Marrill let him slump close for a moment, because he'd have slid to the floor without that support.

Marrill's fast breathing rocked him for a few heartbeats, but the solid form under Colm, restless and writhing, brought him back. Colm sank to his knees and let his cheek rest against Marrill's cock, or rather the wool of his trousers. Did he have the courage to unbutton and discover what he wanted? He moved his cheek back and forth, then pressed his mouth to the fabric and warmed it with his breath and his hand.

Marrill laid his hand flat between Colm's face and his cock. "No," he said.

"Why not?" Colm opened his eyes and tilted his head back. From this angle, Marrill was rather magnificent. His angular face, stern mouth, and dark eyes under furrowed brows gave him the look of an angry warrior.

"You said you didn't want this. Less than a half hour ago." He sounded as fierce and angry as he looked. "I have no desire to prey upon you for my pleasure."

"I'm not your victim." Colm climbed to his feet.

The mood of recklessness that had seized him had been destroyed by talk. He could only do this sort of…activity if he didn't think very much. And now the dreary thoughts came back, but he must not drag Marrill with him. "I don't blame you for anything."

"Are you unhappy, though? About what occurred just now?"

At the moment, he'd gone from elated to a tired sense of shame, even stronger than he'd felt the times he'd touched Barnaby back home. But why were they talking? He longed to go back to that blissful state without thought, only sensation. This was endlessly bleak.

"I'm not interested in making a song and dance of it, sir. I'll be fine." He would be, he always was, and damn the Englishman for appearing to stare into the center of him.

"Then you are. Unhappy, I mean." Marrill shook his head. "I don't want to drive you out of here. I've gotten used to having you here under my roof."

The statement touched Colm more than it should.

"I shall have to go someday, you know." He attempted a smile. "And it'll be a grand day when I do, because then you'll have found the man who's been threatening or even killing your family." He walked over and sat on a chair, leaning to the side to remove a dispatch case and some papers from under his rear. He wasn't sure what would happen next, but he refused to run away. He only prayed that Marrill would want to discuss something other than what had just occurred.

And then he recalled he still hadn't said a thing about the damned dead bird. Was that because part of him still wondered if Quade had managed such a thing? He chewed on his lip and decided any suspicion was nonsense. And if that was merely hope on his part…no. It surely had to be nonsense.

He would do his job now.

He asked, "Did the police come by yesterday?"

"No." Quade's measuring squint directed at Colm was adorable. "Why would they?"

"A thing happened at your brother's widow's house."

"Oh? A thing? What does that mean?"

Colm decided to tell only the barest outline of the story of the bird and the note left with the corpse. He didn't mention any details, leaving out even the type of bird.

"Good God. How very peculiar." Marrill cocked his head to the side. "There have been no females endangered before now. And no threats. Why would anyone try to hurt or threaten Jack's wife?"

Colm spoke carefully, in case Marrill hadn't heard the news. "She is expecting a baby."

Marrill walked over and sat on a wooden chair next to Colm. He took the case and papers from Colm and absently tapped the papers on his thighs to bring them into order. He showed his emotion by tap-tapping them for almost a full two minutes.

"I am glad for her," he said at last. "And for my parents. I suppose that the police might come around to me to ask questions now."

"I wonder that they haven't." He cleared his throat. "Apparently the note is supposed to have come from you."

Quade just laughed. "That's absurd, and so you'll tell them, yes?"

Colm nodded. "Yes, indeed. You haven't been out of my sight." He felt his face grow hot, but Marrill didn't hear the cozy intimacy of the remark.

He said, "I'm grateful that you have warned me, though now I'll be unable to act surprised by the story of the dead bird or my sister-in-law's condition."

"Yes, you must tell the police you'd heard a whiff of the gossip already," Colm said. "That's why I didn't want to give you too many facts. Wouldn't look good if you repeated details known only by the murderer, or whoever sent it, or members of Mrs Marrill's household." He grinned and added, "Or an Irish ex-policeman who'd been asking a lot of questions."

Marrill studied him a long moment, a glowing look on his face. Just as Colm began to wonder if perhaps that warm expression meant they'd return to kissing and such, Marrill asked, "You really do believe I'm not a murderer? You said as much when you first walked into this apartment."

"Yes, I'm convinced you're not guilty." Colm picked a bit of fluff from the lapel of his new gray sackcloth coat. Maybe this sort of conversation was not an improvement, not if he talked about the files his cousin wanted to keep secret, that letter sent to the police.

Marrill said, "You know I didn't deliver the dead bird to my sister-in-law since you are a constant watchdog, but how are you so very sure I'm not the killer?"

"Murderers don't kiss like that," Colm said. Just saying those words embarrassed him. He must be bright red. He'd meant to be silly in order to change the subject. He didn't want to talk about the murders—and that was what they were—with Marrill until he understood the whole thing better.

"That's nonsense about kisses and you know it." Quade's smile was warm. "You're not the sort of man to be influenced by such things."

Colm wasn't sure that was true. Every part of him, body and mind, felt influenced by Quade's touch—a sobering thought that he'd wrapped himself tight in this man's life. Of course, at home, he'd grown used to investigating criminal activity carried out by people he knew. That was the way of life when one was a policeman of small villages.

"Come now. Tell me why you think I'm innocent," Quade barked, such a relief that he behaved in his normal manner. "Have you learned more from the police or your cousin than you've told me?"

"Getting to know you confirmed my suspicion that you're no murderer." He felt his face heat, once again, at the thought of getting to know Marrill.

But for once, the gentleman wasn't allowing his thoughts to turn lewd. Marrill folded his arms. "Please explain what you mean."

"All right. You could live with gold and velvet." Colm waved a finger in a circle to indicate the room and its piles of books. "Mind you, this apartment looks fine to me, but I've seen what passes for luxury over at Mr. Sloan's place, so I know the difference. Your da is rolling in riches, or so I hear, but you stay away from your family's money."

"Hasn't it occurred to you that my father didn't offer any of his wealth to me?"

"Yes, you and he are not the best of friends, but I know you get paid for your work, and you do have some money of your own inherited from your mam's father."

"You've been investigating me?"

"I read a file," Colm admitted. He didn't mention leafing through the bills.

"My grandfather's money is in a trust still. Ah well, I suppose I'm impressed by your research. But I can tell you are hiding something from me. Spit it out, Kelly. It's my life we're currently discussing."

Colm looked down at the lapels of his jacket rather than meet Marrill's glare. He was hiding the fact of the other letter sent to the police, but surely his gentleman couldn't see that in him? When had Colm's face become so easy to read?

"You're right. First of all, it's a bit more than instinct that tells me you're not the murderer."

"And you'll tell me?" Marrill was pleading, and that was more than Colm could bear.

"Yes, of course. The way I thought was this. From what I understand, the deaths might be connected. Why would anyone kill the members of one family? We already talked about money. So many years of planning such a careful crime could be madness, perhaps. Does insanity run in your family?"

Marrill shook his head. "No. Or rather, I am considered the eccentric son…" His voice trailed off. He cleared his throat. "That was my role when there were more of us."

Colm considered moving closer to him, to at least lay a consoling hand on his shoulder, but he wasn't sure if his touch would be welcomed. He straightened in his chair and put his hands on his knees. "To continue, if we rule out madness, and we shall, I think it more likely the deaths might be to make sure fewer people share the family fortune. Each man or boy killed means more money back into a big pot. So d'you see? Why, if profit is the reason for the deaths, you, Mr. Marrill, don't fit that picture of a killer. You don't care that much about wealth. That is to say, riches don't seem to matter much to you. And yes, I could see that the minute I walked in. Take away that reason to kill, and what do we have? For a man such as yourself? Not very much, I believe."

"Yes, I have thought about this as well. And I mean there is…my father," Marrill said slowly. "But that makes no sense. If he is guilty, why would he hire you? And why would he kill his own sons? Why? My grandfather's money surely couldn't be worth so much death."

Confusion filled his voice, and Colm hated the devastated look on Marrill's face.

"And you haven't wondered about your da? He might have insisted you have a guard so he'd have a way to prove he cared for your safety even as he went after you somehow."

Marrill wrinkled his nose. "I suppose I strike you as a fool. I think I really did believe my father had to be innocent."

And he spoke as if that belief were dead. But a second later, Marrill shook his head. "No, no. I still can't believe it of him. Your arguments in my favor work when applied to him as well. He's not prone to strong emotion and is hardly a madman. He has never spoken of money troubles. And these are his own family members, his own sons, who've died."

For a moment, Colm again saw the mask of hatred that members of his own family had worn that night he'd been driven from his village. Family didn't mean safety.

Marrill gave a frustrated sigh and shook his head. "No," he said as if arguing with himself. "I have other ideas."

God, Colm again wished he could tell him about the letter and the rest, but he had to stay true to his promise to his cousin at least for a little while longer. At least until they found that damned Pennick the valet.

Colm broke the silence with babble, hoping to make their talk seem nothing more than an exercise or a game, or, better still, hoping to change the subject. "Of course, I could be wrong that you're indifferent to money. I imagine you'd buy more heavy law books, the more obscure the better. Or build a bigger library? Have you seen Mr. Sloan's library? I never knew such a thing existed."

Marrill's throat worked as he swallowed. "I haven't," he said at last.

"Do you know Sloan? Seems like this London is vast, but I'm told it's more like a village for you wealthy folk."

"You did an awful lot of reading the last few days, didn't you, Kelly."

"That I have, but I'm not speaking of my reading. But do you know Sloan?"

"No." He showed Colm his rare smile. "My family wouldn't associate with his because his background is rather murky and his foster father was the wrong sort of barrister."

"Why's his background murky?"

The good humor on Marrill's face vanished. "His family was murdered. Quite a sensational affair. Now I suppose that's one of the greatest differences between Sloan and myself—he couldn't have been a suspect since he was a small child at the time his family members died, and they died all at once in a very obvious, horrible scene."

"What a dreadful story." Colm wondered if Patrick knew the details of Sloan's past. Probably, since he was an investigator and such very good friends with Mr. Sloan.

"Despite that scandalous story, my father is more impressed by him than I'd thought, since he went to Sloan to hire Patrick Kelly's services." Marrill wouldn't be distracted from the topic of his own family's misfortunes for long. "What have you learned about my family?"

As Colm tried to think of a way to speak of the letter sent to the police, without mentioning his cousin or the actual letter, Marrill distracted them both by rising from his chair and accidently kicking a pile of books over. As he leaned to restack them, he said, "And much as I've liked pretending that these deaths were all just an amazing coincidence, or that the police know what they're about, I've been thinking about it myself. For all that I would rather finish editing this book about tort reform, I must find answers."

"Well." Time to bring out poor Jack. "There is a theory. I happen to know that it's been suggested that the guilty party was your recently deceased brother, God rest his soul. Grant you, it came from an unreliable source."

"Jack?" Marrill straightened. "Why would anyone think he'd be responsible?"

That confirmed Marrill hadn't heard about the letter. Alas, if Colm told him about the letter and Patrick found out, Patrick would pitch Colm out on his arse and deservedly so.

Colm picked through the thoughts he'd gathered from research he'd done on the Marrill family—basic history and nothing more.

Hesitantly, Colm said, "Your brother Jack was ambitious. He married for money, yes?"

"That was true. He had more expensive tastes than I or my father. But he was hardly a monster and quite fond of his wife, Mary, and she adored him. And he got his money with her. No need for our family's fortune." He paused and bit the edge of his fingernail, and in an angry tone as if arguing with someone, said, "But, yes, I know! Some men never feel they have enough money."

"I'd understood he'd do what he could to succeed. And there had been some accusations leveled against him when he was younger."

"Nonsense." Marrill dropped back into the chair.

Colm was about to mention the jilted fiancée of a friend or the broken windows at the college, but Marrill's face had grown stormy again. For a man who claimed to be distant from his family, he did seem prone to defending them. Colm liked him even better for that.

"His youthful idiocy hardly makes him a murderer." Marrill's voice was icy. "I don't see Jack as some sort of Macbeth, slaying those who stand between him and a fortune."

"Though it's an explanation," Colm said.

"But he died. Like the others, he's gone. And I'm still alive." Quade tilted his head back and stared at the ceiling, wearing that devastated look again, the one that made Colm want to shove out walls and kick down doors to make the world a place that wouldn't suffocate his Mr. Marrill.

But he knew Marrill would rather hear the truth, or as much as Colm could offer. "The theory might be that he was out to kill all between him and a fortune, and before he got to you, he was stung by a bee."

Marrill shifted his attention from the ceiling to Colm. "Bah. Nonsense."

"If that version were true, you'd no longer be in danger and the whole nightmare would be over. And that bird sent along was just…" Colm shrugged, unable to say what the hell was the purpose of the bird. "But you agree that Jack Marrill was an ambitious man, yes?"

"Jack," Marrill muttered. "Yes, all right, it is a theory. Ruthlessness runs in the Marrill blood."

He sounded sour, poor thing. And really, this wasn't going to help them discover the truth. Colm clapped his hands twice. "Come on. This sitting about is no good. Didn't you have to work on that book? Take a trip to the library?"

"Yes." Marrill rose to his feet. But he immediately collapsed in the chair again. "Do you know, I think I'd rather get answers. I have thought so since Jack's funeral, and now I must do more than sit about."

"Beg pardon? Isn't that why we'll visit the library?"

"Answers outside of a book or notes for once. I can't…I don't want to live with this cloud anymore. And with that damned bird and that note… At any rate, if there is finally more being done to find answers, the attention will shine on me. Don't deny it." Marrill rubbed his hand over his head, ruffling the straight locks into a mess.

"I shan't," Colm said. "I wonder why the police are not here to talk to you. They seemed to take the threat of the dead bird seriously." He suspected they were searching for the ex-valet. He hurriedly added, "What will you do? You might hire my cousin to do some hunting for answers. I believe he feels badly he hasn't done more."

"No. I don't think I trust a person who is as thick with my father as Patrick Kelly. I want to hire you."

"Me? Don't forget that, though I haven't met the man, I work for your da. And I don't know this city. The moment I open my mouth to ask questions and my accent comes out, I'll get no answers. No, no, I have a fine job keeping watch over your good self."

"You might leave Herr Dorman here with me."

Was it only a few days ago that Colm had tried to think of a way to flee Marrill's company? Not anymore. "I shan't go off beating the bushes for villains and leave you alone."

Marrill's face lightened again. "Very well, then! The answer is obvious, Mr. Kelly. We'll work together."

Colm tried to think of an argument against the plan. *That's not the way a professional goes about his work* would make Marrill laugh in his face. He'd lost that edge the moment he'd laid his needy hands on the gentleman. The only real reason to dislike the idea was it would likely get Colm in trouble with Patrick Kelly. That didn't seem nearly as important as finding answers for Marrill.

He nodded. "All right. You come with me. You know the finer points of law, don't you? You'd be the one to get us into places. Like that club of yours. I'd say let's move along right away, but I suppose it's best to start with lists."

"Ah, and those are my bailiwick," Marrill said.

They settled on either side of his desk.

"Which list should we start? The places we must visit?"

And now Colm had a moment to fret. How would he say this with diplomacy? "I'd say let's start with the suspects," he said.

It was a relief when Marrill immediately piped up with "My father."

Marrill's scowl grew even more thunderous than it had minutes earlier. He stared down at the pen poised in his long fingers as if he hated it. "He is on my list. I left off my young cousin George. My mother." He looked up from the pen. "I started this list already, after Jack's funeral, and it seemed too…too…" He shook his head. "It's loathsome but necessary. I confirmed with that solicitor I met with the other day that my second cousin inherits from my father if I'm dead. And who is in line after him, I don't know. Do you know from the notes you read?"

"No. Do you have a will?"

He shook his head. "I've never felt the need. Should I die before my father, I have nothing but books, and they're going to the Lincoln's Inn, where, no doubt, they'll be tossed into the dustbin. I'll be dead and gone, so I won't care what goes to His Majesty, though I expect someone might be glad of my grandfather's ten thousand pounds. Ah, and I suppose the rest of my grandfather's inheritance is mine now as well, whatever it might be."

He'd spoken of ten thousand pounds and *the rest of it* as if he talked about sums hardly worth mention. It was more money than everyone in Colm's family had—all of them put together. Colm couldn't help a moment of gawping amazement before he continued, trying to keep his voice steady. "Did all four of you Marrill boys receive that amount? Ten thousand each?"

Marrill put down his pen and frowned thoughtfully. "I don't know. We don't speak of numbers or even of wealth—it is considered vulgar in my family."

"Do you have any idea?"

"The first of my brothers died while my grandfather was still alive, twelve years ago. It's true Joseph's demise made a larger pot for the rest of us, but that death couldn't have been inspired by wealth since we didn't know the terms of Grandfather's will." He sighed and rubbed his forehead. "And as to the question of whether my father has written me out of his will or who'd inherit should I die before my father, I don't know the first."

He leaned back in his chair and linked his hands behind his head as he stretched. "My father has made comments about my new role as his successor, so I expect he hasn't disinherited me. But about that second question, I know that if I died before my father, my second cousin, Wilbur Dunne, will gain my father's money and the lands. I discovered that the other day. See? I am an investigator like you."

"Then Wilbur Dunne must be a suspect."

"No, I doubt it. He's a mild-mannered fellow with funds of his own. Always chasing some enthusiasm or another. And as far as I can figure out, he spends more time outside of England than in it."

Colm tentatively asked, "Nothing will go to your mam?"

"My father is quite traditional. My mother would get a stipend, but not the lands or bulk of the estate."

That was something of a relief, Colm thought. He'd met more than one murderess in his time and hoped Quade's mother wasn't one. "I wonder if your father is mentioned in your remaining first cousin's will. I mean the young boy at school."

"Would a boy like George have a will? I don't, but, then again, after his father and brother died, he came into more wealth than I have."

"Indeed? Do you know how much?" Colm doubted it. He'd never met a man with less interest in money than Marrill. Then again, he'd never spent time with a man who didn't have to scrape and scrimp to get by.

Marrill lowered his arms and rubbed at an inkspot on his shirt cuff. "No, I don't. But botheration, that does explain something… I expect I must be in line for Cousin George's money."

"What does that explain?"

"They won't allow me be alone in the room with him, although perhaps that is due to other reasons."

It took Colm a moment to understand. Did that confirm that Marrill's family knew that he liked men? There was that word *deviant* used in the description of Marill. Colm wanted to ask but only said, "I'm sorry. That seems beyond—"

Marrill cut him off. "No, no need. I'd hardly know what to say to a ten-year-old." Of course he'd come back with a caustic response. Any sort of sympathy directed at Marrill ruffled the gentleman.

Colm knew better than to push. "Do you know where Wilbur Dunne lives?"

"I looked that up last time we were in the library. He's in London, not far from Mayfair. He isn't in the colonnade on The Quadrant on Regent Street, of course but not so far away." He waved a vague hand. "Pillars and balconies. Near the East India shop."

Colm had no notion what Marrill was talking about, but the hand wave and mention of pillars seemed to mean wealth. "That's a fine sort of address, isn't it?"

"Yes, as I said, he inherited money of his own. Though I admit I don't know the number and I can barely recall the man."

"I suppose we should start with your father and your family's estate in…" He tried to recall the name, but England consisted of Liverpool and London. "Where is it again?"

"Kent. Near Canterbury and the Stour."

"Is that Stour a town or a big church as well?"

"A river." Marrill drew in a long breath. "But my father and mother are not there. It's the end of the season, and they're here in London, I expect."

"Ah?" Colm tried not to show his astonishment.

Marrill must have seen. "Yes, I try to stay away from family."

"Stay away from family." Kelly repeated the words as if they were in a language he didn't know. "I can't go near mine, and you don't even want to talk to yours."

He must not have done a good job of hiding his surprise, for Marrill said, "Do recall who hired you. And I believe my father did it to keep me from murdering anyone else." He gave a mirthless laugh. "Which I suppose is better than hiring a murderer to push me in front of a train or stage some other such incident. I'd wondered about that at first, you know. But Patrick Kelly has a good reputation."

"I'm so very sorry," Colm said, then threw away the promise to his cousin not to share. "There was nothing in the notes that said you were a dangerous man. Are you sure that's what he believes? That you're a murderer?"

Marrill wrinkled his nose. "I am not certain about anything when it comes to my father."

"Don't you want to know? It's—" He stopped speaking when he realized this was stepping over the line.

"Go on."

"It's your da. I can't understand not making a try to see him." He didn't sound as bitter as he felt, thank the Lord. For here was

Colm, only hoping he might be able to speak to his mother face-to-face again someday. He chewed on his lower lip and brought himself away from thoughts of self-pity because he'd been banished.

And speaking of banishment, perhaps it was time to throw away all chances of future employment with Patrick. "If you won't talk to your family, we can start with mine. We might pay a call on my cousin Patrick."

He hadn't meant that moment, of course, but Marrill dropped the pen, covered the inkwell, and stood. "Let's go. At once."

CHAPTER EIGHT

Quade had been so intrigued by the thought of visiting Colm's relation that he didn't ask questions until they were inside the hack rolling toward the cousin's house. "A visit to your cousin should be quite interesting, but will he contribute to the information we need? He's been hired by my father, and I'd tried to get answers from that last fellow, the valet before you. He gave me blank looks and said he had no notion what I was talking about."

Several moments passed, and just as Quade supposed Kelly might also say something about having no notion, he spoke, sounding reluctant. "Patrick has some files that we might persuade him to let you see."

"Good," Quade said. "I say, is he your cousin with a noisy radiator and a book about etiquette?"

"That's the boy. He's the one who pays me too." Colm frowned, glanced at Quade, then looked away.

"Go on, what's the matter? I can see you've got something on your mind." Quade liked the fact that he could read Colm easily, whose emotions were displayed on his face more completely than anyone Quade knew. Or perhaps he only watched more carefully.

"I reckon Patrick saved my life. I don't want to repay him by annoying a client. But on the other hand, the most important hand, I mean, the truth is important." Colm muttered something that might have been, "And so are you."

"No reason the client, meaning my father, should find out that you've involved me. I certainly won't tell him. If your cousin Patrick wishes to inform my father, that's his business."

Colm's cousin lived in a terraced house near Grosvenor Square, much like the one Quade's family owned. It was better maintained, and the white stones had been scrubbed clean instead of allowing London's soot to turn them a mellow gray.

As Quade paid the driver, he looked up and down the street, and realized he recognized the location.

"Isn't this is Mr. Sloan's house? Your cousin must be close to him to live here," he said as they walked across the pavement to the elegant front door.

For some reason, that made Colm turn pink.

The butler opened the door almost immediately after they used the shiny brass knocker.

Quade's mood dipped. He wished he'd dressed better—at least changed his ink-spattered shirt or grabbed a hat that didn't have a frayed lining. The sight of a stout butler brought him straight back to his childhood, and he automatically straightened his back and shoulders. He'd never managed to adopt the skill of easy manner with servants, or anyone else, for that matter.

They were led to a waiting room and left to their own company among an extraordinary number of knickknacks and statuary. Rather than take a seat near the fire, Quade walked to a far corner to examine a four-foot-tall faun made of marble. It reminded him of an angel tombstone in the graveyard back in Kent, though the details were remarkably fine.

"This place is like some sort of palace, isn't it?" Colm whispered. "I get a mite scared coming here. Just walking up and down the street around here is like stepping into a fairy tale."

Quade's response had everything to do with his own past and nothing to do with fairy tales. And it wasn't fear, actually; it was the echo of past disappointments—the ones he'd been responsible for. Too quiet, too sour, too ill-at-ease with others, too unable to find an easy topic to converse upon. And now he was going to delve deep into a troubling past. It had to be done. He folded his arms and scowled at the grinning faun.

"We'll get what we need and be gone as soon as we can," Colm said.

Quade turned away from the statue. "Why are you reassuring me as if I were a recalcitrant child?"

"Aha!" Colm beamed at him. "That's it. I couldn't think what you resembled. That's the very thing. Recalcitrant means afraid?"

He had been grinding his teeth, but Colm's comment distracted him. "No, it doesn't. Let me make it clear, I'm not a small child. I am neither frightened nor truculent."

"That's the ticket, Mr. Marrill, just what I learned as a boy myself. When you're angry, there's no room for fear or the other."

The door opened before Quade could think of a suitable response to Colm's nonsense. He immediately discerned which man was Colm's cousin. The Kellys had the same crinkle at the corners of their eyes and mouths when they smiled. But Patrick Kelly's smile wasn't real.

He was obviously quite annoyed with Colm, but professional enough to shake hands with Quade. He even introduced him to his friend Mr. Sloan. Quade knew about the wealthy Sloan, though they'd never met.

The introduction apparently ended Patrick Kelly's patience. He turned to Quade. "Mr. Marrill, I beg your pardon, but I need to speak to my employee."

"That doesn't present a problem for me." Quade decided perhaps Colm was right, and, if it would help the situation, he'd be a sulky child. He walked over to a chair and sat.

"Perhaps you'd care to wait in the library?" Mr. Sloan had followed him and hovered near him now. "I understand you appreciate books."

"I'm staying here, in this room," Quade said. "But don't let me detain you from whatever you're doing. I know we've interrupted your day."

"I shall ring for tea," Mr. Sloan suggested.

"No, no. I don't need anything." Quade crossed his legs and rested his hands on one knee. "Thank you."

Mr. Sloan opened his mouth. Closed it again. He clearly wasn't used to being dismissed by a visitor in his own house.

"Very well. I shall return to my own work." Sloan actually smiled. "Perhaps we will meet again, Mr. Marrill? I do hope so."

Quade doubted that last statement, but gave credit to Sloan, who played polite very smoothly. This close, Sloan's dark hair shone and his smile showed white, even teeth—no wonder the well-dressed gentleman was so popular in society.

After Sloan left, Patrick gave Marrill a glance that was as exasperated as any he'd seen on Colm's face. The raised brows looked very similar.

Marrill pulled some folded manuscript pages of his latest job, the book about tort history, from his inside jacket pocket and held them up for the Kellys to see. "I'll read these," he said.

Patrick dragged Colm to the other side of the room.

Once they'd started in on a furious sotto voce conversation, Quade got up and wandered to the fireplace, still pretending to read. Patrick was too intent on Colm to pay any attention.

"What do you expect me to do?" Patrick asked in a low voice that was just sharp enough to carry. "Why did you bring him here?"

Colm's answer wasn't as easy to hear, but Quade caught the words: "Marrill file."

"I thought I made it clear that this is not what I hired you to do," Patrick said.

"You made that clear as glass, yes, indeed. Of course, even though I'm doing more work than was described in my job, I won't expect any extra in my pay packet." Colm's earnest reassurance was loud and probably designed to make Quade grin. Nice to see him pull that nonsensical misunderstanding routine on someone else.

It didn't help Patrick's anger. "You have no idea what else is going on in this matter, which, by the way, is none of your business." He pursed his lips and was silent for a long moment. "I think I made it clear when I gave you work that if you bungled an investigation, or disrupted my good relationship with the London police, or if you disturb our client, I will dismiss you immediately."

"Indeed, you did." Again, Colm showed easy acceptance.

Quade wanted to interrupt on his behalf, but remained silent to hear the rest. He didn't even dare put away the papers in case the rustle should alert Patrick Kelly to the fact that he was stalking them.

Patrick demanded, "Then why are you blundering around, possibly interrupting a case?"

Colm said, "I thought the police had abandoned any inquires since Jack Marrill had died. Am I wrong? Did that dead bird start them up again?"

"What makes you think I would share even that information? Damnation, Colm. You were with the police, don't you understand levels of command?"

Colm seemed to ignore him as he went on. "They've done naught about investigating the dead bird, so far as I can tell, although the police were hanging around the widow's place."

"Never mind that. I told you I'd take care of finding out what I could. Why the hell did you bring…" At that moment, Patrick glanced around and noticed Quade listening. Patrick's glower looked familiar. Quade had seen Colm's full lips gone thin in the past.

He began to speak again, but low enough that Quade couldn't hear.

Quade had had enough. He interrupted, calling out as he walked over to them, "I asked Colm Kelly to do some work for me. He's going to help me in my inquiries, and I beg of you, Mr. Kelly, do not attempt to convince me that what happens in the Marrill family is none of my business."

Patrick swore. He glared at Quade and then at Colm.

"Very well. If he works for you, he does not work for me."

Colm's mouth went into that thin line as well.

"What the devil does that mean?" Quade said.

"Nothing as far as you're concerned, except I beg pardon because you do know I've been retained to keep you under watch, Mr. Marrill. I shall have to hire someone else."

"No." Quade realized he'd shouted the word. He paused and tried again. "You do that and I'll have that new man arrested for trespassing. Your employee Mr. Kelly has done a good job keeping me from harm's way, even during difficult circumstances." Christ, had Colm made a report about that drunken episode in the club? "You should be lauding him for his work, not turning him out. And if I choose to hire him to do work that does not in any way conflict with your employment, I'd say it was really none of your business."

Patrick's eyebrows went up.

Silence fell, interrupted only by the soft tick of a clock somewhere in the room.

"It seems you're as passionate about him as he is about you."

Quade longed to demand what Patrick meant by that provocative statement. No, on second thought, he didn't want to know the answer. He walked back to his chair and sat again.

"Patrick, have pity on the gentleman. He's merely tired of hanging about waiting and waiting, and I'm not talking about myself now. It hasn't been easy, always being on edge in case there's another event," Colm said. He turned to Quade. "Begging your pardon for speaking for you, Mr. Marrill, but I want my employer to understand that waiting for an attack—ach, and one from an unknown enemy—creates what you might call tension."

Quade thought of the days of strain between the two of them, an awareness and tension so thick, he could wrap desire around himself like a blanket. *It hasn't been easy*, Colm said. *It* had nothing to do with any bloody outside enemy. "The next event" for Quade and Colm had nothing to do with murder.

He shifted in his chair as a flash of memory to the moment he finally got his hands and mouth on Colm on that thick cock of his, all hot and hard… His mouth watered at the thought of finally tasting him. This was hardly the time to indulge in lurid imagery, he reminded himself.

There was never a good time. Not during the long nights, so close to Colm.

Colm was still talking. "And then there's the question of how long will his da pay for protection?"

"For as long as it's needed," Patrick said.

Again, Quade dragged his mind away from thoughts of touching Colm. "That's absurd. When my father spoke to you, did he seem to know how long that would be?" Quade asked. "I think I ought to know if he indicated some understanding of the situation, don't you?"

"And you can't ask him?" Patrick asked.

Quade had in the past and intended to again, but he said, "I'm asking you."

Patrick's expressive brows went up again. "Very well. I agree that you have the right to know details that my *employee* has no right to share." He glared at Colm. "And you, Colm Kelly. I cannot believe you stood in this very house and solemnly promised not to share details of the letter sent to the police."

Silence fell.

Colm wore his best innocent smile. He blinked slowly. No that wasn't a smile, it was a smirk. And the blink was more like a wink for Quade than something directed at Patrick.

Quade suddenly understood the reference wasn't to the bird incident. This was something else. He asked, "Letter? What do you mean?"

Patrick shut his eyes and muttered something under his breath that might have been *oh shit.*

"I have no idea what you're referring to, Mr. Kelly," Quade said. "But I shall, very soon. I think you'll have to tell me."

A half hour later, they sat in the office. Colm admitted he had divulged the fact of the bird to Quade.

"But he didn't even tell me it was one of her pigeons from Mary's dovecote," Quade said resentfully. "It could have been a parrot or starling for all he said. Now I demand to know the rest."

Patrick refused to allow Quade to see the files, but he read aloud from them in his thick American accent. "These are from my notes. The letter was an anonymous note delivered to the police soon before Easter. It claimed Jack had murdered several members of your family, his brothers, uncle, and cousin. The letter was unsigned, but I suppose certain facts—no, before you ask, I don't know what they are—indicated it was from a servant who had been dismissed and nursed a grudge. Several of your brother's servants were interviewed very discreetly to discover if they knew of anyone who might dislike Marrill, and they all named a man called Pennick, a valet Jack Marrill had turned out without a reference. At any rate, whether or not it was Pennick, whoever sent the letter definitely accused Jack of murder."

Quade's stomach dipped and contracted with a familiar squeeze of helpless rage. *Murder*. The word had been spoken aloud, had been used by the police. Why hadn't anyone told him? Why did they speak of murder with his family's servants and not him?

He squeezed his hands together and forced himself to concentrate. "Could that valet have been guilty of…the crimes?" He tried to remember his brother's valet, a moonfaced man with greased-back dark hair. He sighed and rubbed his eyes, thinking about the years of death haunting his family. "No, Pennick can't have been responsible for all the deaths. I believe the man was fired when Jack found him stealing his clothes. But he was hired less than three years ago. And the trouble began almost a decade ago."

"Your oldest brother died six years ago," Patrick said. "When I think about what I've learned, if there are any actual troubles, I'd say they started then."

Quade said with some relief, "Yes, that makes sense. That could mean my youngest brother's death was not murder. He died nearly twelve years ago."

Patrick said, "Pennick is likely not responsible for all the crimes—though my contacts at the police believe he left the pigeon at Mrs. Marrill's house, and that was still part of his mania against your late brother."

"What did Pennick say when they interviewed him?"

"Welch, my friend, actually asked me to keep an eye open for him, and, in fact, I have a man looking. No one has been able to find Mr. Pennick for quite some time, and yes, that's vague, I know, but it's exactly what Welch told me. I think Welch is keeping about my search for the man secret from the other officers. The police won't devote their own official resources to find Pennick. And Welch is the sort of guy who keeps his cards close to his chest, I think you'd say."

Quade still held hope the stories he'd been telling himself for years now were true and there was only the one murder, his poor cousin who was hit by over the head—and the deed was committed by strangers.

He'd cling to that belief as long as he could, even as he tried to find answers. He said, "They did bother to investigate the matter before Jack's death, conducting interviews. Why would anyone pay heed to the words of a disgruntled ex-servant? You'd best tell me what was so amazing and sensational—why the existence of a letter disparaging Jack must be kept secret from me." He felt another spurt of outrage.

Colm hadn't said anything to him. Colm, his…friend.

Patrick flipped through the pages, obviously buying time while he considered what he should say.

"Mr. Kelly? Why was it kept a secret?"

Patrick sighed. "My desire to keep quiet about it was simply a matter of how I came by the knowledge of the letter."

"Is that all? Why didn't you allow Colm to tell me about it?"

He heard a soft protest from Colm but kept on speaking. "And why is it even worth mentioning now? I can tell that it is."

Patrick steepled his fingers. "The answer to that is difficult to explain."

Colm said, "No, it's not really, Cousin Patrick." He looked at Quade. "The letter informed the police about a gruesome souvenir."

"Also a dead bird?" Quade demanded.

"No it was a blunt object that might have been used in an attack." Patrick must have decided to stop holding back.

Suddenly, the words poured out, but he was more like a man excitedly discussing the details an interesting cricket match than a murder. He rested his hands on the folder of papers. "Your cousin Cyril Marrill was twenty-two and a man about town—found bludgeoned after a long night of revelry. And the item in question was allegedly related to that incident."

"I recall Cyril's death," Quade said impatiently. "What was the item in question, if you please."

"The letter led the police to a possible weapon in the garden shed of Jack's London house." Patrick shuffled through the notes. "There were other details, interesting ones."

Quade had difficulty holding on to his temper as he leaned forward. "And?"

"The day after the letter arrived, police fetched the item from the garden shed—"

"What the hell was the goddamned item in—"

"It was a pry bar, and it had blood and hair on it. There was talk of unearthing the body of Cyril Marrill to match the hair color and the injury and so on, but, then, less than a week later, Jack died."

He leaned over the desk, showing more animation. In fact, he fairly bristled with excitement.

"There was still the attack on Cyril Marrill to figure out, even with Jack out of the picture. The only reason the valet didn't end up being accused of Cyril's murder was simply that he was not in town when it occurred. They'd managed to get that much out of Pennick, and verified it before he vanished." Patrick Kelly talked about the murder with animation as if it were a puzzle.

Quade could only see his dead brother and his murdered cousin, Cyril, a silly young man but full of life and interest as he juggled tobacco and a pipe and described the splendid, revivifying qualities of a good bowl of tobacco. An ass, but a friendly, vivacious one that Quade knew better than his own brothers—and a person he still missed. And to imply that Jack would kill that good-natured fool… Quade realized he made a small sound that could be considered a growl.

Colm hitched his chair a bit closer to him, and his foot somehow found Quade's.

Quade tried, unsuccessfully, to calm his heartbeat and breath. Colm got up, walked to the far corner of the room, and returned with a glass of something brown he put in front of Quade. Whisky—but Quade still took a sip. "And did anyone ask himself why a valet would be lurking around a garden shed?"

The two men raised their brows at him. Apparently the Kelly cousins didn't understand the role of a valet in a household. "Never mind. Did my father know about the suspicion someone tried to lay on Jack?"

"I don't know who does or doesn't know about the letter or the investigation. I couldn't ask Welch because, to be honest, I wasn't supposed to know about it myself. I have no idea what your father thought about the potential weapon's discovery or if he even knew of it."

"Did you try to find out?" Quade demanded.

"Yes. I did ask a couple of questions during my initial interview, and he seemed uninterested in discussing the matter with me. In fact, he informed me more than once that my agency was hired to protect the parties in question, not to sneak about. But I assume his reaction would be the same as yours. It was a preposterous idea invented by a dismissed servant with a grudge." He rubbed his chin with his palm, the same thing Colm did when turning over a problem. "Did anyone in your family know? I expect the police had to tell Jack Marrill when they visited and removed the evidence. Have you spoken to your sister-in-law?"

He thought back to the conversations he'd had with Mary. "She never mentioned the letter, but she's always been a quiet lady. After Jack's death, she took to her bed. And she's been unwell. Now I know why, with a baby on the way."

“She told you that?” Patrick asked.

Colm jumped in. “She might not be a gabber, but the staff certainly know all about that letter the police got. The cook made reference to anonymous notes yesterday.”

Patrick waved a hand, an imperious motion to stop the questions and comments, a motion that reminded Quade of a professor stopping interruptions during a lecture.

“To sum up, the anonymous letter was delivered to the police,” Patrick said. “The police made a call and did a search and found an iron bar. The household staff, the gardener in particular, claimed the bar was placed there by an outsider. And there was some evidence that was true.”

“How would they determine that the servants were telling the truth?”

Patrick glanced down at the notes. “There was a leak in the shed roof close to where the bar was found at the very back of the shed—rain water must have trickled in for weeks or months before the police found that spot. The pry bar showed no rust like other iron objects. The dust on the floor showed disturbances where footsteps had been rubbed out.”

Colm, the over-eager student who wouldn’t stop interrupting the professor, spoke up. “If you check the next page of your notes, there’s the bit you said about how the police kept the whole thing as quiet as possible.”

Patrick nodded. “Jack’s parents and his widow might know about the weapon found in the London house shed, but I strongly suspect they were spared the details about the claims made about Jack.”

“Strongly suspect,” Quade grumbled. “Based on what?”

“The man in charge of looking into the matter, Mr. Granby, decided it had to be the valet who sent the letter. Granby said the accusations were false. He has a very high opinion of wealthy and respectable old families and doesn’t like to be intrusive.” His tone made it clear he didn’t share Granby’s opinion. He said, “They were still deciding how to proceed when Jack Marrill was stung and died. Granby wouldn’t go poking about annoying a grieving family, particularly when it was felt that Jack Marrill’s death ended the matter.”

"And now what do the police say with the new note? Do they think it's over?" Quade demanded.

"I expect Welch is finally openly and actively hunting for the missing valet. But keep in mind, Pennick's not a suspect in the attack of your cousin, who, as I told you, was murdered when the valet was not in London."

"How Pennick got his hands on the potential murder weapon, that should still be of interest to the police," Colm muttered. "Why would they leave all these incidents pass as if they were nothing?"

"And weren't you going to help me to understand all this?" Quade rose to his feet, too restless to sit. "And as for you, Colm Kelly, why did you stay silent about this first letter? Were you paid off?" he demanded.

"In a manner of speaking, yes." As always, Colm remained unruffled as a pond on a still summer day.

Usually, his lack of sturm und drang calmed Quade, but now he felt a sharp blaze of anger. "Why? Why would you not tell me…" He glanced into those hazel eyes that watched him steadily. *Me, your friend*, he silently finished.

Quade had moved close enough to Colm that he could touch him, stroke the fine gold stubble on his jaw, or give that face a good blow. He was hardly used to such strong emotions—and how odd to have such strong conflicting desires at the same time.

"My cousin is my employer, and he told me not to mention it to you." Colm tilted his head and examined Patrick. "I expect he wasn't even supposed to learn the details of the valet. The way Patrick talked about the letter, it sounded as if he didn't have time to read it, which could have meant he sneaked a look. Read something upside-down maybe? And took notes after? Ha, he is a rascal."

Patrick sniffed disdainfully but didn't answer.

Quade still felt as if he'd been betrayed by a best friend.

Something of his anger must have shown on his face, because Colm turned his gaze on Quade, his face unusually solemn. "But now that you know, and you're demanding answers, I'll help you. No more secrets."

"Even if your cousin says not to?" Quade scowled at Patrick, silently daring him to speak up.

Colm's customary half smile returned. "Yes, even then. Even if he dismisses me for doing so."

Now his calm eased Quade's heart. He knew Colm wasn't lying—and not only because he said the words in front of his employer, but because he trusted Colm.

Patrick grumbled, "Here now, didn't I say you'd convinced me? Stop with your dramatics, both of you. It's not the end of the earth."

But their particular unspoken fight about *it* hadn't been about the godforsaken anonymous letter, Quade knew. If Colm had said he would side with Patrick instead of Quade, something important would have been harmed. Something, *It* again. Craving, desire, lust, and now friendship and trust must be added to the list. They'd be alphabetically arranged as always in his mind, so that meant the words were twisted in with the others into a tangle that was growing larger and harder to unknot with each passing moment.

Quade sat down again. "Very well, if you're helping me, perhaps you have suggestions on what we might do next."

"We could speak to your da. Wait, I wonder how we can at least make sure the letter came from that man, Pennick. Oh, and yes, I want to see that actual letter." Colm made an apologetic, comical face at Patrick. "Ach. So we'll have to disturb the police after all."

Quade didn't really want to cause trouble between the cousins, especially now he had Colm on his side. "Perhaps seeing the letter is unnecessary, that is if Patrick Kelly can recall the contents."

Patrick blew out a long breath that puffed his cheeks. "Alas, Cousin Colm is absolutely correct. I only jotted notes, and I can't even recall if there were any misspellings. Damnation, getting our hands on the note could have been useful. And the other letter for a comparison."

Quade asked, "What more would there be than the words on the page?"

"Plenty to see." Colm spoke up before Patrick could answer. "Did the same person write both letters? Was the hand educated? Feminine? Was the note a hasty scrawl or careful copy? And what it's written on might say something. I mean was the paper foolscap or fine stationery?"

Patrick gave him an approving nod. "I see the RIC has trained you well. Good thinking."

"I read novels. I like Miss Braddon's work."

Quade glared at him. "Oh, for goodness sake, why are you so unwilling to take credit for your cleverness?"

Patrick raised his brows and tilted his head, definitely intrigued at Quade's outburst.

Quade hurriedly continued, "Then we're agreed that the three of us will go to the police?"

Patrick shook his head. "Not you, sir. I shall, since I'm the one with contacts there."

"But I should see the letter. I might recognize that hand writing or the paper." Quade was tired of passively waiting for answers. By God, he'd go talk to his father as well.

"No," Patrick said. "I'll go alone. In fact, I shan't go at all if you insist that on tagging along."

Those words seemed familiar, and Quade realized years ago he'd heard similar tagging along after comments from his older brothers…his dead and gone brothers. "I must do something," he said. "And the fact that I'm a possible source of information can't be ignored. The police haven't come round to interview me, for pity's sake. And they should be suspicious of me."

Colm nodded slowly. He rose to his feet. "Let's go."

"What are *you* doing?" Patrick practically bellowed.

Colm only calmly jerked a thumb in Quade's direction and said, "He's right."

"If you won't come with me, I'll go to the police on my own and shall insist on seeing the letter. Letters, I mean," Quade said to Patrick. He took pity on the obviously unhappy man. "If they ask me how I came to know of the first letter's existence, I shan't name you."

He had no idea whom to approach or how to find out, of course, and he doubted Colm did, but his threat worked.

Patrick gave a harsh bark of laughter. "Fine. You win. Let's go."

Quade waited to feel a sense of triumph but wasn't surprised when he felt nothing of the sort. He dreaded what they would discover, which might well be nothing at all.

CHAPTER NINE

Patrick's friend Welch, a middle-aged fellow with graying hair and a drooping mustache, wasn't dressed like a policeman. He wore a sagging blue suit and sat behind a desk. When he looked up, Welch seemed pleased to see Patrick, until he noticed the others. He pushed back his chair as Patrick introduced Colm and Marrill.

He rose to his feet and squinted at Marrill. "Mr. Marrill? Quade Marrill?"

"Yes, I expect you know the name. The police interviewed me before. And now I'm here to find out about the notes and evidence you have relating to my family."

Colm admired how his Marrill had no interest in pleasantries and nonsense when he was focused. He'd been that way since Colm had first met him, but in the last day or so, he'd turned sharp, not mean, more the well-honed blade ready to be used.

Marrill continued, "There were accusations directed at my late brother Jack Marrill. I'm particularly interested in them. Since he's recently deceased, surely you won't mind sharing that information?"

The officer pushed his chin up out of his stiff collar, showing the world an impressive display of nose hairs. "If there is anything…" Welch hesitated and rolled his shoulders back as if relieving some burden. "That is to say…that sort of thing is not available to the public. And I'm not sure how you came to know of it at all."

Patrick watched the exchange, wearing a face covered with confusion mixed with curiosity. Of course, he wasn't supposed to know about the letter that he'd read on the sly.

"Kelly?" Welch narrowed his eyes at Patrick, who only shrugged, a look of hurt bafflement on his face.

Patrick said, "You know I'm interested in the case, but I didn't suggest coming here. Still, it's not a big surprise that Mr. Marrill is interested as well."

Not a confession, not a lie—Cousin Patrick was adept at evasion.

Marrill rapped the desk with his knuckles. "I would like to know why you didn't ask me about that note sent to my brother's widow."

Welch gave a surprised chuckle. "That note to Mrs. Jack Marrill implied that you were a threat. You're saying you want to be considered a crazy devil, then?"

"Of course not. But someone clearly wants to point the finger at me. Why haven't you asked me any questions?"

"Take a seat." Welch settled himself into a chair. The other ignored the suggestion and paced around the small office.

Welch tapped a pipe onto a tray and then repacked it from a pouch that lay open on his desk, most of which seemed covered with a fine dust of tobacco and ash. "I believe we have a person in mind for that bit of ugliness, sir. No need to disturb your family what's already been disturbed enough."

Patrick said, "You can't tell us who?"

At the same time, Colm said, "You're looking for that valet Pennick, aren't you?"

Welch busied himself by fiddling with the pipe's bowl. "I can't tell you that since I'm not in charge of the case."

It was as good as a yes.

It took some more cajoling, but eventually, Welch rose from his chair with the air of a martyr and led them down the stairs to the storage rooms, where they discovered nothing except that the police department was shockingly careless.

Patrick, Quade, and Welch stood in front of the counter and argued.

Colm ached to join in the battle, but Quade was doing a good job for himself, so he leaned against a wall and formed an audience along with the fat policeman who sat behind the counter and toyed with the ends of his waxed mustaches and watched. Only the cop's fingertips and eyes moved. He wouldn't move unless ordered to, and he apparently enjoyed the show.

"But the case about my cousin Cyril's death isn't closed, is it? And the blasted note from the other day? Why would a piece of paper be in the locker and not on someone's desk?" Quade paced back and forth at the front of the storage room. "The letter that arrived at Mrs. Marrill's house on the breast of the pigeon is certainly fresh and not down here. Wouldn't you want to compare that note to the others?"

Welch made a snorting sound. "Interesting that you know about that dead bird. But I expect it wasn't because you sent it. Our officer said someone was sneaking about gossiping with the cook. That'd be you people?"

"Yes," Colm said immediately. He pushed away from the wall. "'Twas I alone. I work for Mr. Kelly, but I didn't ask for permission from him. Just went ahead and talked to the lady on my own."

Welch didn't look particularly upset. "Ah well, it's considered a separate incident, unrelated to that pry bar. A prank, if you will." Somehow, he gave the impression that he sure didn't consider it separate or a prank at all, but the higher ups weren't interested in his opinion. "The case is still open, but no one is working on it at the moment. Granby…" He shook his head. Whoever this Granby might be, he didn't impress Welch or Patrick.

The man behind the counter spoke up at last. "Shifting storage to another building soon. Running out of space here, aren't we. Bit disorganized at the moment."

"What we are looking for is a simple piece of paper and an envelope, and it's evidence that's only a few months old," Patrick said. "Just the papers and the iron rod with blood and hair. You must have that?"

Welch gave up the battle. He pulled out his notebook, scribbled something on a page, and ripped out the page. He handed it to the man behind the counter. "That's the case number."

"I 'spect we'll find it." The uniformed officer let go of the ends of his mustache and shuffled back and along the shelves, muttering to himself.

He appeared a few minutes later clutching the bar, which had been wrapped in cloth. He put it down on the table, then matched the paper tag dangling from it to the number Patrick's friend had handed him.

Welch carefully unwrapped it on top of a white cloth. At least he seemed to know what he was doing.

Marrill peered at it. "Where is the hair and blood?"

The cop unhooked a paraffin lamp hanging over the desk and carefully brought it down, just above the bar. "Huh. There's a bit, I think." He pointed. "Could be rust, though."

Patrick moved closer and stared down. "No hair, as far as I can see. Where did that go?"

Colm felt slightly sick, not at the sight of a potential murder weapon, but that the whole search for the truth seemed to be taking them nowhere. He'd been called to testify before the magistrates in criminal cases in Ireland, and he knew well enough how to store and keep evidence for a trial.

These big city Londoners apparently didn't.

He wished he could move closer to Marrill, who leaned over the bar as if it could give up its secrets. Had someone destroyed the evidence on purpose?

Patrick was angry too. "Where the hell is the rest? The papers are gone?"

"All right, Kelly, don't get peevish. I have a few spare moments now and can hunt for that letter. Those letters," Welch said, pushing away from the wall. "They might be upstairs in the investigating officer's desk to go with the recent threat. And perhaps if there was hair collected from the bar, it would be preserved separately. I can give you at least a few more minutes of my time to look."

Patrick's friend led them back into his office, a small room that was jammed with papers and books. The stacks of papers probably felt like home to Marrill—though his apartment didn't smell like pipe and cigar smoke and sweat, and this room most definitely did.

Ten minutes later, Welch had found nothing and the man in charge of the case was not on the premises. He'd apparently gone off to look into some other mysterious complaint unrelated to the Marrill family.

"You are saying that Granby is off doing something else." Marrill sounded as frustrated but not raging. "Does that mean that the Marrill family investigation isn't important?"

"No, sir, it is, of course. We do have other investigations in our laps." Welch examined Marrill for a moment, then added, "We're officially calling what has occurred your family a series of unfortunate coincidences, but we're also on alert. Granby takes on cases of extortion and fraud, and the letter sent to us seemed to fit the category. We don't believe the first letter was anything more than an ex-servant trying to cast blame on the man who fired him. The rod with the blood and hair and all—well, that didn't prove anything. As for the bird…" He shrugged. "That might be him. One of Jack Marrill's neighbors is a cranky eccentric, and we're speaking to him as well."

Patrick spoke up. "But if Pennick got hold of that bar, then why isn't he on all the lists relating to the Marrill family?"

"There is but one such list. The only murder investigated was that of Cyril Marrill, and he was robbed in a dangerous dark street where another man had been done to death the same way less than a month earlier. We've had officers patrolling the area, and the footpads are staying away."

Marrill began, "What about my uncle, he—"

"Died of natural causes," Welch said.

Marrill shook his head, his eyes bright, but Colm suspected he was too angry or upset to speak.

Colm wanted to say something but was grateful when Patrick took up Marrill's questioning. He'd gone from a reluctant participant to someone who wanted answers. "Jeremiah Marrill allegedly died of a heart attack, but there wasn't an autopsy to discover if poison was employed."

"He had a dicky heart. His son had been murdered." Welch put down the pipe and rose to his feet, impatient at last. "Come now, Kelly. If these other deaths are more than unfortunate accidents or illness, which I doubt, then they've been planned and carried out by someone with more brains than that Pennick. The whole attempt to pin the blame on Jack Marrill was clumsy work, and we are certain it was Pennick."

"And that damned pigeon?"

"I'm not sure why you're so keen to find crime there, Mr. Marrill, sir, since you're the obvious suspect. It's likely Pennick or some other ghoulish person trying to frighten the poor widow." He wiped some tobacco from his suit. "Now I think we're done here."

He showed them the way down a narrow hall that had pipes for the gas lighting recently installed. Smoke smudged walls showed where the old paraffin lamps had hung.

As they walked, Welch spoke to Patrick in a voice probably not meant to reach Colm and Marrill. "Don't bring any more civilians to gawk at us, man, or I'll be uninterested in working with you in the future. Don't know what you're up to, dragging in a gent who is wrapped as tight as a mummy in this matter."

"Say, does that mean you're admitting there is a matter? You and I both know an attack a couple of months ago was too—"

Before Patrick could finish his sentence, Welch called him a vile name. He lowered his voice, then muttered something about "Bloody Granby…footpads again. You'd think an attack would be enough."

Patrick held his hands up shoulder height, surrendering. "All right. Never mind that."

He glanced back at Colm and Marrill walking side by side, then told Welch, "I need to talk to you about that robbery I was asked to look into last month. Your boys have been looking into it too, right? I'd like to compare notes."

The robbery apparently also had nothing to do with Marrill and his family. After that peevish outburst from Welch, the subject of Quade's dead family members and the strange notes had probably already been dismissed from Patrick's and Welch's minds.

Colm walked a little faster. "But you'll still look for the missing valet," he demanded of Welch.

Welch came to a stop at a small alcove overlooking a stable yard. The window was open, and the breeze, with its smell of horse, was fresh relief from carbolic, sweat, and pipe smoke. "Yes, we're looking into it. Now that note went to Mrs. Jack Marrill, we're going to poke around ourselves. Even Mr. Granby agrees."

Even Mr. Granby? But Patrick looked at Colm and gave the tiniest of shrugs along with a head shake. Colm didn't know his cousin well, but he suspected that meant Patrick wanted him to stay quiet and to send the message he wasn't giving up either.

"Are you satisfied, Mr. Marrill? I promise to do my best." Welch's reassuring manner didn't seem as honest as his annoyance had less than five minutes earlier.

Marrill shook his head and shifted from foot to foot. "I'm done here."

Patrick asked, "Would you wait for me, Mr. Marrill? I'll only be a few minutes, and I'd be glad to buy you a cup of tea."

"No. No need." With that typical blunt and distracted response, Marrill headed down the corridor, and Colm hurried after him.

"Where are you going?" Colm asked when he caught up.

"To speak to my father."

"Are you sure that's a good plan?"

Marrill stopped and gave him a cold, flat look. "It was your bloody idea."

"Of course." He didn't add, *that was before you seemed so angry.*

Marrill sniffed, then strode toward the stairs. Patrick jogged up behind them. He grabbed and held Colm's arm. "Listen. If he's going to visit his father, then you need to be very careful. Remember you represent our company, and stay quiet. You do know how to do that, hey?"

"Have to go." Colm shook his arm loose with an apology and ran after Marrill, calling, "Here, now, wait, sir. I'm still your guard."

They climbed down the clanking wrought iron spiral staircase toward the front door of the police station.

"I'll surely annoy you again by asking, but I must. Do you think it is a good plan to talk to your da? Right this moment when you're angry enough to grind your teeth? I can hear that, you know."

To his relief, Marrill slowed. As he considered the question, his rage seemed to drain away. "I want this done. Once I get the usual cold shoulder from him, perhaps I'll be able to return to my work because I'll have done all I could. If the police don't find Pennick, I'll hire yet another inquiry agent to find Jack's pestilential ex-valet."

"As long as you don't get rid of me."

Quade touched his arm, and his mouth quirked into a half smile. "I didn't hire you, remember?"

They took a hansom, which barreled through the streets at an alarming pace. Despite his duties as an alert watch-guard, Colm had to shut his eyes several times in alarm. When they nearly hit a slow-moving dray, he groaned a protest.

"You'll get used to the traffic." Marrill must have been watching him.

"I doubt it. I don't think I'm suited for city life."

Marrill asked, "And where do you see yourself in a year or so?"

"Alive? More than that, I don't know."

"Do you think you will you return to your family in Ireland?"

He shook his head.

"I suppose that was a rude question." He peered at Colm. Marrill actually seemed worried about Colm's feelings.

"Not at all."

Marrill moved closer to him. "I think you could thrive wherever you landed. A pragmatic fellow probably does."

That nosier and less anxious version of Marrill had returned, so all was right. The man always made him laugh, especially when he threw in his big words.

Colm grabbed at the handhold as they jolted over some rough road. "That first part, I suppose I should say thank you. But what is a pragmatic fellow when he's at home?"

"Logical, sensible. You don't allow emotion to rule your life."

"Oh, nonsense."

"But you rarely get angry or upset." Marrill sounded nearly angry again. "It hardly seems natural."

"Bah," Colm said. "I have no spleen."

"Is your lack of strong response intentional, or do you work at staying calm?"

"Calm and Colm—maybe I mixed the words as a lad, eh? Made me grow up with stunted anger." This conversation made him uncomfortable. It felt as if Marrill was trying to get under his skin or maybe peel something away. For a man who claimed to be bad at seeing others, Marrill was good at flaying apart a person's defenses.

Colm tried to concentrate on the moment and his surroundings—when he was unsettled, trying to simply observe was best. But that proved not much better. He watched Marrill's strong white teeth worrying the side of his thumb, a habit of discomfiture or concentration, Marrill had once told him.

It seemed the discomfort wouldn't go away even when the talking stopped. Slowing his pounding heart was impossible because Marrill was there, so close he could smell him, the familiar scent of books and Marrill. He could see the small hairs at Marrill's wrists, the scrape above his collar from the razor. He could see the rise and fall of his breath. Unlike Colm's, it was slow and steady. They'd reversed roles, perhaps. But no, because Marrill let his hand drop and stared back at him as well. Not so indifferent at the moment after all.

Colm forced his gaze away and out the window.

The sight of a gorgeous bridge towering over the Thames managed to distract him. He did like the city as long as he didn't pay attention to what the rushing horses were about to run over or smash into. "How much farther are we going?"

"Only a couple of miles. London is not very large." Marrill moved away again, thank the Lord.

"Don't be daft. I can see it's enormous, Mr. Marrill. You mustn't try to fool me any longer," Colm drawled in his best country accent.

Marrill's smile was like his anger and his fear—large and genuine.

The Marrill townhouse reminded Colm of the home Cousin Patrick shared with Mr. Sloan, although this place was less well scrubbed and perhaps slightly more forbidding. The iron rail surrounding the entrance and front windows gave it the look of a fortress. The black paint on the iron bars was peeling, and the brass knocker on the door was a bit green.

Did they need more servants? Weren't they dreadfully wealthy? Perhaps the neglect came from being a family in mourning rather than a lack of funds. Colm wished he could ask Marrill, but the man had grown as straight as a badly made tin soldier.

Marrill's attempt to appear indifferent didn't fool Colm, who could see he practically vibrated with the need to be unconcerned.

The butler who answered the door recognized Marrill and seemed glad enough to see him, though his brows slanted up in surprise.

Colm was again grateful for his education with Patrick. He handed over his hat and coat without a word or sign that he disliked being parted from his possessions or that the being who took them was an actual person. And the fact that Colm wore nice clothes and didn't open his mouth to show off his accent meant that the butler didn't give him a single disapproving sidelong glance. That was a change since he'd arrived in England.

"Mr. Marrill is in the dining room, sir."

"Will you announce me?" Marrill sounded as bored as could be.

"Certainly, if you wish it, sir." The butler clearly thought the son of the house was allowed to run about the place freely.

"Yes. I wish it, and we'll wait in the drawing room. Unless my mother is there?"

"No, sir. Mrs. Marrill is not at home. I'll summon the maid with tea."

"No need, thank you. We'll just wait."

They walked into the room, and the butler left, softly shutting the door behind him. "I shouldn't have done that," Marrill said regretfully. "I forgot to find out if you're hungry or thirsty."

"That's all right, Mr. Marrill."

"I'm Quade, you know."

Colm loved that he'd offered his name, but he said, "Perhaps when we're alone. Not here, Mr. Marrill."

"At any rate, I should learn to ask if you want food. I get so caught…" He shook his head. "I beg your pardon. I am trying to do better."

"I don't understand. Do better with what?"

Quade was quiet a moment before answering slowly. "I don't always understand why people respond the way they do. The easiest way to cope with such misunderstandings is to pretend it didn't happen or it doesn't matter. Ignoring others is a simple solution to a thing that frustrates me." He looked around the room, he looked at his hands. He looked everywhere but at Colm. "I don't want to ignore you."

Someone must have chided him too hard, or hurt him, Colm thought and wondered why that thought hadn't occurred to him before. Of course, an injured man would do his best to hide, roll up like a hedgehog, and show his spines should anyone come near.

And now he was slowly, consciously unrolling just for Colm. It was a gift that made his breath catch in his throat.

"Thank you, sir. But you don't need to guess with me. I am direct. Recall that I went and dragged you out of your home that day I was hungry?"

Again, that big smile. "The day I got stinking drunk."

"Ah, but I had a good meal that night. One of the best I've ever enjoyed."

"I find it hard to imagine anyone would mistake club cooking for genuine haute cuisine."

"Another one of those differences between us."

"I shall have to take you to somewhere worth eating a meal in someday." He touched Colm's shoulder. "Thank you for coming here today." His hand trembled.

Colm reached up and grabbed his bare hand. Quade's fingers were icy. Colm asked "Is this so terrible? Let's go. We can go have a reviving pint and return."

Naturally, at that moment, the door opened. The two of them were too close together and Colm had hold of Marrill's hand. He thought of the moment when he'd found Sloan and Patrick not so very long ago.

Fortunately, the man coming through the door didn't appear to notice. That could have been a sign he was Marrill senior—he was so focused inwardly, he might not see what was in front of his face. He had the same slender build and the same plank-straight hair as Quade, but graying, and his shoulders were slightly rounded. He didn't offer his hand or any other sort of greeting—also like Quade, or perhaps it was the other way around.

"To what do I owe the honor?" he asked Quade. "Your mother is not here. She's paying calls." He seemed to notice Colm at last. "I beg your pardon. I'm Marrill." And now he came forward with his hand out.

Colm shot a glance at Marrill junior, who didn't say anything. So, of course, Colm had to shake hands.

"I'm Kelly, sir. At your service."

"You're Irish?"

So much for his attempt to hide his accent.

"Don't you recognize the surname? *This* is the man you hired, Father." Quade sounded immensely satisfied as if glad he'd tricked his father into shaking hands with a servant. Colm felt a surge of resentment at Quade for tricking his father and for making him the reason for an unpleasant encounter.

But Mr. Marrill only blinked once, twice. To give the man credit, he didn't recoil in shock or whip out his handkerchief and rub at the hand that had shaken Colm's.

Colm turned and glared at Quade. "I should wait outside the room."

"No," Mr. Marrill senior said quickly. "No need. Please." He backed away from them and stood near the empty fireplace.

Colm wondered what ailed him, and then realized the truth of it. Marrill senior's hand rested lightly on the fireplace poker. God above, he behaved as if he were afraid of his own son. As if he'd thought Quade guilty.

Quade's eyes narrowed—so he'd apparently noticed his father's reluctance to let Colm leave as well.

An uncomfortable silence fell. Was it up to Colm to break it? No indeed, he'd act the meek servant just as Patrick and Sloan's staff had tried to teach him. Best not sit down and certainly not speak unless he'd been spoken to.

He moved to the area near the other side of the fireplace that Quade faced. That way, he'd be behind Marrill senior and maybe these two would be freer with their words, if he could be that lucky. This was an echo of the visit he'd paid on Patrick, when Marrill—Quade, he'd grow used to calling him—had lurked in the room as Colm and Patrick talked.

But Quade didn't speak. He drummed the fingers of one hand against one thigh, as if trying to recall the rhythm of a song or type something in telegraphic code.

His father pulled out his watch, looked at it, wound it a few times, and tucked it away again. "Your mother should return in an hour," he announced.

"I don't expect to pay a long visit."

His father pursed his lips but didn't protest. More silent moments passed. Colm rocked back and forth, heel toe, to stop himself from breaking in with comments about the weather or London sights. Patrick had warned him, and for once, he'd pay heed to his instructions.

Quade's father walked to a wooden chair and settled on the edge of the seat. "Might I enquire as to the nature of your call?"

Colm winced. They'd come for a reason, and, knowing his Quade, the son wouldn't be diplomatic. Sure enough, he said, "The deaths in our family. Or perhaps it's best to call them what they are: murders. We haven't spoken of them, you've ignored my questions about them, but now it's different. I heard of a letter."

His father scowled. "Letter?"

"From Jack's valet. Ex-valet. The letter was delivered to the police, and it accused Jack of criminal activity."

Marrill senior's back had gone stiff and straight.

"Do you know what I'm talking about?" Quade demanded.

"I had heard rumors, yes."

"Did you see it?"

"Why are you asking me about this?"

"I want to know what's going on. Who's responsible for these…things." Did he mean the murders or the rumors? Colm supposed Quade didn't know either.

Marrill senior raised his hand as if warding off his son. "The valet. You said as much. That's the end of it." He stared at Quade. "Please." It sounded like an actual plea.

"Yes, I know you don't believe we should discuss these matters." Quade's voice grew in volume. "And until recently, I would have been just as glad to ignore the topic. But since Jack's death. I've come to think a lack of action is a mistaken course for me. I mean to say, I have waited for others to find the answers for me. You sent help to me, and he's been of enormous assistance."

"I beg your pardon?"

"Kelly. I'm talking about Kelly."

His father turned his head to look at Colm as if he'd forgotten he was standing there.

"What has he to do with the matter? He's to keep watch over you."

"Yes, and that reminds me of another point he brought up. How long will his services be needed? I can't have a guard all my life."

His father turned in the chair and glowered at Colm before returning his attention to Quade. "Oh? Indeed? I hardly think it a matter for discussion at the moment." He left off the phrase *with the help present*, but his pointed glance at Colm made it clear enough.

Quade made a small sound of frustration. "Why are you unwilling to find an answer, Father? Or talk to me about your suspicions?"

The older man only shook his head.

Quade rose to his feet. "One wonders if perhaps the reason you're reluctant to discuss the matter is that you already know who is responsible for the deaths in our family."

Oh Jesus, Mary, and Joseph, this was not going well. Colm clamped his lips shut, put his hands behind his back, and pretended to be a piece of furniture.

Mr. Marrill stood up now too. "What makes you think it proper or wise to bring up those deaths? It is not your place to drag such painful topics into my drawing room, as if you're some sort of cat presenting a dead mole to the household."

"How does one gain the right to discuss them? My brothers, my uncle, my cousin. They're gone, Father. It's not a coincidence, and you know it, or you wouldn't have hired Colm."

"That's his first name, is it? Are you on such good terms with him?"

"Why yes, I am. I trust him, and I do not trust you."

His father blinked and drew in a sharp breath. "You, sirrah, are rude, and this call is like your letters, another instance of you…you stepping out of bounds. You have no right."

"Yes, I do. I need to speak of the murders, we all do, and I have the right to lead a life I feel best—"

"No, you don't any longer." His father's voice had dropped. He sounded almost anguished. "Because you're the last of my heirs, you'll have another path to follow. That is… Unless it becomes clear that you are the culprit."

"I am most certainly not guilty of—"

His father raised his voice to speak over him. "Unless you are proved to be a criminal, you shall inherit everything."

Quade shifted uneasily. "I don't want to."

"You can't lead any sort of life of reading dull books and sorting through your precious notes about them."

Colm had enough of this man's anger. "What is the trouble, sir? Quade—Master Marrill, I mean—clearly has no interest in your fortune, which should ease your mind about his innocence." Honestly how many people hadn't made this simple leap of understanding?

Mr. Marrill made a strangled, angry sound.

Colm changed his tone to something coaxing. "But sir, is there more you haven't mentioned? What else is the matter?"

Mr. Marrill twisted in his chair, his complexion purple. It didn't speak well of Colm that instead of worrying about the poor man, his first thought was that if he died of an apoplectic fit during this visit, Quade would be under suspicion of murder. Again.

"Beg pardon, sir." He tried once more. "But perhaps we might be able to help? Or I could ask Mr. Kelly to look into the matter?"

It was a guess on his part that Marrill senior was hiding something from them. Clearly, Quade didn't understand that Colm was only guessing, because he demanded, "At least tell me what it is, Father."

Mr. Marrill didn't answer immediately.

Quade cleared his throat and made an obvious effort to sound more conciliatory. "Tell me, please."

"Do you not know?" His father stared at him. For a long moment, neither spoke.

Then Mr. Marrill stretched out his legs, winced, and rubbed his thigh. "Not long before Jack's passing, we were in London."

Surprised, Colm forgot his resolution to stay silent. "I thought you were in Kent from January until March?"

Marrill waved a hand impatiently. "It was a short visit. We were in London for a number of reasons."

He rubbed his side absently and went on. "Someone put a cloth over my head, a bag. I was smashed over the head and kicked. The attacker managed to injure my legs."

"Your limp," Quade breathed.

His father's mouth thinned, then he continued. "There was only one man attacking me, and I managed to get free. He had a knife and slashed at my arm, cutting me, then struck me with some sort of club. It reminded me of…" For the first time, his voice lost energy.

"Cyril," Quade said softly.

His father grunted and didn't speak.

Quade said, "What did the police say? Surely you mentioned the other crimes in our family."

His father avoided his gaze and scowled at Colm as if he'd asked the question. "First the police told me they believed it was the work of an ex-servant of Jack's, a valet. They told me they suspected he was trying to make Jack look like he was a villain. But after they found my watch and a knife in the possession of a man who had assaulted other gentlemen, Mr. Granby informed me they were done. They had an easily solved crime. No need to look further."

"Why didn't you tell me?"

It took his father a long time to answer. "Ah. I'd supposed it was that valet, Pennick, and that's what I told them. I'd thought he was guilty of it all, because how else would he have gotten that bar he put in Jack's garden shed?"

"And why didn't you tell me about that bar and letter?"

"It wasn't your business. The next time you and I met was hardly the time to exchange gossip."

"After Jack, after he…yes," Quade said. "But you might have written."

"Nonsense. It didn't matter about the letter and the bar and what have you. That wasn't the man who attacked me. The authorities searched for Pennick and tracked him to Wales. He was in Wales the day I was attacked."

That was where he'd been during Cyril Marrill's murder as well. "They did some work after all," Quade muttered. "They seemed like a damned feckless lot."

Colm felt a spark of indignation as well. Patrick didn't have the attack on Mr. Arthur Marrill listed in his files either. Had Welch not told him? Why would they want to keep it a secret from Quade? And how many more Marrills had been attacked?

Quade asked, "All right, I understand why you didn't tell me about the letter Pennick sent to the police."

"Big of you," his father said. He had the same dry manner as Quade, or the other way around, Colm supposed.

Quade shifted in his chair but didn't lose his temper. He only asked, "Did Pennick say anything else?"

"Far as I know, they didn't actually find him, only found where he'd been staying in Wales."

"That's a pity. But, Father, you haven't answered my question. Why didn't you tell me you were attacked and nearly beaten to death?"

"Hardly that," his father said. "I recovered quickly."

"The policeman Welch didn't want me to know either. But why didn't you tell me?" This repetition sounded less angry and more hopeless. Colm wanted to touch him, just a reassuring brush across the shoulders, and actually took a step forward, but Quade's eyes narrowed and Colm came no closer.

At long last, the truth burst out. And it was just as Colm supposed. Arthur Marrill's words were low, far more appalling than a shout. "Do you want me to say this again and again? It was none of your business. Or so I hope and pray. Hoped and prayed every day. Because…you could well be deeply involved in that attack."

"Father," Quade gasped.

That broken word stirred Colm, who couldn't stand it any longer. "Mr. Marrill. Your son had naught to do with any murders."

The older Mr. Marrill, whose back was already impossibly straight, seemed to stiffen even more. "You. Get out."

"Ah, you're not afraid to be alone with your son. That's good. You know he's not guilty." Colm, who should have known better—and who almost always did—Colm, who'd kept his mouth shut whilst being called the most hideous names, couldn't stop pushing the man who'd put that devastated look on Quade's face.

"This is none of your concern. You are shockingly insolent."

"Yes, that's true. But to think I trust Quade Marrill more'n his own Da does…That is more shocking, I'd say."

Mr. Marrill's face went white. "I shall contact Mr. Kelly immediately and have you removed from your position. You clearly have no understanding of what you've been hired to do."

"Again, you likely have the right of it." Colm's stomach had congealed. He would be cast out again. But he'd grown too angry at the insults to Quade to keep his gob shut. "But neither do you, as a father. A parent ought to talk to his child, discuss the matter, before passing judgment."

"You have no notion what I should do."

Colm opened his mouth, but before some other damned fool thing could emerge, Quade said gently, "Thank you, Mr. Kelly. But please go."

He walked out of the room, remembering to close the door softly behind—a good servant at last. He nearly ran into a giant of a man he hadn't noticed before, lurking just outside the room. The man was dressed in a badly fitting uniform, probably that of a footman.

He choked back the shout of surprise and, after a moment or two of waiting for his heart to dislodge itself from his throat, asked, "You one of Kelly's men?"

"Know him, don't work for him." The man had a peculiar accent, like Patrick's.

"You're American?"

The man nodded.

"If you're not with Kelly, what are you doing here?"

"He recommended me. I'm here to watch the old guy. You're watching the young one. Keep your voice down. He don't want the staff here to know a thing about it."

Colm wondered how old man Marrill managed to explain the roughneck's presence to his staff. Chances were he didn't bother. He seemed quite capable of ignoring any or all questions. Speaking of which… "Did Mr. Marrill tell you about that attack? A bag over the head."

"Not the old guy, but Kelly told me about it. Old guy is the most closemouthed fellow on earth."

"Patrick was only hiding that detail from me, then," Colm grumbled. "And here I thought he'd told me it all."

"He doesn't like to spread information far and wide. Anyway, from what I hear, that's not going to be your problem much longer, since you're out of a job."

"Listening at the door, were you?"

The big man, who had only a fuzz of hair on his head and a nose that had been smashed more than once, looked about ten years younger when he grinned. "You bet. Say, listen, you are a fool."

"Don't I know it."

"But I'll be sure to tell Kelly the old guy lost his temper for no good reason. Mr. Marrill does that often enough. For all that he likes secrets and staying mute, he's got some hot blood. The boss will shift you to some other work, maybe, away from this family."

"That's kind of you." Colm slumped against the paneled wood of the corridor and stared up at an ancient portrait of some Marrill ancestor that glared back at him. “I’m to blame for this visit. I coaxed Mr. Marrill, the younger, I mean, to go after the truth.”

“These guys.” The other bodyguard gave a disgusted snort. “They can’t stand showing fear or some such twaddle. Yah, stiff upper lip. Scared ninnies.”

Colm considered protesting that his Mr. Marrill was no such thing, but he’d already been moved once to make an ass of himself in the last few minutes.

The big man moved close to the door again and even laid his ear against it. After a moment, he pulled away. “They’re talking too quiet now.”

Colm waited and made plans should he lose his job. He prayed he might stay with Quade, at least until he found another position. That attack on Arthur Marrill was too much. Someone was killing off Marrills, and he’d walk away only if Quade told him to go.

CHAPTER TEN

Quade hardly listened to his father snarling under his breath about the intrusion of strangers. He hardly even cared that his father had finally admitted he thought Quade might be guilty.

He was far too caught up by the way Calm Colm Kelly had lost his characteristic sangfroid and acted like an idiot in defense of Quade. And why had he poured out emotion on such a neutral subject as Quade's father? True, his father had always rather intimidated him, but now Quade wondered why. Perhaps watching Colm attempt to spar with his father had made a difference. A knight attacking a fireless, aging dragon on his behalf.

"I fail to see why you're amused." His father's cold voice didn't stir the usual resentment and dismay.

"Not at you, Father." He made an effort to stop smiling. "I made a mistake in coming here."

"That Irish want-to-be detective poured nonsense in your ear."

Now Quade did laugh and explained, "He was a police sergeant in the guards in Ireland."

His father's eyes widened, but he didn't say anything.

"Do you honestly think I killed my brothers and uncle and cousin?" For once, he managed to ask the question, and remarkably calmly too.

His father remained silent.

"You told Kelly to leave the room, and, as he pointed out, that must mean you're not afraid of me."

"I realized the house is full of witnesses. Whoever is doing this is not stupid or hasty."

"And I'm not stupid, but I hardly plan so many years in advance."

His father's expression almost lightened. "It is not an easy time," he said at last. "The things you have said to me."

"What do you mean?" Quade asked.

His father only shook his head, and the grim set returned to his brow and pinched mouth. The lines of disappointment, rage, and sorrow had set, and this was now his mien.

"You said that right after Jack's funeral, that I complained. I don't think I have. Why do you think that?"

"Your letters are filled with vague threats and distortions."

"No, they aren't. I fail to understand why you say things like that." His tone sounded menacing, even to him, when really, Quade only wanted to go to his father, embrace him. He gave up trying to push the matter. "We are not enemies, Father. I promise you. Can you show me these letters? I have sent only three since Jack's death."

"I am speaking of letters before that incident."

"May I see them?"

"No. I burned them."

"I wrote nothing that required such a strong response. I wonder what's going on."

His father looked puzzled but still wary.

"You don't believe me?" Quade demanded.

"I am weary, Quade." It was the first time he'd used his name in a very long time. "I think the best thing to do is to pretend this visit never took place. We can only hope to get past this deeply unpleasant time without further incidents."

"No, that's ridiculous. We can't go about our business as if everything is as it ought to be. Not if someone is possibly trying to kill us."

His father's laugh held no humor. "Who could it be? The only one with anything to gain is Wilbur Dunne, who'll inherit should we all perish. He has no need of wealth. Furthermore, he is a weak-willed creature without the brains to come up with any sort of evil schemes."

"I suppose I should be glad you believe me smart enough to be a scheming murderer."

His father's glare returned, but he spoke mildly enough. "I think it best if you leave. I need to write a note to Mr. Kelly telling him his employee's services are no longer required. Now that I think of it, that Irishman"—he waved a hand at the door—"is also named Kelly, so the investigator apparently hired an incompetent relation. Bah. I'll have to find a replacement elsewhere." And with that, Father, ever the brisk and efficient planner, returned.

"No, don't bother. I shan't allow any new man into my home." Quade walked to the door.

"You shall accept a replacement or—"

Quade interrupted. "Or what? You'll cut off my stipend? I have been supporting myself for these five years at least. I have no need of your funds. You have no threat to hang over my head." He should have had a sense of triumph, but he only felt hollowed out. And perhaps that was appropriate as he carved his father out of his life.

"It is in your best interest to have protection," his father began.

"And now you seem less entirely convinced I'm guilty after all? Good. You and I are both confused."

His father shook his head. "Protection," he began again.

"Yes, I'll hire my Mr. Kelly." *His,* yes. "I suspect much of your dissatisfaction with him is that he does work for me rather than you."

"The upstart was supposed to keep watch and nothing else, not insert himself into our family's matters."

"It's too late now to hide from the truth. He and I will find it." Quade longed to tell his father to go to hell for thinking the worst of him and for hiding—and for trying to force him to hide as well—but decided to try for Colm's manner. He breathed in and out, once, twice, then said, "I'll bid you good day. I hope you're doing more than attempting to set a watchdog on me, Father. I certainly am." He paused, hand on the doorknob. "I shall write if I discover anything that might interest you. I promise not to bother you in person again. Please give Mother my regards."

His father's scowl grew worried. "She might wonder that you didn't stay to see her. At least leave word."

"Give her my regards and feel free to tell her why I didn't stay."

He walked out and didn't slam the door behind him.

Quade waited impatiently as Colm said goodbye to a large man hulking in the corridor just outside the drawing room. He wanted to race from the house, run as fast as he could, but he settled on a brisk stride.

"I'm sorry I behaved badly," Colm said when he caught up.

Quade broke into a trot to get across the road before a coach ran him over. "You did nothing wrong. I did nothing wrong."

"You didn't, that's certain," Colm said heartily. "Me, that's a different story. I spoke out of turn to your father. Where to next?"

Quade said, "You know you're no longer employed as my guard."

Colm looked at him sideways, as if trying to gauge his mood. A small smile touched the corners of his mouth.

"What is it, Colm? I can tell you have some ridiculousness you want to share."

"No such thing, sir! Hardly ridiculous that I get such pleasure out of doing the job of watching you, I'll do it for free."

That was flirtation. Quade's anger at his father dissipated—it was difficult to nurse an emotional injury when he had Colm Kelly at his side. Quade's steps slowed. "Your cousin might give you different work, and I'll tell him so. I hope he understands and finds another job for you."

"Me as well, but only after I know you're safe."

Quade stopped abruptly and turned to face Colm, who nearly ran into him. "Thank you," Quade said. "You have no idea how glad I am to have you with me." He swallowed and swallowed again. His nose and eyes prickled, and he looked up at the gray sky to stop any sort of tearful nonsense.

"Aw, Mr. Marrill, I so want to embrace you," Colm said softly. "Damn." He stepped close, seized Quade for a brief hug, and gave him a few hearty pats on the back.

"Now I'd best step back." His breath was warm on Quade's ear. "I need to do my job whilst I still have it."

Quade was the one to step back and away from Colm's arms. "I'll pay you. At the moment, I should feed you."

"Are you hungry?"

The thought of food made him feel sick. "I would like a beer. And after that, I'll call upon my cousin Wilbur."

Colm said, "Huh, will we now."

His simple amusement restored Quade's spirits more than he'd thought possible. No matter what happened, he had Colm Kelly in his corner. He set off walking again. "I promise, one beer only. Don't give me that look, Mr. Kelly. That incident at the club was unique. I don't think I've ever been so rat-arsed before. After that, I shall call on my cousin Wilbur. You've annoyed my relation, I've annoyed yours.

Perhaps the two of us can work together and truly make Wilbur angry."

They went to a pub very close to his father's house. Kelly looked around the place with interest. "There are more people in here than fit in two of the villages I patrolled," he said.

Quade led him to a table in the middle of the room.

"Not that one." Kelly moved to another table in a dark corner, then sat with his back against the wall. "Still doing my job," he reminded Quade.

The server brought them pints and a plate of pickles and greasy, shriveled cheese. Kelly ate the cheese with obvious pleasure.

"It's rather disgusting," Quade said.

"Tastes fine to me."

Quade drank some beer. "Do you miss your home?"

Kelly nodded. "The people. The quiet of it, yes, and the fields and the ocean. But I hear there are fields and commons like the country not so far from here."

"I'm sorry you had to run away from Ireland."

"My own fault. I should have let well enough alone. I had developed feelings of the wrong sort for someone who didn't take well to hearing them." Kelly sounded as composed as ever.

"You're saying that in addition to losing your home, position, and contact with your family, you also lost love."

Kelly was quiet. He reached for his beer and drank much of it. "Ah well. It's not all lost after all. And I have heard from my mam. My sister's letter had a message from her."

"How strange you refuse to allow yourself to rage." Oh, bother. Not the way to reply. Quade should have said something less provocative in response.

Kelly leaned on the table and spoke sotto voce. "Didn't you yourself say mourning does no good for a man? When we talked about your family, your brothers, you said as much."

Had he? Quade couldn't recall saying the words out loud. "There is something of a difference. I can't reach into the grave and pull back my family," he said.

"I can't reach across the Irish Sea and expect to receive embraces from mine." Kelly still sounded pensive. Another person might would have been snarling with rage by now at Quade's intrusion.

"Do you know, you haven't lost your temper with me," Quade said.

Kelly's smile lit his face, and as usual, Quade had an oddly physical response to it. "Is that what you're doing? Trying to prod me into anger?"

"Perhaps, a bit." Quade sipped the beer, which was too flat for his taste. "My brother once told me that if reincarnation is a true thing, in my last life I'd have been one of those insects that can't help buzzing around and biting others over and over."

"A gadfly is generally a good thing. The world needs 'em, as Mr. Socrates said."

"Gracious, you know philosophy?"

Kelly shrugged. "We had a fine grammar school in my village. The local priest loved teaching and only had a few boys to practice with. He and the lady teacher set out to make us all into scholars, forcing us to recite whenever they cornered any of us, even on a Sunday or in the fields."

"Did you enjoy school?"

"Generally we lads ran off or hid when we saw Father Duncan coming. But I did develop a taste for reading. My da said it was a waste of good daylight, but it delighted my mother that all her children can read and speak fine English too. Modern world, she said, though I doubt she'd imagine such a thing as this London."

He wore a fond expression as he gazed out at the businessmen and clerks at the end of their workday. Colm's smile faltered and vanished. "Two men are coming this way. I wonder… They seem familiar. Do you know them?"

"Oh no. That's Melton and Crispin. They're from my club."

"Argh," Colm said softly. "The one with the bulging eyes and the slicked-back hair and the wolf-y smile."

"That's Crispin. What about him?"

"He tried to get me to box for him."

"What?" Before Quade could get an answer, the two gentlemen were hailing them and flooding the air with their words.

"Hullo, hullo, hullo," Melton called, as if spotting the fox across the hunting field. "We saw you leaving your father's."

"I'm just across the road from Mr. Marrill now." Crispin took up the next line smoothly, as if the two formed a music hall crosstalk act. "Took a lease on Tumbalt's place. Not nearly as pleasant as your family's house, but it's a good neighborhood, don't you think? I'm going to be married soon, and I thought I'd best get shot of bachelor's quarters."

Melton interrupted, less smoothly this time. "We'd just been discussing what to do about you at any rate, Marrill, and here you are."

"May we join you?" They each pulled out a chair and sat before Quade could protest.

"What can I do for you gentlemen?" he asked.

"As the American poet says, let the dead Past bury its dead. That is to say, the committee has gone over that incident." Melton gave an embarrassed fake cough. "Fault on both sides, so on and so forth. We wanted to assure you that you might come back any time you wish, Marrill. Er, perhaps it would be best if…"

Crispin shot a quick glance at Colm. "Not to say visitors aren't welcome, of course. A short stay in the visitor's parlor?"

"That's fine, of course," the other said. "In moderation. Meals…" It was his turn to let his voice trailed off.

The other nodded. "That is to say, best not."

"If my friend isn't welcome, then I'm not interested." Quade rose to his feet and beckoned to Colm. "You should take heed of men like Mr. Grace. He has been nothing but polite to Mr. Kelly."

"I beg your pardon, who?"

"Mr. Grace. Or perhaps he's returned to his own club. I wouldn't be surprised."

"A familiar name," Crispin said.

"Of course. That skinny chappie. Doesn't dress well, does he. And old." Melton made a face. "Reminds me of my father-in-law-to-be, though my relation-to-be at least knows how to buy proper suits, though his shoes are quite worn through—"

Crispin interrupted. "Grace? Grace, yes. I can't recall who vouched for him."

"Aha! That's just the sort of thing members said at the last meeting. Vouchsafing needs to be done by multiple members. One would feel far more secure if more than a single member vouchsafed."

"Surely not."

"And the new members must wear a button of some sort, don't you agree? Or perhaps a green buttonhole for their first week? But not a carnation. I cannot abide carnations."

Quade had had enough of their nonsense. "Mr. Grace isn't a permanent member."

"Weren't there dues and whatnot?" Melton asked no one in particular.

"I should say! Yes, of course." Crispin touched the middle of his mustache, apparently lost in thought about buttonholes. "We're going to raise them soon enough, by the by. The lesser element won't be encouraged to remain, all in all a good thing. Some of the dreary suits I've seen infesting the place… No style is bad enough, but shoddily made is too, too much." He clicked his tongue.

Quade realized he didn't actually miss his club much after all. He put on his hat. "Good day to you both. Feel free to contact me again if you have different news."

He and Colm left. He strode toward his apartment so quickly, he was soon out of breath.

"Aren't we going to Wilbur Dunne's house?" Colm said.

Quade looked around. "We're going in the wrong direction. I forgot."

Colm caught up with him. He wasn't out of breath, of course. "We're nearly home. Might as well at least stop there."

"A man can face only so much confrontation in one day."

* * *

When they returned to the house, a literal confrontation occurred. As they started up the stairs to Mrs. Eldred's house, a man came out the front door.

The evening was chilly and damp, colder than even a usual early spring day, so it wasn't entirely strange that the man wore a muffler up around his face and neck and his hat pushed low on his head.

He must not have seen them, for he thumped hard enough into Marrill that he knocked him off his feet. Marrill stumbled hard on the stairs and might have gotten badly hurt if Colm hadn't caught him. After Colm finished steadying Marrill, he turned and trotted back down the stairs.

"Where are you going?" Marrill called.

"I think that man attacked you."

"I think we have spent too much time worrying about people coming after me." Marrill came down the stairs slowly. He rubbed his leg, which must have hit something during his near fall.

Colm stared after the figure walking briskly away, not running but not looking back. Wasn't that an odd response? "He didn't even stop to see if you'd been injured," Colm growled. He began to trot after the swiftly walking man.

"Come back," Marrill called. "He's hardly running off, just preoccupied. And I'm fine."

"Why didn't he stay to see if you were all right after smashing into you?" Colm looked back and forth between the disappearing figure and Marrill and decided to follow the one he was to protect. He kept talking as they entered the building.

"I can see myself doing something very much like that," Marrill said. "I've given the cut direct to people I know by not noticing as I pass them on the street."

Colm joined him. "Why was he in the building? Didn't you say the other tenant, Mr. Malthus, is in the country? And he's certainly not someone visiting Mrs. Eldred."

Marrill climbed the wide inside stairs to the apartment. Colm called after him, "Don't touch anything if it looks as if someone broke in."

Marrill opened the door. "It's unlocked."

Colm raced up at those words. "No, I'm almost certain I locked it. Just wait." He pointed. "Go stand down there, please."

Marill grunted something but obeyed and went back down the stairs.

Colm slid through the apartment slowly, opening each door, examining each room before he ran down to join Marrill, who was talking with Sally, the maid, who was wide-eyed with interest.

She absently twisted her apron in both hands. "No, no one's called on anyone in the house today, sir. At least none that used the knocker. I'd know too. I haven't been out at all."

"Nothing looks disturbed in the apartment, sir," Colm said. "Will you come see?"

He and Marrill walked through the rooms, looking up and down at everything. Nothing was out of order. Of course, with the usual piles of books and papers it appeared as if it had been mildly ransacked.

"Nothing gone," Marrill reported. "And the place hasn't even been disturbed that I can see. So if he was a burglar, he gave up quickly."

"What did you notice about the man?"

Marrill blinked, then shook his head. "Nothing more than the fact that he has a very sharp elbow, which he jammed into me. He might have been about to fall and flung an arm out."

It had looked aggressive to Colm, perhaps even an attack, but Marrill wore that tight, closed expression that meant he didn't want to argue. Fair enough.

Colm chewed his lip and thought. "He didn't smell like a poor man."

"I didn't distinguish any sort of scent."

"Yes, that's what I mean. He can afford clean clothes and baths. But he wasn't well enough dressed to be a rich one. He wore more clothes than a man should in this weather. It's chilly, but hardly mid-winter."

They made another half-hearted search through the rooms, but nothing seemed out of place. The sugar jar with the household funds still sat on the shelf next to the stove.

Colm added some coal to the stove and put a kettle on to boil. Marrill returned from the office where he'd been sorting through papers. "Nothing amiss there," he announced. "How did he manage to unlock our door?"

Colm liked that phrase, *our* door.

He sighed and admitted the truth. "Ach, maybe I remember wrong and I didn't lock it when we left. We ran out quick-like, all on fire to see my cousin. Seems like days ago, doesn't it?"

Marrill gave a small huff of unamused laughter. He walked to cupboard and got out the loose tea Colm had ordered. Though he preferred coffee, Marrill sometimes drank tea and seemed to have the knack of making it well. Colm's was always too weak, or so Marrill claimed.

Colm watched Marrill, in shirtsleeves, move about the kitchen. They'd fallen into the funny ways of a household with neither a servant nor master. It would look peculiar to anyone other than them, Colm supposed. The informality and ease suited him.

As he measured tea leaves into a pot, Marrill said, "I can't help thinking of that blasted Pennick and the nasty notes. Break-ins and whatnot. And the notes my father burned."

Colm nodded. "We should look take a very careful look around to see if anything is missing or if something has been added."

"Added? Oh, you mean like the pry bar."

"It'll be easier to search in daylight. We can look tomorrow morning," Colm said.

"Tomorrow, we visit my cousin."

Colm grimaced. "I'd ask if you're sure that's a good plan, but you sound far too much like a barracks commander to question."

"Am I so commanding?" Marrill sounded pleased.

"No, it's more that you are that stubborn."

"That will have to do, I suppose. And you'll coax and wheedle me if you think I'm wrong. Or just flat-out refuse to allow me out of your sight, then tell me you won't go with me. Being polite all the while, of course."

"Yes, toadying to you even, if necessary," Colm agreed comfortably. "That about sums it up." He sipped his tea and felt happier than he should have.

"I like sitting here with you," he said. "Just the two of us alone."

Their eyes met. Marrill went very still, and the tension of his body crackled straight into Colm, as if it had been an invisible line of something that was always there but usually could be ignored, but oh no—not when each of their bodies woke to lust at the very same moment. So much want and need between them, it drowned out everything else. Colm awkwardly looked down and tried to take another sip of tea, but it only tasted like desire.

"Ah," Marrill said. "I wondered if you… If it was a problem. Because it was before."

Now it was, of course, because Colm had proved to be stupid enough to say something out loud about the two of them alone.

Damn, it this was just like the incident with Liam, when Colm couldn't just enjoy the ache of unfulfilled desire and keep it to himself. Except that the threat here came from actually acting out his dreams instead of being ejected from his life.

He forced a smile onto his face. "No, no, not a problem at all." He'd pretend he didn't understand, though he could see well enough how quickly Marrill breathed and how his fingers touched the edge of his cup. And Colm couldn't stop himself from staring, studying each bit of the man across from him. He took in Marrill's fingers on the cup, his shoulders in the well-made cotton shirt, up to his mouth, and his eyes—which stared back.

Colm put his cup down deliberately and rose to his feet. "Best lock up, then." He fled the kitchen like a coward, and Marrill didn't protest.

Colm locked their front door and, just to be certain, placed a chair against it. He checked the windows and the back entrance to the apartment. By the time he was done, Marrill had gone into his room and shut the door.

Disappointment washed through Colm. He'd been the one to walk away from the kitchen. And now what could he want?

That night he'd rushed into Marrill's room thinking they were under attack by dragons—his memory had captured the image of a rumpled bit of hair over Marrill's forehead, the texture of his skin. And if he went into that room now, would he hope for more cozy conversation? Perhaps a nice chat with Marrill whilst sitting on the edge of his bed? Not likely, not without rousing something he wasn't sure he could allow out of either of them.

Colm stared at the blank white door barring the way into Marrill's room. He stood in the corridor far longer than a sane man should.

CHAPTER ELEVEN

The next morning, worries attacked Quade. Colm insisted on serving breakfast before they set out visiting Wilbur Dunne, but nothing tasted right to Quade. The porridge was lumpy, and, far worse, the coffee he'd made tasted like acid.

"It's confoundedly bitter," he complained to Colm. "And it's a brand-new batch roasted by the grocer very recently."

"Coffee always tastes bitter. 'Tis the devil's brew."

Quade emptied the cup and pot out the back window and, more stealthily, since Colm had made the food, hid the porridge leftovers. No doubt he suffered from nerves after confronting his father, and now he would have to speak to a cousin he barely knew. It didn't help that he'd spent much of the night thinking about going into Colm's room. And imagining Colm in his bed. And wondering if he'd mind just talking, with only the warm comfort of another body next to his. The warmth of skin… Quade rubbed his eyes, dry from lack of sleep, and straightened his tie before setting out to pay a call on Dunne.

Wilbur Dunne's house was large and crumbling a bit around the edges. So perhaps Cousin Wilbur wasn't as wealthy as Quade had thought.

But once the butler had ushered him into a drawing room, he changed his mind. The décor was a mix of ancient Egypt and Grecian. Quade walked to a wall tile and touched the chipped bottom of the square, marble, not plaster.

"I think that the wall tiles and statues were not imitations. These are like the Elgin marbles," he told Colm.

"Oh?" Colm peered into an open sarcophagus. "This is a coffin, isn't it. Strange bit of furniture to have about the house."

"The Egyptian material is not uncommon, but the friezes and the statuary are. I wonder if it's legal for him to own some of these?"

The door opened, and Colm leapt to stand in front of him, moving so quickly, Quade felt a breeze as Colm sprang into a protector's position. He'd been too caught up in his own thoughts to notice Colm was on edge, or more likely, Colm hid his strong responses until they were necessary.

Wilbur Dunne strolled in. He'd gained some weight since the last time Quade had seen him. He was on the edge of stout, and his face had lost some of its sharper edges. His carefully arranged light brown locks covered the thinning hair on his forehead and pate.

"This is an unexpected pleasure," Wilbur said. His face was flushed as if he'd been drinking or running fast.

"Yes, I would have sent round word or invited you to look in on me, but my home is not an ideal place to entertain visitors." Quade hoped he sounded convincing. It wasn't a lie, after all.

"I am glad to see you, of course. But, er… Well. How are you? I should ask that." It was as if he'd lost some script for unexpected visitors and had forgotten his lines. Quade could sympathize. Perhaps awkwardness was a family quirk.

Quade could save them all the scrabbling for proper conversation, and Colm might relax a little, if he came right out and made accusations. But, then again, they'd be turned out at once. Best to go slowly.

Wilbur was regarding Colm with a tight, puzzled smile. "And who have we here, Cousin Quade?"

Quade said, "This is Colm Kelly. He has been in my father's employment until very recently. Now he works for me."

"Oh, indeed! In what capacity?"

Quade was attempting to come up with some innocuous title when Colm spoke up. "I'm his guard. People have tried to kill members of his immediate family. I'll stop anyone who comes after Mr. Marrill." He sounded nothing like his usual easy-going self. With his shoulders back and the unexpected glare in his eyes, he seemed to have transformed into a snarling creature. A watchdog and not a tame pet lapdog after all. And a cold Colm seemed a more effective version of Quade at his most aggressively annoying.

Wilbur gave a startled snort of laughter at the obvious challenge to try something. He retreated to a bell pull. "Gracious me. Well, well. That's certainly interesting, isn't it? But I beg you, stand down. Cousin Quade, you take a seat. I shall…yes, of course, I'll ring for tea."

When the butler arrived, Wilbur ordered service for all three of them. "Perhaps not the thing a chap such as yourself is accustomed to," he said to Colm. "One never knows what is proper in this case. I've never had a guard to tea before, other than my sister's husband, of course, but his is a different situation, of course. He's in the Coldstream. Queen's guard of course. You'd know that even if you are Irish, I expect?" His tone was friendly, not belligerent, and any awkwardness had vanished.

Quade had forgotten how affable Wilbur always seemed, and he seemed even softer than ever. It was impossible to imagine those plump white hands holding a bar and striking a man on the head. And now he recalled that Wilbur had a fear of horses. Also impossible to think he might be the sort to direct a team off a cliff. Of course, he might employ someone, but how would he go about finding such a man?

They sat and discussed the antiquities on display in the drawing room—or rather, Wilbur droned on about them. Even Quade, who appreciated minutia, felt dozy after a few minutes. His cousin had a mania for antiquities he couldn't recall hearing about before.

"Have you been a collector for long?" he asked.

There was a considerable pause as if Wilbur hadn't heard. Just before Quade could answer, Wilbur said, "Six years, thereabouts." He changed the subject after that, back to the quality of the statues he'd recently acquired.

He didn't ask after Quade's family or even Quade himself. Over the next quarter hour, they talked of the weather, of the horse races, of some act of parliament pertaining to imports, but not a word about the family that had only recently lost a son.

Quade dragged out the topic himself. "I was surprised not to see you at my brother's funeral."

Wilbur winced. "That was a dreadful business," he said. "Alas, I was not in England at the time to offer support to your family in its time of need. I've been going on expeditions to Egypt in the last few years. The last was almost a year long. Surely you knew about my travels? I produced a volume concerning the things I've seen. I thought I'd sent a copy to your family."

He rose to his feet, hurried to a bookshelf, and returned with a large, pale green leather-bound volume, which he thrust into Quade's hands. "Please, keep it by all means. I hope you enjoy it." He looked across the room to where a large grandfather clock ticked. "Now I must bid you goodbye because I have an appointment in less than an hour." He moved toward the door.

Quade felt a wave of suspicion and frustration. Why on earth hadn't Wilbur said or asked a thing about Jack? Quade refused to move from the room until his cousin addressed his concerns.

Judging from his response to Colm's announcement of his position as bodyguard, Wilbur must have at least heard the rumors of the Marrill family woes. Instead of showing interest, he had hurriedly changed the subject. He might have been genteelly discreet, of course.

Time for Quade to be direct and rude. "Cousin Wilbur, why haven't you asked about the attacks on my family?"

Wilbur blinked. He licked his lips. "Such a question to ask, Quade. You wish for honesty?"

"Yes, please."

He drew in a long breath, his chest rising high before he answered. "You and I are not close, and I hardly feel it is my place to tell you such things but, very well. I think you are wrong to be so fearful. The awful things that have occurred seem entirely unrelated. I didn't like to speak of these matters at any time, and particularly not now."

"Why not?" Quade asked.

"Perhaps because your, ah, guard is here with us. I'd prefer to speak alone."

"Just say what you mean."

His cousin's smile was false. "Since you insist, I do not like to cause offense, cousin, but I believe your family has had a terrible streak of bad luck and nothing more. And why you would wish to talk with me…" His voice trailed off. His mouth opened wider, rather comically round, then snapped shut.

He rose to his feet, his eyes wide with shock, as if Quade had just taken a swing at him. "Is that the reason you visited today? To find out if I'm trying to kill you?" His voice went high. Was he truly astonished to find out he was a suspect?

Since that was indeed why they'd paid the call, Quade only shrugged.

"It is past time for you to leave." Wilbur's voice was ragged with strong emotion—rage? Fear?

"Thank you for the tea," Quade remembered to say. Colm didn't speak. He did give a perfect bow, respectful without a touch of mockery.

When they walked out and around the corner to a busier street, Colm insisted on hailing a hackney, an act he also performed with skill.

Despite his claim that he would never adjust to life in the city, he was quickly transforming from rural constable to a citizen of London. Quade felt a pang. Perhaps once he'd adjusted to the city, Colm would see how clumsy Quade actually was. Although he'd never tried to pass himself as a sophisticate, Quade had had moments when he'd been able to explain life in London to Colm. Those moments would end soon.

Quade took his seat in the carriage and wondered why he should care so very much what a man of Kelly's breeding thought. The brief flash of snobbery almost made him laugh out loud. He had been raised not to notice the lower class beyond a civil greeting. His family and their servants lived in the same house, but each seemed to negotiate a separate world, one he hadn't entered since he was a small boy with a nanny. He'd sometimes sneaked to the kitchen and annoyed Cook for treats, but once he'd gone off to school, he'd outgrown that life and those forays downstairs.

"I'm sorry about what took place today," Colm said. "My cousin and Mr. Marrill were absolutely right. I stepped out of bounds and shan't do it again."

"Ha, you might have been listening to my thoughts about proper order and that sort of rot."

"I can only say I'm sorry, sir."

Quade shoved him hard with his shoulder. "No need to call me sir when we're alone. That genie has escaped captivity. And as for the rest of it, utter nonsense. I consider you a friend, and I don't put boundaries on friendship."

"Hmm." Colm suddenly looked amused—no, that was a leer on his face.

Quade snorted. "I'm not sure what you are thinking, but I meant conversation. No boundaries on what we can say to each other."

The smirk vanished. Colm gave a slow, thoughtful nod. "Of course. Thank you for that."

"As for more than that," Quade lowered his voice. "Propriety flew away the moment we touched."

Colm's leer had returned. "At first I was mortified, but now, when I think of it…"

"Do you think of it?"

"Too much." Colm reddened, but the smile didn't vanish. "You've changed me, I think."

"I know you transformed me, though into what, I'm not certain. I suspect I know when the metamorphosis took place, the moment you entered my apartment. One doesn't pay close attention to domestic staff. But you…" He shook his head. "I noticed you when you came through my door. Before that—I think I knew something transformative was coming up the stairs when I heard your boots."

"Who knew clomping old boots could do such a thing?"

"Not I. But I know it's true."

"Ach, Quade." The words were nearly a whisper. It was Colm's surrender.

There'd been a charge in the air that sparked through Quade, and it had exploded when they'd touched. And would catch and spark again any minute. A carriage, even a closed hack, was not the place to allow a surge that would result in a conflagration.

So many days, and those long nights. They would not last. Quade looked at Colm's eyes, his slightly parted lips, and knew the fight had ended for them both.

Quade gave a shaky laugh. "When we're alone."

They made it up the stairs and even managed to shut the door. In seconds, Colm had Quade in his strong arms and pressed him to the wall.

Quade reveled in the unyielding body against his, particularly the very hard ridge of Colm's penis moving against him, scraping his own through their nuisance clothing.

Their kisses were extravagant, openmouthed expressions of hunger that only grew deeper as the kisses did as well.

The passion in those sloppy kisses grew and ebbed, and as they became more delicate, he worried that would be the last time their lips touched. He nudged in closer and tilted to get a better angle for their mouths.

Don't speak, he silently admonished them both. Not a word. He closed his eyes too and concentrated on the sensation of the hard body under his hands and the heat of the breath touching his neck. He'd twisted so now he pushed Colm against the wall, but that meant he couldn't easily touch his buttocks or back.

Pulling away, he reached for Colm's hand but didn't look him in the face. If their eyes met, he might see something he didn't want to. No distractions and as few chances for Colm to reach for regret as possible.

As he tugged Colm down the hall, he thought of what he might say if the protesting started. *Just let me touch you, then. No? Then please let me look. I'm begging. I'm starved. I need this. Please, please. Just once, let me see?* But Colm's hand gripped his in return. No need to grovel or plead.

They went into his room and undressed, fumbling at their own clothes, without speaking.

Quade paused now and again to watch Colm body's revealed. His skin was pale, the dim light caught the gleam of hair on Colm's arms and legs. The hair on his legs was darker, though Quade stopped paying attention to that detail when he saw that cock, ruddy and thick, in a nest of the dark hair.

He put both hands over his own more slender member.

"Don't," Colm whispered. "I want to see you all."

The times he'd lain with Barnaby, Colm had savored some of the details: the warmth, the breathing, the weight and heft of another person on his skin. But most of the times he'd gone to the other man's house, he'd kept his eyes shut as much as possible and only went in the dark. He had been too aware of all they did, and the shame had lingered along with Colm—along with each of Barnaby's groans.

Colm heard them clearly because he'd been too quiet, letting Barnaby touch him and do nearly all the work in their encounters. His orgasms had been powerful, but the rest of the experience could not jolt his mind out of the shame that felt like a miasma—and then the shame had only increased when he saw how eager Barnaby was before, touching him with trembling fingers, and how truly moved Barnaby was after. He'd beg Colm to stay, and of course, he wouldn't.

The thoughts came into his mind for a moment or two, but most of the time he lay in that bed, he could only pay attention to one thing: Quade Marrill.

With Marrill, Colm could no more stop himself from stroking and tasting and moaning with pleasure than he could stop himself breathing for long. He had to return those hungry kisses with his own starved ones. He had to lick his way down to that elegant cock, to lap it and take it in his mouth. He had no choice in the matter.

He hadn't known he could be that greedy for sensation. And he scarcely noticed when his need to get as close as possible made him clumsy. Even the ache in his jaw as he sucked on Quade's cock was arousing.

With Marrill, Colm's eagerness wasn't a race to the point of release. Each kiss and touch was its own reward. And if he closed his eyes, it was only an instinct to hold back too much sensation. He'd open them again at once because he had to admire Quade's face in the dim light and to watch his features contort in pleasure and amazement.

He lay as close as he could to Quade, his head resting against the taut flesh near Quade's jutting hipbone. The slippery hot member in his fingers was harder than granite, and Colm loved watching the effect even the smallest touch had, keeping his eyes on Quade as he slid the pads of his fingers over the head of Quade's cock, or lapped his tongue over the elegant rounded crown. Watching Quade was more than enough until Quade reached down and wrapped his hand tight around Colm's cock—a masterful grip. Quade's palm was soft from his life of leisure, and that hand with those deft fingers was as sweet a thing to touch Colm in his life, almost as astounding as Quade's mouth.

Colm gasped, and his attention suddenly moved, dividing between giving pleasure, taking it, giving it, taking it and, then taking and taking, thrusting into Quade's palm.

He couldn't do more than hold on with the pleasure tightening through him, but managed to do that much, keep his hand on Quade. Colm muzzily noticed that even as his own balls and body coiled up, the cock in his hand grew. Quade's head went back, his mouth open in a nearly silent groan.

"Me too," Colm said and found himself chanting. "Me too, yes, please, you and me too. God, yes, me too."

Silly words, and he couldn't care a whit as his body went up and the pleasure gave and took. Gave until it only took and took, until he exploded in Quade's firm grip. Afterward, a fast and unpleasant change usually took place in his heart, regret replacing eagerness, but he didn't drop into the usual melancholy now. And the softness in Quade's eyes lasted even past the minutes after their release.

Colm slithered up, along Quade's body, not moving away from the warmth he still enjoyed, until they lay in each other's arms, facing each other.

"Hallo," Quade said as he stroked Colm's hair, then combed his fingers through it. Once, Barnaby had done something similar, and Colm had wiggled away, uninterested in affection, more concentrating on arousal. Amazing what a difference this need for touch that didn't vanish after orgasm brought to his outlook.

Within moments, lust and longing woke—almost immediately after they were sated—and he found himself stroking Quade's body again, leaning close to Quade's neck so he could breathe in that scent of paper and expensive soap.

"I crave you," he whispered into Quade's ear, and the shiver that rolled down Quade's body felt like a gift.

Their kisses were slower and touches more deliberate, but Colm's attention never wavered. He was in that bed with Quade, mind and body.

They rested together on the bed. Dawn turned the wall red.

The real world would return, and it was time to discuss the Marrill dragons. They would have to talk and compare notes.

He put his hands behind his head and began. "Your cousin. He has that expensive hobby."

"Yes." Quade clearly had been lying in silence, thinking of the same topic. "I wonder if we, or perhaps your cousin Patrick, can find out if he's in debt? Or under some sort of financial pressure?"

"I suppose he might." Colm turned onto his side and laid a hand on Quade's chest to feel the soft rise and fall his breath. Colm asked, "Do you want to go back to your club? I expect you're tired of only me for company." And didn't he sound like a sad lamb with that comment.

"No, I'm not, you wretch."

Colm closed his eyes and smiled. He'd never experienced such intimacy and bone-deep pleasure. If he should die tomorrow, he would have lived as fully as he could at long last. This must be what made men pie-eyed and peculiar about women.

He asked, "Have you ever…ah…done something with a woman?"

"Once. Long ago. Have you?"

"Mm. No more'n kisses, though. It was pleasant, but this…" He lifted his head and gazed into Quade's sleepy eyes. "Much greater than pleasant."

It would be time for the maid to appear. They rose from the bed and cleaned up the room and themselves.

Colm expected there to be awkwardness when they left the cocoon of protected space, of the bed. But Quade had to finish a project and returned to work. He didn't seem to change much at all, a relief overall. The only difference was he'd look up and smile into Colm's eyes. He even climbed to his feet and backed Colm into a corner for a kiss.

Once, when Colm said his feet hurt from all the walking they'd done the day before, Quade demanded he strip off his shoes and socks. He examined each toe and rubbed them and Colm's feet. And within a few minutes, Quade had put his hot mouth on Colm's toes. A few minutes after that, the rubbing had spread to other parts of Colm's body, and they were at it again, sucking and rubbing naked. And, then, within an hour, Quade had put on his clothes and was back at his desk.

Uncomplicated but with added kisses was most definitely the way one should conduct a furtive, illegal love affair, Colm decided.

CHAPTER TWELVE

The roles of lovers fell on them as easily as if they'd practiced or even discussed the matter, though in truth, they didn't speak of their feelings. Quade didn't mind as much as he'd thought, perhaps because he could read Colm far more naturally than he'd managed with anyone in the past.

Quade considered going back to the club to find Billbrook or Hoyt. When he called on Mary, she wasn't home to him. That was both a relief and a disappointment. He left a calling card and a note wishing her well—a shorter version of the letters he'd sent her in the last month with no mention of dead birds or threats, though he longed to bring them up.

Colm sent off a list of questions to Patrick, mostly about the young cousin and Wilbur Dunne's finances, but also about the father. He included a line about how Mr. Quade Marrill would pay Patrick for his work, which he thought would annoy Patrick nicely.

Quade spent a couple of hours working on his book. "I have a deadline," he told Colm as he rose from his chair to stretch. "You protect me from intruders and murderers."

"It's not funny." Colm beckoned to him before he could resettle to his manuscript. "At least let me show you some not-very-gentlemanly moves to defend yourself, all right?"

Within a few seconds, the wrestling had turned very interesting indeed.

A half hour later, they lay in bed together, naked and sated.

"Have you ever, ah, gone inside a person?" Quade asked as he stroked Colm's chest.

Colm grabbed his hand and kissed it. "You are curious about my life."

"Yes. Have you?"

Colm rolled onto his back. "A man named Barnaby. He's older than I, at least ten years. And he loved to have me go into his body." Colm fell silent, his eyes gone distant.

"It stirs you to recall it?"

"No. Thinking of him mortifies me—of what we did together."

This must be why people didn't pry into the past. The chagrin hit Quade far harder than he would have guessed. "Why are you disturbed by what you did with him? Do you feel this way about what we've done together?"

"No, no." Colm waved his hand in the air as if shooing off a fly. "Not at all."

"It appears you are inconsistent."

"Used to be, yes. I craved touch, but the thought of it, especially after, made me cringe too. Not anymore, not with you."

"Good." Quade could breathe again. "Although why with him?"

"You are a pest."

"I admit to the charge. Still, it is interesting to discover why you worried in the past."

"The difference is I used him. He might have wanted more companionship than just…" He made a crude gesture with his fist of one hand and his finger of the other.

Marrill rolled onto his stomach and gazed into Colm's face. He wouldn't pretend it didn't matter. "Did you enjoy what you did together?"

"Oh indeed. He had a nice enough form, and another person's utter pleasure can make a man excited, no matter Barnaby wasn't the man I dreamed of. I knew that I wasn't risking anything with him. And he was content with what we had. Every couple of months, I'd stop by for a cup of tea and end up plunging into him." Colm sighed and stared up at the ceiling. "I hope no one ever figured out what he and I did together, because poor old Barnaby couldn't leave his little cottage by the sea. He had no sense of adventure, beyond wanting my cock."

"Why do you feel guilty?"

"Because." He winced, paused, then spoke in a rush. "I cared deeply for someone else while I did all this with Barnaby."

Quade wondered what bad memory haunted him, but waited in silence for the rest of the story.

After a few heartbeats of silence, Colm said, "Even after Barnaby confessed to me that he thought of me often. It was a declaration of love, and he'd worked hard to say those words. I didn't answer properly, only made a joke about him surely having better uses of his time. Poor man, so timid and alone. I thought of him more often as I lay in bed recovering from my beating than I ever had before."

"Why?"

"Oh, his bravery in coming to the point with me after all that time. More than that, as I lay on the bed I thought that if I'd just been content with what he and I had, I'd have been able to stay in my villages."

Quade considered thumping him on the head— not so very hard, only enough of a blow to distract him from nonsense. "You, unlike Barnaby, are capable of adventure. It's a pity you had to leave your comfortable life, but it's not an utter disaster."

"Oh, aye. Yes." He wrinkled his nose. "No need to sound so stuffy, lad. Those were the thoughts I had as I lay recovering. Now, if I were to reflect upon the matter, I'd say thank goodness I made an arse of myself and was driven from my village, because this is how I could find my way to Quade Marrill. This is what makes me entirely happy. Time with you."

Quade had to touch him and decided to thump Colm after all, a light one. He loved the way those eyes lightened when Colm laughed at him.

Breathing hard, Quade said, "Yes, a part I hadn't known was missing, found and slotted into place."

From whence could such sentimental words have sprung? He hoped it didn't sound treacly to Colm, and it didn't, thank goodness.

"Well, if that's an invitation." Colm snickered. "I'd be happy to slot my part into your place."

"Good Lord. And to think you were so embarrassed, so entirely horrified when we first kissed."

"Yes."

"Why have you changed?"

"Time? I don't know. One grows used to sin? Or perhaps you wake up one morning to realize it wasn't sin after all because no one is injured? The father of the parish told me that lust is sinful when it comes unaccompanied by anything more than animal hunger."

"He was talking of marriage, I imagine. That's certainly not our lot."

"Yes, I know. I suppose it's prideful to think we'll know the devil, should he come calling. But I expect that the devil can't keep real, genuine affection in his collection of weapons."

Despite the warmth the words "real affection" gave Quade, he persisted. "Aren't you worried those are just clever justifications?"

"Ho, now why should I be any different from anyone else? Justifications are what people always have. I saw that often enough. I had a trainer in the barracks who said it was our business to stay out of most people's business and it would save the public's money. If it helps them sleep at night and be happy in the day and doesn't harm anyone else, leave it go. I expect God is at least as kindly as that policeman, and certainly a deal busier."

Quade leafed through the large green volume that his cousin had given him. "I believe he must have paid to have this produced."

"Oh?"

"Yes, and this book is expensive. Look at these handsome engravings. They are not the work of an amateur artist." He held it up to show Colm the intricate maps and drawings of the temples and other places his cousin had apparently plundered to make his collection. "I expect the drawings and maps were commissioned for this project. He must have money."

"Must have had—that is the what-you-may-call-it."

"What do you mean?"

"In the past."

"Ah, of course. You mean past tense. You wonder if he's used up his inheritance on his adventures and this book."

"That's it." Colm sighed. "Oh, for a true education."

Quade gave a dismissive snort and returned to reading a harrowing account of a desert sandstorm during an expedition. "He seems so caught up in this work. It's rather like a mania. He surely spends every waking moment thinking about antiquities and how to find them. I find it difficult to imagine he had the time or interest to arrange murders as well. And he'd have to find others to do the deeds for him because he's never been in the country when my relations—ha, *his* relations—died."

Someone knocked on the door, far louder and more insistent knocking than the maid's small taps.

Colm was the only one of them with footwear. He had a certain pride in those shoes of his, Quade realized with a stab of fondness as he hunted around the floor for his own shoes. He put them on and was buttoning his waistcoat as he walked out to the corridor.

Colm's cousin Patrick had come to call without waiting for an invitation, and now pushed past Colm when he spotted Quade.

"You've come to answer my questions," Colm said. "You could have sent word."

"No. That's not why I'm here." He jammed his hat under his arm, pulled out his watch and glanced at it.

"Won't you come in?"

"I don't have time. That valet, Pennick. They've found him."

"What does he say?"

"Nothing. He's dead. And there's some indication that you're the culprit, Mr. Marrill."

"I beg your pardon?" Quade said. "Slow down."

"Welch just sent round word about the fate of your brother's ex-servant. Pennick's head was bashed in, and he was dumped into the Thames. And when his rooms were searched this morning, they found some indications that you and he had a connection."

"No." Colm took a few steps to stand between Quade and Patrick Kelly. It reminded Quade of a young collie dog he'd had as a child that would guard him when strangers approached.

Patrick rolled his eyes and sidestepped neatly so they stood in a triangle. "Of course, no. And Cousin Colm, you've been following him day and night, haven't you?"

"Yes, day and night."

Quade glanced at Colm and pressed his lips tight at the thought of the nights lately. But they had serious business to discuss.

Colm returned his look for a brief second, then asked. "How long ago was he murdered?"

"How would I know that?" Patrick paused. "No, wait, come to think of it, Welch's messenger said something about the disgusting state of the fish-nibbled body, so I'd guess it must have been in the water more than a day."

Colm interrupted, barking out the question, "You said there was a connection. What sort of evidence?"

"In his rooms, some letters Pennick wrote mentioning you and pay you'd given him to implicate your brother Jack."

Quade gasped. "That's a lie."

Patrick went on as if he hadn't spoken. "As well as several sheets from a manuscript that apparently was something you're working on, Mr Marrill."

"A manuscript? Which one?"

"I have no idea." He looked toward the door. "But you'll find out soon enough. I expect the police will be here any minute."

"Why did you come?"

Patrick hesitated. "Why? Naturally, I'd want to advise my employee."

Colm said, "But I thought I'm no longer employed by you."

"Who told you that?"

"Mr. Marrill senior fired me."

"Ye gods and little fishes, I pay you, he doesn't. I'd better go now before the police come knocking. I'm surprised they aren't here already."

Patrick bade them goodbye. He clapped his hat on his head as he trotted down the stairs and out the front door.

"He's moving faster than ever I saw him go." Colm snapped his fingers. "Ach. I forgot to thank him and get answers to those questions." He closed the door. "Manuscript pages. Now we know at least one thing that thin man who bowled you over might have stolen while we were out. That's twice he's tried to make others look like the killers."

Quade went into his room and Colm followed.

They began the hunt again for anything that might have been left behind. Colm yanked books off shelves and shook them. Quade leafed through piles of papers, examining each.

Colm went to hands and knees to look behind his old enemy the radiator. He found a piece of glass.

Quade frowned at it. "Laura broke a glass a month ago. Must be that." He started sorting through another manuscript, looking for missing pages. "I'll wager that wasn't the valet we spotted coming down the stairs. The person who ran into me."

"Oh?" Colm shuffled over to look under the bed. "Aside from the fact that Pennick might have been dead at the time, what else convinces you?"

"I recall him as a plump, short fellow. He might not be plump any longer but I don't think he could have grown taller. Perhaps Pennick came up with the original plan of murdering someone in my family, God knows why. He was supposed to place the blame on Jack, or perhaps he came up with that on his own. It would be ironic if he shared that plan with his own killer who's done the same thing."

"Perhaps." Colm squinted thoughtfully and scratched his cheek. "Hmm. Of course we might be wrong and that visitor had nothing to do with any of this. Though I say it is all a piece. And I still say our door had been locked."

"Does that mean our guest was an experienced house breaker?"

"Doesn't take much to unlock a door." Colm scoffed. He rose to his feet and brushed off his trousers.

Quade eyed him. "You're all over dust."

"Hardly, though I see what you mean. Ach, I've grown so used to clean floors. Amazing how fast a man could adjust to a change in the world."

Quade supposed their condition might shift in another dramatic fashion. For instance, they might end up imprisoned in tiny, dank cells—if not for murder, then for the way they carried on together.

That ship had sailed, and would likely keep right on sailing around the world and back again. He forced himself to remain calm as they examined the rooms for another five minutes before the pounding on the door began.

"Ah, more callers."

"I'll answer," Colm said. "I'll be a servant now."

"You hardly look like one."

"Never mind that."

Quade waved a hand. "And I'll act like a recluse with a great deal of unfinished work. In other words, unlike you, I'll behave naturally."

"Sure." Colm gave an exaggerated tug at his forelock, then hurried to the door.

Quade sank into his favorite chair and, to look occupied, grabbed a book. The voices in the hall sounded reasonably civil, so that was to the good.

The police entered the foyer of the flat. Quade wouldn't invite them to sit down, so they crowded in.

Welch repeated the story of the death of Pennick, leaving out details like the bashed head and fish-nibbled body. There was no mention of the bird left at his sister-in-law's house. Quade considered bringing it up but decided to let Welch talk. The other policemen might not know the details.

"And we found these in his home." Welch produced the manuscript pages, six messy pages neatly bound in a ribbon—a glossary.

Quade stared down at it. "That's from a book I finished ages ago." When he walked away, they trailed after him. He went to the bookcase next to the door and pulled down a volume about the formation of the courts of chancery. "Yes, this is the one. It was published last year. I held on to the notes until it was published." He flipped to the front of the book. "In the summer."

He handed the book to Welch, who held it close to the light and squinted. The man needed glasses.

Quade explained, "After a book is finished, I only save the final notes. Once it's published, I throw out most of the earlier copies I've made. Otherwise, this place would become cluttered." He glanced at Colm, who'd just made a small choking sound, and added, "Even more cluttered."

One of the other men, who hadn't been introduced, said, "So you threw away these pages?"

Quade nodded. "Someone must have pulled them from the dustbin ages ago, months, I'd say. This plan, or whatever it might be, was hatched quite a time ago."

"Possibly Pennick," Welch said. The other man scowled at him.

"My brother dismissed Pennick several months before I disposed of the notes. But why would he bother with me?"

"We believe he'd been practicing your handwriting. That was in the folder as well. I think he'd kept all the pieces together."

"Why would he do that?" And a moment later, he understood. Perhaps Pennick had been forging notes that were supposed to be from Quade. Did he send them to Hoyt and Mary too perhaps?

"We discovered samples of several sorts of handwriting in his apartment. We haven't checked yet, but we think one might have been your father's and another your late brother, that is Jack Marrill. Pennick simply copied the samples."

"It wouldn't work if he were alive to come to trial. Imitating handwriting?" Quade pondered the idea of forgery. Would it hold up in modern scientific law? He muttered, "Michon's study is interesting—he calls it graphology, makes it sound like a science, eh? Bah. Such a thing is hardly useful in any sort of criminal case Although, hang on a minute. There was that case in the United States, the Howland will forgery case. Pierce, that was the man. He used mathematics to analyze signatures and—" He realized everyone was staring at him, and his face went hot. "So Pennick imitated our handwriting. Why would he bother to hold on to the damned things?"

"Perhaps he'd been hired and kept the work he'd done to show he'd performed the task." Colm stopped, then added, "Or someone else put it in his place? Or he'd kept the evidence so he'd get more money from his employer."

"Extortion, you mean?" Welch sneered. "That is far-fetched even for a man who believes in fairies."

Quade couldn't believe Welch's absurd dig and gave a startled laugh. "Are you referring to the fact that Mr. Kelly is Irish? By God, Welch, you should be ashamed."

Colm laid a hand on Quade's arm an obvious signal of *please don't worry* or maybe the light touch communicated *shut your idiot mouth, Quade*. Before Quade could say more, Colm said, "It's important to figure out why the man is dead. If one assumes it wasn't a random attack, and I don't, then Pennick was killed for a reason."

Quade twitched away, chagrined by his own outburst. Perhaps Welch had been trying to unsettle him and Colm. The detective wasn't stupid and wouldn't poke at them just to be annoying. Quade decided he could act as coolheaded as Colm. He said, "I say find out why he was killed and maybe we'll figure out why members of my family keep dying." No, he should have kept quiet. He was too loud, and his voice quavered too much.

Welch and the other man directed hard stares at him. He finally noticed that the other younger uniformed policemen standing in his apartment looked very much as if they were waiting for orders. All attention turned to him.

Welch spoke up. "You seem upset, sir."

"Did you not hear me? People in my family have died, and I don't understand why that is happening." Quade squeezed his hands into a tight fists in an attempt to calm himself. "Now this person is dead as well, another connection to my family."

Probably best not to point that out, he realized even as he plowed on. "But if you are thinking I might be a suspect in his death, no. That's ridiculous."

"Ah?" Welch made an encouraging sound. *Say more.*

Quade knew Welch wanted him to look like a fool, or worse, guilty, but took the bait even so. "We had nothing to do with each other. You know Pennick took those notes from my dustbin for his own peculiar reasons. I don't think I held a conversation with the man. In fact, I didn't see him more than once when he worked for my brother at the family hall. Jack and I weren't close, and I had no reason to visit his home." He wondered if that admission that he was distant from Jack sounded as bad to Welch as it did to him.

Welch eyed him with that myopic squint. He might need glasses, but it seemed as if the policeman was peering under Quade's skin. "You weren't close to your brother?"

"I cared about him. I—I loved him like a brother." Quade swallowed hard because he realized this was true. "But he and I had very different sorts of lives."

"Oh?"

"I'm sure you know more about him by now. Before he was married, even after…" He clamped his mouth shut.

"Go on," Welch ordered him. Quade shifted from foot to foot and considered suggesting they sit down, but decided that would only give the man an excuse to hang about the apartment.

Welch said, "Tell me what you are hinting about your late brother."

He was right, Quade's comment had been insinuating, and poor old Jack deserved better, though there had been that rumor Colm mentioned, so it wasn't news to the police. "He was rather rackety. Wild oats and so on." Quade tried to laugh.

"What does that mean?"

"When he was younger, he was banned from several music halls, and I think there were some other claims made against him. Something about broken windows. I didn't know the details, but you surely do by now."

"It wasn't part of the investigation," Welch said. Perhaps he did know what Quade was talking about and that was an evasion. "His death was due to natural causes."

A bee sting on a chilly day, Quade thought, but he was bound and determined to keep his bloody mouth closed.

And after all, Jack might well have been killed by a bee or wasp. He'd had a terrible response to an earlier sting, and there had been hives not so very far away from the Marrills' estate, in a pasture past a copse of trees. Quade's father had ordered the hives smashed to pieces after Jack's death.

Quade had thought that action interesting for two reasons: their father showed strong emotion, and he seemed to believe the doctor's pronouncement of the cause of Jack's death.

Now Quade wondered if that order for destruction had been for show. A barn door slammed publicly shut after the horse had escaped just to make it clear that you believed the horse had come from that particular barn.

His father might be lying about many things, like burning letters.

"You should visit my father. Demand to see any correspondence from me."

"I beg your pardon?"

"He has accused me of being emotional and upset when I don't think I have been. Would this idiot Pennick have written to him pretending to be me? Why would he do such a thing? He disliked my brother, not the rest of us. I think." He dropped his voice to add, "Though there was that note delivered to poor Mary."

Welch gave a dubious grunt. Again with the flights of imagination, it seemed to say.

Quade fell silent and wondered how it would be if he came to see his father again. Would there be more hiding from the emotional turmoil, or was this enough to get him to speak?

Welch was asking him a question. “Do you think your brother’s habits had something to do with the valet’s dislike of him?”

“I have no idea,” Quade said. “Pennick was fired, after all. Perhaps Pennick was insane and he went after other people the way he did Jack. Maybe one of them killed him off. Did you find any notes practicing other people’s handwriting? Other than my family members?”

Welch ignored his question. “You talked about rumors you heard when you were young. Surely you must have had some reason to mention Jack Marrill’s wild oats.”

“I shouldn’t think so. I was repeating nonsense I’d heard when I was young. Very young,” he added. “The vaguest of rumors I’d heard whilst at school.”

“Do you suppose Pennick’s strange note and the evidence planted in the garden shed has to do with those wild oats?”

Quade rubbed his chin and wished he’d shaved. He expected he looked even more disreputable and shabby than usual, and that wouldn’t help his reliability in the policeman’s eyes. Welch seemed far sharper than he had when they’d gone to the station. Perhaps he’d actually hunt down some answers.

“You should find out, I think.” Quade gave up being circumspect about Jack. “If the valet had been a pretty young girl, a maidservant perhaps, your theory about Jack’s habits might be accurate. A female servant might have cause to dislike my brother.”

“Oh?” Welch folded his arms. He waited for a few long moments before prompting “Who would know the details of Jack’s more recent, shall we call it, caddish activity? His widow?”

Quade shook his head. “Perhaps nothing went on.”

“But would she tell us?”

“I’m not sure. One gets the impression she would turn a blind eye to his activities.” As did the whole family.

“You sound envious, Mr. Marrill. Perhaps you wished you were your brother.”

Quade gave a startled laugh. “Dead so young? Of a bee sting?”

“No, in pleasanter surroundings and able to enjoy life with a wife willing to overlook your excesses. His widow is an attractive lady." The man looked delighted at this thought. "Colm Kelly went round after the bird incident. It could be that you sent him there because you'd frightened her by killing her bird and leaving that message. You wanted to see if she required comforting."

"That's utter nonsense. If you're going by Mr. Kelly, you'll know that he's been guarding me constantly except that one day. And you'll know I had no notion about Mr. Kelly's visit to her house," Quade said, "Furthermore, I have no desire for a levirate marriage."

"A what sort of marriage?"

"Read your Bible, Mr. Welch. I'm not going to marry my brother's widow." He almost mentioned Hamlet, but decided he didn't want to be linked with that particular murderous brother, Claudius. "I don't think I can help you at all, Inspector."

Welch gave him that sneer of a smile and remained silent for what might have been a full minute. He went mute often enough it must be intentional, but Quade wasn't going to make any more silly remarks. He shifted, and so did Colm, who managed to brush Quade's knuckles with his own. That touch felt like reassurance.

Broad-shouldered Colm stood close, breathing slowly and exuding just the sort of peaceful strength Quade envied. He made a conscious effort to match his breath and stillness. There. Even the most nervous energy could be quelled, or perhaps only disguised.

At last Welch pulled out a watch and looked at it. "I would love to get more information from you, Mr. Marrill, but I believe you're not interested in cooperating."

"Why do you say that?"

Welch ignored him and gestured impatiently at the door. "Kelly, you come with me."

"Here now, what do you want from him?" Quade's attempt at calm took flight faster than a flock of nervous starlings when a hawk cried out.

Welch said, "He's not a suspect in any of this. I want to talk about anything he might have seen or heard. Perhaps I'd like to check what you said about his activity and yours."

Suddenly treating Colm as if he were some sort of colleague? Welch switched tactics easily. He certainly was smarter than he'd seemed before—or perhaps more interested in the case at hand. A murder might have woken him up.

Colm shoved his hands into his pockets. "Since all I've witnessed has been as an agent, I don't think I can do that without my employer present." He glanced at Quade with his eyebrows raised, in some sort of silent appeal probably. In a question of law, Quade might know the answers.

Colm's argument wasn't the worst attempt to get out of an interrogation, but it wouldn't do. The law didn't offer the privilege of confidentiality to Colm as it would a barrister.

Unfortunately, Welch knew that—or more likely he didn't care. "Come on, don't be a fool. If you don't cooperate, I'll tell Patrick Kelly you were obstructing justice. In our dealings, he needs me more than I need him, and he'll take my side in this matter, I imagine."

"Indeed, he probably will. And what a fine idea it is, to ask him." Colm gave him his brightest smile, and Quade found himself smiling too. Even Colm's falsely merry face brightened one's spirits.

"All right, Inspector Welch, let's follow your fine plan. If I'm not under arrest, I'll go with you to talk with my cousin. Shall we go at once see Patrick?" Colm sounded as if this were his idea of a lovely plan. "We can hammer all this out together. More than one mind, after all. We do want to discover the truth of the matter."

Cozening Irishman—nothing like Quade, who'd want to use a hammer when the lightest touch would make a better and faster outcome.

God bless Colm, he was a finer gentleman than Quade could ever hope to be. How would he convince his Irishman to stay once this peculiar episode ended? The death haunting Quade's family—or still stalking it, perhaps—God, that was a dreary truth. How odd to think the dark time had led to his discovery of Colm the brightest moment in his life so far. Brighter even than the man's smile.

"Inspector, if you still want me to come along and add my own impressions and ideas, I shall." Quade put in a note of reluctance in his offer, as if he was doing Welch a favor, though he longed to go because he had no intention of allowing Welch or anyone else intimidate Colm—if such a thing were possible.

Welch squinted in his direction. "I thought you said you had no ideas?"

"Something might come bubbling up to the surface."

"Meet us at the station in a half hour. I want to talk to Kelly on his own at the moment. And no, Mr. Kelly, we're not visiting Patrick." He eyed Colm. "I know part of your job is to protect Mr. Marrill, so I'll leave behind two of my men to accompany him and keep him…safe."

Instead of ignoring them as he usually would, Quade offered the two officers who guarded him a cup of tea. They refused it and stared straight ahead in that expressionless manner of bored policemen everywhere. He abandoned the idea of trying to coax information from them and slouched back into his office. He stood in the middle of the floor, eyeing the shelves of books, wondering if any contained points of law that might help Colm if the police started to push him. *You're the one in trouble*, an imaginary Colm pointed out.

He found one of the notes he'd scribbled whilst sitting with Colm. *Who hired Pennick? Did he work on his own?*

Quade wondered if the police would share any of that information with him or, more likely, Patrick Kelly. Colm could probably coax that information out of his cousin. Quade would have to wait.

He sat at his desk and began to make another new list, of everyone he knew who might also have met Pennick. Just to jostle his memory, he made lists of names he could dredge up from the past, all the gossip about his brother. He could recall a few scrapes and a boy named Bassett who had challenged Jack to a fight for an insult of some sort. Jack had laughed about that. And he'd laughed about the girls as well.

Quade rolled the pen between his fingers and tried to ransack his memory for all those girls' names. There had been one named Honor, or was it Virtue, Grace or Patience? That pious name was the one he'd heard about at school. There was also Mabel, a maidservant who'd been turned out soon after Quade's third term at school had begun. He'd heard whispers that she'd been increasing. Would the London police send word to Kent and find out details of the Marrill family from the people who knew them?

His father would hate that. Quade paused a moment. They'd said they might have found a sample of his father's handwriting. Would someone be calling upon Arthur Marrill and asking him uncomfortable questions? He wished he could see that.

No, more than that, Quade wished he could visit his father and speak easily with him, perhaps finally learn what he knew—but that would likely be another painful and useless attempt.

When enough time had passed and his paper held more than three dozen names, he recorked the ink, put the paper in his pocket, and went out to find his guards. "I think we might leave now?"

One of the policemen agreed that was what he understood as well.

"Very well," Quade said. "Let's go find my servant—and your master."

CHAPTER THIRTEEN

A carriage waited for Welch just down the street under a tree. It wasn't exactly a Black Maria but it looked grim indeed, and a shiver of uncertainty hit Colm as he climbed in. The two men accompanying them went in the front, up on a box. For a moment, Colm wondered if he were to be locked alone inside but then Welch followed him and, with some trouble, hauled himself into the murky interior that reeked of sweat and tobacco. Welch sat with his back to the horses and fished a pipe from his inside jacket.

Colm wasn't sure he wanted to be trapped in a small space filled with foul smoke, but decided he'd best ignore minor discomforts. The flash of the match shed some light for a moment in the dim carriage. After a puff or two on his pipe, Welch seemed to relax and even grow chummy.

"Tell me anything you can think of about his lordship."

"Who, sir?"

"Mr. Marrill. I think of him like that after his visit to my office."

Colm wondered why people persisted in thinking of Quade as a high and mighty. He just held back his smiles and was uncomfortable around strangers.

Welch went on. "He's good-looking. Tell me, is he a devil with the ladies?"

"Not so I've noticed."

"Who does he spend his time with? Have you seen anything even remotely of interest to me?"

Colm desperately tried to come up with facts Welch might consider useful and that would turn his attention away from Quade. "He's more like a monk than a normal man. He works all the time." *Except when he's sucking me off.* "No women, no carousing."

Welch gave a dissatisfied hum and puffed harder at the pipe.

Colm tried again. If he wanted information from Welch, he'd have to give some, and he'd best not appear charmed by Marrill. "He's been sad about his family, I do believe that. Upset. And, um, I don't think he's used to drinking, that is, he doesn't have a good head for alcohol."

"Oh? Does he grow angry when he drinks?" Welch sounded too eager, like a man following a scent to prey. Perhaps he'd had heard from the people at the club.

Colm said, "Not really."

"Is he in debt? Does he gamble?"

"I don't think so. Not a man to spend much on clothes or anything but books."

"Yes, he's not fashionable, for all that his apartment must cost more than my own little house. He doesn't have the dash of his late brother or even his father." Welch sounded disappointed.

"You've talked to his father?"

Welch fiddled with the curtains of the carriage until more light streamed in. "Yes, he proved even more useless than your Mr. Marrill. A prickly, closemouthed sort of gentleman."

Now that he no longer felt as if he sat in a coffin, and Welch seemed more amiable, Colm relaxed. He asked, "The older Mr. Marrill had nothing to say about Pennick or his death? Or his relations' deaths?"

"If he any ideas, he wouldn't share them with the police. He couldn't order us to leave, but I could see he wanted to." Welch's pipe went out, and he squinted into the bowl. "He did tell us to keep away from his nephew, but to go ahead and let his remaining son have it with both barrels."

"Did he now?"

"Not in those words. He picked his way around with a raft of fancy phrases. But I believe he thinks Quade is somehow responsible for all that's gone on. He suggested we see if he's paid out money to—to ruffians, that was the word he used." He relit the pipe and sucked at it so hard, he had a coughing fit. That gave Colm time to silently examine his own anger to that load of shite. The urge to storm over to Marrill's fancy house and scream sense into him shocked Colm—far more than the fact the man thought his own son guilty. After all, Colm had figured that soon after meeting the man. But he hadn't expected Mr. Marrill to throw his son to the wolves.

Welch must have seen Colm's fury. "You don't agree?"

"No. I don't."

Welch squinted at him. "Tell me this. Why should I believe you and not his father who knows him?"

Colm breathed in and out once before answering. "I am an outsider. I got no dog in this fight." Ha-ha to that, he thought. "I know I have spent more time with Mr. Quade Marrill in the last month or so than his father has for years. Unlike poor Mr… Here now, what is the senior Marrill's Christian name?"

"Arthur."

"Thanks for that. Unlike poor Mr. Arthur Marrill, my mind is not warped by bereavement over the loss of three children, a brother, and a nephew." He considered his final argument and decided why not. "And I was trained by the Royal Irish Constabulary on methods of policing and investigation."

As he'd expected, Welch made a rude noise at that last one. Ah well, good to know where one stood in the local coppers' eyes.

"All right, Officer Well-Trained Irishman, tell me what you do think." He pulled out his watch and held it up to the window. "We're going to go once around the park and after that, it'll be back to Mr. Granby, my colleague. He's the bloke who's more an expert on the Marrills."

"Do you know, I'd suggest that you find out if your friend Granby has been taking some extra money on the side. Begging your pardon for insulting an officer, but he's not done a good job on this case."

He braced himself in case Welch struck him for insulting an officer. But the man didn't even grow upset. "Just you stop right there with that talk. No."

"How are you sure?"

"Because I've taken a bit of a look, and don't you say anything even to that cousin of yours, by the by. Granby's done nothing so vile as being paid off to look the other way. He just has some airs and maybe social aspirations, fancies himself a gentleman, which is a useless attitude for a cop."

Colm raised his eyebrows.

Welch explained. "He seems to think servants and the like aren't as reliable as the middle-class or gentry."

The like probably meant Irish, so Colm had best talk fast—and to Welch.

"You've interviewed Mr. Wilbur Dunne? He's the one man who'd profit from the deaths in the Marrill family."

"We're aware of him. He's not a suspect. He has been abroad during all the events that might or might not have been crimes."

"A man can hire help even when he's far away."

Welch sniffed. "He'd have to have hired more than one person to help—at the very least, Pennick to kill the cousin, and after that, well, someone else to kill Pennick. Mr. Dunne contracted a fever during his travels. Now he's got a weak heart and can't go about smashing men and dumping them in the river. Still, you've got a good notion. There's a lot of money at stake, and I do like money as a reason to kill." Welch's grin showed a few gaps in his molars, which gave him a wicked appearance of a carved turnip jack-o'-lantern. "I wouldn't mind talking to him myself, but we'd best see what Granby says. If he declines interviewing the gentleman again, I might go on my own. Or better still, I'd send our friend Patrick Kelly. He owes me a few favors. And I think I will be looking harder into Jack Marrill's past like his brother suggested."

For the first time, Colm had a sense that Welch actually cared about solving crimes. He returned the grin.

Welch asked, "Can you think of anyone else we might look into? Anyone you might have met?"

"There was a man we'd thought had come to rob Mr. Marrill. He rushed off as if he were in a violent haste, but we never did see results of his visit."

"Tell me about him," he ordered.

"Yes, indeed, I wrote something down." He pulled out his little incident book and ripped out the pages with his notes. "I don't need these, so you can keep them."

He glanced down at the writing. "You're practically a novelist with this description."

"Well. I was a bit shaken. And I've listed the other people Mr. Marrill talked to. Members of Mr. Marrill's club, several librarians." Colm thought back to their afternoons in the library and told Welch about the argument with a man over some Latin translation. "But none of them seemed the sort to hold a years-long grudge as this might be.

I'd say the thing to do is look back in time. When did that first Marrill male die? See what happened about that time."

"The very first Marrill boy drowned, but that was likely a true accident." He wrinkled his forehead, now resembling a basset hound even with the impressive mustache. "I have the list back at the office with the dates and details. Until this Mr. Pennick was found, I wasn't so wrapped up in the case, except as a favor to Patrick Kelly and to annoy Granby." He sighed and poked at the inside of his pipe with a burnt wooden match. Something must have gone wrong with the pipe, but he didn't try to light it again, to Colm's great relief.

"We'll go meet Mr. Granby and Mr. Marrill—your Quade Marrill, I mean—back at the station. And I've sent round word to Patrick Kelly again." He shoved the pipe back into his jacket pocket. "And when we appeared, you weren't surprised to see us. I wonder if he stopped by to tell you that we'd planned to call?"

Colm didn't answer. He pretended to be fascinated by a scene outside. And to be sure, it was a rather interesting scene to watch. Usually when he went around the town, he was with Quade and he concentrated on possible danger, or on not staring at the lanky form striding along in front of himself. Welch settled back into his seat with a sigh. "We'll see," he murmured darkly. Colm pretended not to hear.

***

Quade went to his office to grab a sheaf of paper and pencil. He wished he had written down the notes he'd made in a more orderly fashion. As he went to a shelf to fetch another pencil, he noticed the drawer to the sideboard lay open. And as he walked to the drawer, something tiny and bright glimmered on the floor. He stooped and picked up a shard of glass from the carpet.

"This is the second piece we've found. I should think the maid would have picked up all the pieces before now," he told one of the policemen. Then again, the light from the window was at a particular angle it hadn't been during their previous hunts through the apartment.

"What are you doing?" the policeman demanded.

Quade got down on the floor and crawled around. At the edge of the carpet, he discovered another, even smaller, shard.

"The glass the maid broke shattered closer to the window." He rested on his heels, then continued to crawl again. In the footspace of the desk, he found another tiny piece.

He discovered the source of broken glass in the top drawer of the desk, the one he never used. There lay picture of the Marrill brothers facedown inside the drawer. It wasn't obvious until he turned over the framed picture that the front glass had been shattered. "Good Lord," he said.

The policeman moved quickly. "What is that?"

"It is a photograph on albumen paper," he said. "I'd thought we were ridiculous to worry about that thin man, the visitor, but he must have been here."

With a shiver of anger, not fear, he gingerly fished the photo from the drawer. Each of his brothers' faces was scratched off. His own was intact. On the back was a single word. He traced it with his finger.

"Is this word new or has it always been there? Sons," he said to no one in particular. "My father hadn't commissioned the picture, so that might be from my mother?"

He thought of his mother, starched and remote. The idea that she might have anything to do with anything so messy and unpleasant as murder, much less be responsible the deaths of her own children, was absurd.

And truly, even that first thought, that she'd shrink away from a mess, was hardly fair to the poor lady. She wasn't a cozy, demonstrative mother, but Quade felt certain she had a regard for her family.

Suddenly, he wished he could visit her in the country, not in London. He hadn't called his parents' house "home" since he was in school, but he wished he might go there now, at once. Or perhaps he really wanted to return to the time when he wasn't the only remaining son, when the photograph in his hand hadn't been gouged and wasn't a *memento mori* or a threat.

Why? Who had done this? Why? The useless questions wouldn't stop crowding his brain; indignation shoving out any sort of cool contemplation that would help him think clearly.

"Best leave that glass in place, Mr. Marrill. We'll want Mr. Welch to see."

He rose to his feet and carefully stepped away. "I wasn't thinking when I picked up the photograph. I apologize."

"I guess it's too late to worry about you touching it. We'll bring it with us," the fatter, older cop said. "Do you know who might have done this? Are we sure it wasn't the maid?"

He thought of Sally and shook his head. The marks on the photograph were made by a malignant person.

"Any chance it could be the man who's been living here with you?"

"Colm? Colm Kelly?" Colm did know where the photo had been stored, but that was absurd. Quade held back an obscene remark and only said, "Not him. I believe it was the work of a-a person, a man." Colm had been right. They'd had an unwelcome visitor.

They gave him a patient look. The mutilated photograph had shaken him more than he'd suspected. He licked his lips and tried again. "That is to say it was someone I didn't recognize. He came rushing out of this house."

That sounded ridiculous even to him, but the policeman didn't roll his eyes. He only said, "Aha."

To Quade's relief, he pulled a small notebook from a pocket in his frock coat and began asking Quade questions about the man who might have been an intruder after all.

To be believed in this situation, or at least to have someone act as if he weren't insane or lying, was a blessing and allowed Quade to think again.

He said, "I didn't get a sense of his age, though he moved briskly, and what I saw of his eyes—light colored, I think—were clear. He seemed tall, but he was coming down the stairs at me." He closed his eyes. "Is this why he entered my home—to deface my family portrait? That makes no sense. He didn't take the manuscript that Pennick had—that was thrown away ages ago. But why else? Why? But someone came in, and now that's true, I suppose I should look for more signs."

"It might have been someone other than that gentleman. Anyone you can think of who's come in here? I mean guests, servants, deliverymen, grocers' boys, anyone." The policeman widened his murky blue eyes. "Oh, now, a friend of that dead valet, perhaps?"

"I don't recall any visitors between the last time I saw the photo intact and today. I rarely entertain at home. But there was a German, Herr Dorman," Quade said. "Patrick Kelly would know about him. He worked as a substitute guard when Colm Kelly had a day off. But isn't this the sort of questioning the inspector would perform?"

"Aye." The policeman flashed him a smile that didn't seem genuine and tucked away his notebook. "Should we go?"

"Not yet. I wish to look carefully one more time."

"It's been days since that incident, hasn't it? You'd have noticed something by now," the muttonchop policeman argued. "We'd best be going."

"Yes, it's true time has passed, but…" He held up the photo and waved it. Proof he hadn't looked well enough. "Until now, I don't think I believed that any uninvited guest had been in our…my apartment." The policemen looked at each other, exchanging silent communication. Were they supposed to bring him in by a particular time? Or had they noticed his use of the word "our."

"I shan't take long," Quade said.

"Right, sir."

Quade walked around the apartment one more time, looking through drawers and into cupboards one more time. The two policemen trailed after him, silently watching. He found nothing new or different.

When they left the house, the policemen walked on either side of him. He considered taking off at a dead run to see if they'd chase him down. They were protecting him, he reminded himself. He wasn't a prisoner, he hoped.

"We might stop for a pint," he suggested. That seemed a less dangerous way to discover how tightly under their control he was.

The cops exchanged looks again. "Best to meet with the inspector," the muttonchopped one said. "We can give you a cuppa tea."

He was about to argue, just to find out what limits they'd put on him when he stopped dead on the pavement. "Tea." He shook his head, touched his lips, recalling that bitter taste, the nausea, and the slightly dizzy sensation he'd thought were simply nerves. "Coffee."

"Sir?"

"The coffee. It tasted foul, even acidic, and I threw it out after only one sip. I was sure something had gone wrong with it." He stared up at the sky, his fingers still tapping his lower lip. "Can coffee go bad? I buy a roasted variety."

"Mr. Marrill, are you saying you suspect that an individual has tampered with your coffee?"

"Yes. I was going to throw the beans out, then decided to save the package to complain to the grocer."

He turned on his heel and marched back up the granite steps and then into the house. The maid and cook had been peering out the door. One yelped, the other said, "Beg pardon," and both vanished before the three men rushed up the stairs again.

Now that was like the man he'd run into, but they'd all stopped to speak. They didn't just rush off in silence—the way he'd just done.

Quade went into the kitchen, straight to the muslin sack that held the coffee beans. He opened the top and held out the sack. "Smell this," he demanded.

"Smells fine to me," the muttonchopped policeman said disdainfully. "Do you suspect someone is trying to poison you, Mr. Marrill?"

"If you're worried, we'd best bring it with us," the fat one said between gasps, still out of breath from the swift climb back up the stairs.

They finally marched back out into the rather fine day, and the fat policeman insisted they hire a hack. "The department will pay for it."

At the front of the station, they had to wait for several policemen to file out the door before they could enter.

"A smaller entrance makes sense if you should be under siege," Quade remarked, which drew odd stares from both of his escorts.

They made their way past the man standing guard at the heavy piece of oak furniture that was something like a counter or desk.

Quade recalled the grubby back halls and offices were less impressive. Only a few steps in and he could hear the clang and shouts of the holding cells and the bells ringing—calling tubes, he imagined.

The policemen led Quade into the same small office he'd visited before, piled with paper and books.

Colm stood in the back corner while Welch leaned over the cluttered desk, leafing through some papers. Quade sidled over to stand next to Colm. He wondered how the scent of leather and outdoors emanated from his friend, even after all this time in London.

"Did you learn anything from the inspector?" He spoke in a low voice, in part so he wouldn't be overheard, but mostly so he had the excuse to lean even closer to Colm.

"Not very much." He hesitated. "They have questioned your father."

"And what did they learn?"

Colm shrugged and didn't smile or look into Quade's face.

Quade tapped him on the forearm. "I can read you by now, Mr. Kelly. You know more than you want to say."

Before Colm could respond, a man wearing a yellow waistcoat and flannel trousers entered the room. He carried a straw boater and looked as if he were ready for a lazy afternoon punting on some slow-flowing river.

"Welch, I hope you're not messing about with my paperwork." The gentleman tossed his hat on a coatrack.

"This is Inspector Granby," Welch told them glumly as if saying *don't blame me for this idiot*. "Have you met Granby, Mr. Marrill?"

"No, we haven't met. A pleasure, I'm sure," Granby announced. He stuck out his hand for Quade to shake. "I am sorry that you have been inconvenienced, but Welch insisted that scoundrel Pennick's death might be connected to your family somehow."

Of course it did, you moron, but for once, Quade didn't speak his thoughts. "The police didn't visit me at your behest?"

"Mine? Oh, no, no. That story of mayhem overlapping your world is Welch's bugaboo."

Quade tried to catch Welch's eye, but he was pretending to read some papers he held in his hands.

"Do you have any suspects in the murder of my brother's ex-valet?"

"After Pennick left your brother's service, he apparently ran with a very disreputable crowd. Very rough scoundrels. I'm far more inclined to believe one of them did him in rather than anyone in your family."

Quade hadn't heard the expression *did him in*, but he understood its meaning too well. "Inclined to believe is not the same thing as completely convinced," Quade said. "You, or perhaps Welch, were right to summon me here."

Granby laughed. "Yes, I'd heard you were blunt, sir. And quite a scholar, I understand?"

Quade wasn't sure how to answer that, so he only gave a small bow. He wondered if it was time to bring up the coffee. "I understood that you have been looking into any strange occurrences to do with my family even before Pennick was found."

"Indeed, I have been looking into the matters affecting your family, Mr. Marrill." Granby pursed his lips and looked solemn. "The misfortunes are terrible indeed, but fate alone is to blame. We have no reason to believe the hand of man was part of any death other than Cyril Marrill's."

Colm made a small sound of disbelief or protest.

Granby turned to him. "Sir? How is you are involved?"

"He is Mr. Kelly, my friend and valued advisor," Quade said. He wondered if should have let Colm speak for himself, but Colm's beaming smile directed at him was reassuring.

Welch said, "He works with another Mr. Kelly, that American inquiry agent."

"Him." Granby wrinkled his nose. "I'm not sure that qualifies as an encomium."

Quade wasn't going to let the conversation wander. "I might not be able to help you learn the truth of Pennick's murder, but there have been some odd things happening with me and I would like to talk about them now." He launched into the description of the man who might or might not have tried to knock him down.

Mr. Granby said, "A man coming down some stairs in a hurry hardly constitutes an attack."

"Yes, I understand that." Quade glanced around at the men crowding the office. The policemen who'd accompanied him stood near the door. "These officers have the objects that show possible signs of an intruder."

The mutton-chopped man put the photo on the desk and stepped back, moving smartly and respectfully as any policemen delivering evidence in a trial.

Quade pointed to the edge of the paper. "Someone came into my house, broke the frame and glass on this photo, and ruined the picture with those marks on my brothers' faces." There, that came out perfectly dispassionately.

Colm was far less calm. He started up. "That's the picture from in the drawer, isn't it, sir?"

Granby scowled at Colm, perhaps surprised by the accent. He examined the picture. "When did this happen?"

How long ago had Colm forced Quade to gaze into the photographic faces of his brothers? "Sometime in the last month," he said.

"And who, besides Mr. Kelly here, knew you had that photograph in a drawer?"

"The maid, I suppose. Anyone who hunted through my office." Which was no one.

"And who would have had the time to do that in the last month?"

"Not many people," he admitted. "But more than the photograph, there's also a matter of my coffee. Something is wrong with it."

"Oh, indeed? Your coffee?" Mr. Granby shook his head slowly with the air of a disappointed tutor coping with an unsatisfactory scholar. "Of course one must make allowances for the fact that you're upset. And I suppose we should all like to find out why the late Mr. Pennick had a sample of your handwriting, but yours is not the only strange collection of notes we found in his residence. But perhaps you should look closer to home to find out why your coffee tastes bad. The grocer's, for instance? Start there rather than wasting the time of busy men."

Quade had already had enough of the man's condescending attitude. "I am not making that up, you patronizing—"

Colm grabbed his arm hard, with both hands, startling Quade enough to stop him from making a fool of himself. A good friend, Colm Kelly. But the Irishman had gone pale and his eyes were too wide—far more astonishment than the situation called for.

"What's wrong?" Quade asked, concerned.

"My sainted stars, you complained and felt poorly after one sip. And I thought nothing of it. I'm a sad excuse for a guard. The coffee!" His face had gone red, and he still clutched Quade's arm.

He dragged Marrill out of the office, throwing a "Pardon" to the assembled policemen.

In the dingy hall, he spoke low and fast. "Good God, Quade—Mr. Marrill—you know."

"About the coffee being poisoned? It is just an impression." He rubbed his chin, trying to come up with something that wouldn't give blasted Granby ammunition, but he didn't want to lie to Colm. "I'm not certain but the taste was quite bitter. I know it is supposed to be a bitter beverage, and I was shaken when I found the picture, I admit, but—"

Now it was Colm's turn to interrupt. "If it is true and the coffee has been tampered with, you know the man they must find. I mean at least one of the people."

Quade glared at him. "What do you mean?"

"The gentleman from your club. The one we met recently."

"Melton or Crispin? They're asses, but hardly interested in going after the Marrill family. Why would they do such a thing? And if we are going to reach for a theory to cover all the reasons my family have died in the past ten years, well, those two won't work. They're younger than I. They'd have to have been bloodthirsty schoolboys."

"No, no, not them." He paced back and forth along the edge of the corridor, agitated. "He asked that you don't drink tea but prefer coffee. He was most interested in it. And you told him about where we lived and, aw Jaysus, he's a thin man as well. Mr. Grace."

"Grace?" A chill struck Quade with that single word. *Grace.* The gentleman was certainly old enough to have carried out a peculiar campaign for a decade. Quade slowly reached into his pocket for the pages he'd scribbled on.

"Grace," he said again as he unfolded the paper and looked down the list. There were the first names of the women that he'd heard linked with Jack's name: Anne, Mabel, Honor, Patience—only now he remembered the whispered rumors. The name hadn't been Patience and Honor; it had been Grace.

He liked Mr. Grace, and he didn't like many people, and the idea was too vague. He automatically added, "This is nonsense. There is no proof."

"None so far," Colm agreed. He halted his pacing in front of Quade and reached out to touch his arm. "But it can't be ignored. You don't mingle with many people, Mr. Marrill. Only a very few come into your life."

Funny that at a moment like this, Colm's offhand comment still held a sting. Quade asked, "Do I detect pity in your voice?"

"No, why would you think that? Just means less clutter to wade through." In a low voice, Colm added, "Makes what I want to do with you easier as well." Did he actually wink?

He should have known Colm wouldn't look at him with pity. What was more, Colm didn't possess the habit of trying to turn a person into something he wasn't.

Quade cleared his throat and returned to the more important conversation. "Mr. Grace, though. That is nonsense, I swear it."

"I hope so," Colm said. "And I'll sleep better knowing that the coffee is just badly cooked or whatever 'tis they do with the stuff."

Mr. Welch poked his large face into the hall. "Mr. Marrill, Mr. Kelly, would you please take a seat and tell us what you're discussing?"

They shuffled back into the office.

Granby, sitting at his desk, examining his cufflinks heaved an exaggerated sigh. "Is this necessary for us to hear?"

"Yes," Colm said.

Quade looked into Colm's suddenly serious eyes, more gray at the moment than usual, and agreed, "I think we must. I shall tell you all the details I have. Kelly, you go first."

***

Colm and then Quade described all the interactions they'd had with Mr. Grace. While they spoke, Patrick knocked on the open door and entered.

Mr. Welch gave Patrick a nod, then continued with his questions. "And Mr. Grace was a member of your club?"

"Perhaps? Though he said he was the member of another club that was under repair."

Colm interrupted. "Those other two, the younger gents Melton and Crispin, said that he'd paid the dues and was a part of your club with the one, whatever it may be called." His frown cleared. "Vouchsafing, that's the word."

Welch gave Colm a frown before returning his attention to Quade. "You said you struck him in the face one day? And he still was friendly with you after that?"

"Yes. I am bit hazy on details but…" Quade shot a glance at Colm and rubbed his cheek. "Grace is forgiving. He didn't seem to hold that against me. He seems a kind man, but one who has been ill. One can see he's suffered."

Welch looked down at the notepad he rested on the edge of the desk. He flipped back several pages. "I might ask your father, Mr. Arthur Marrill, about Mr. Grace."

"What the devil? Why?" Granby spoke up at last. "That makes no sense. Bad enough that you're acting on virtually no evidence, you'd be disturbing a gentleman who's recently bereaved."

"You're likely right, but we'd best check it," Welch said with an air of false reluctance. He swiveled on his chair and leaned toward Quade. "Grace and your father are of the same generation?"

At Quade's nod, Welch continued. "So if there's any past connection, any history with Grace and the Marrill family, Arthur would be the one to ask. I shall check with your club, but I'd be grateful for a good description of Mr. Grace."

Before Quade could speak, Granby harrumphed and said, "What can you mean? You do know this conspiracy sounds ridiculous. Did the Irishman start this?"

Colm said affably, “Perhaps it’s all ridiculous, but it’s worth a visit. If there’s a years-long grudge, perhaps Mr. Arthur Marrill is the only one who could help.”

“Fairy tales, nothing but faint hopes for answers.”

“That’s twice now you officers have implied that Mr. Kelly—” Quade began, but Colm interrupted him.

“Possibly you’re correct, Mr. Granby,” Colm said, agreeable as always. “But every wisp must be followed, eh?”

“What would you know of real investigations? I am fed to the teeth with this desire to see that the crimes are connected. Random acts strung together neatly to satisfy your need for answers, Mr. Marrill. I have other work to do. Actual police work.” Granby stalked out of the office, bumping into Patrick, who stood in the doorway, watching.

“I beg your pardon, gentlemen,” Welch said, and adjusted his tied that had slid sideways on his too high and tight collar. “I’m sure my colleague will take a stroll and return to us in a few minutes.”

Patrick crossed the room to take the chair next to Colm. “Granby fancies himself a high-strung artist,” he said in a low voice. “He dislikes anyone trampling on his ideas.”

Welch pulled out his pipe and began fiddling with it. “Perhaps he’s right about fairy tales, but indeed we must check all paths, even the fanciful ones.”

“Especially when those paths are the only ones we have,” Colm said to Quade.

“We shall wait to see if the coffee has been tampered with,” Welch said.

Quade said, “I don’t need to wait.”

“Beg pardon?” Welch rose to his feet.

“I may visit my father any time I wish, after all.”

“Damnation! This again,” Patrick said, with some heat. “Going off half-cocked and barging about the place. I’ve met the gentleman, and he won’t thank you.”

“Shockingly enough, I know my father even better than you do, Mr. Kelly, and you sound like Inspector Granby,” Marrill said. “Are you coming, Colm?”

***

Colm didn't want to argue with Quade, particularly when they had witnesses."Sure. I'll come, but only if you wait a bit."

Quade said, "I beg your pardon," in the frostiest voice.

Colm didn't bother to answer. He tugged at Quade's sleeve, and without a word, Quade followed him out into the hall. Again. Colm did feel a bit absurd with the back and forth, but he'd rather not talk under the interested gaze of Patrick, two policemen, or Welch.

Quade said, "Are you agreeing we should leave at once? Good."

"No. I dragged you out because I think you are in the mood to argue. I volunteer for the role, but I didn't want to do that in front of the others. And you already squabbled with your father."

Quade sniffed and thought for a moment. "Not really arguing. One simply wonders why we should hold off on a visit? For what am I to wait? I want to find out what happened as soon as possible."

Colm rested his hand on Quade's shoulder, to reassure him or slow him down, even Colm wasn't sure which. The muscles were hard as a rock but seemed to relax a little under his palm. Colm said, "We should first discover if that coffee has been poisoned., then we make a plan based on what they find." His Quade proved such a contradiction—a methodical and careful man with his papers and lists who tended to rush out when in a temper.

"Of course you're right. You are far too often, Kelly. Dammit. Those procedures might require days." Quade's face screwed up. He muttered, "Marsh, Stas-Otto."

Colm leaned close enough to pick up the random words. "Muttering to yourself again. What are you saying?"

"I'll contact my friend Hemner in Berlin, but I want to remember the tests I've read about in legal documents, the protocols for discovering poisons, though those were from the bodies of victims. To be honest, it's far too easy to come up with lists of the poisons themselves. Arsenic, belladonna, cyanide, strychnine."

"You do like lists."

"Yes, alphabetizing helps me think and to calm down." He heaved a sigh. "I expect I'm rather odd."

"Yes," Colm said happily. He wanted to seize Quade's hand and draw him close. He settled for that light touch the shoulder again. "You are just the sort of odd I like. Come, perhaps the others will help us find an answer."

"Not bloody likely," Quade said, and they walked back through the door.

Welch must have been listening. "I understand that you are anxious to get to the bottom of this, Mr. Marrill, but I assure you that we are taking this seriously. Your coffee will be tested as quickly as possible."

Quade frowned at the sack of beans that sat on a desk. "Very well, I suppose I trust you and that'll be faster than sending it off to Berlin."

Welch drew his head back, clearly ready to be offended by the grudging comment, but Colm spoke before he could.

"Is that big American still watching Mr. Arthur Marrill?" Colm asked his cousin.

"Yes, he'd tell me if he'd been shown the door. He's reliable," Patrick said.

"Good." Colm turned to Marrill and gave a little flourish with his hand as if conjuring good news from the air just for him. "Then there is no reason to rush over to the Arthur Marrills' house and set them in a pother until we know more."

"Yes, fine," Quade grumbled.

Patrick Kelly cleared his throat. "I beg your pardon, sir, for trying to dictate how you speak to members of your own family."

Quade gave him a puzzled scowl. Colm wondered if he couldn't comprehend apologies, or simply didn't know how to answer them.

"You and Welch are right that I shouldn't go off half-cocked and thoroughly annoyed," Quade said at last. "But I'm not sitting about like a lump, here or at home. I've done that for far too long. No more waiting for you or anyone else to get to the bottom of this."

"Sir, I assure you that leaving it in the hands of experts is the right answer."

Deep in thought, Quade ignored him—perhaps didn't even notice his comment. "We'll go to the club. I have some questions for… Hang on a moment. Maybe some of the blasted coffee can go to Hemner."

Patrick rolled his eyes at Welch, but Quade ignored them both. He pushed a chair out of the way and went to speak to the cops. Colm caught a few words about effective tests. Marrill took out a pencil and paper and, leaning over Granby's crowded desk, began scribbling. Welch, playing with his pipe, looked on with an expression of long-suffering patience, the same he wore when Granby spoke.

Colm leaned against the wall, next to a framed picture of Queen Victoria. He exchanged glances with Her Majesty before turning his attention to his cousin. "I'm going with him, though that club of his might not allow me to enter, for all that I'm dressed more like a gentleman."

"Is that the one where you brawled?" Patrick asked.

Colm heaved a sigh. "No need to remind me. Yes, that's it."

"Ha, that place. I've been there as a guest. I've heard it was once a fine establishment but now it's down at the heels."

Colm had thought the men's club as elegant a spot as any he'd ever seen, even comparable to Sloan's townhouse, but he decided not to admit that to Patrick.

"To keep him safe as possible, get Quade Marrill to come by my place, right? Sloan's house, I mean. As soon as you can. I'll tell him the same. I'm not sure what you or he are planning to do. Can you tell me, Colm?"

Colm laughed. "As if I knew?"

"You said you'd done detective work in Ireland. Do some now and find out what your man is up to."

Colm recalled his last big "case," solved after he'd followed a path of gossip and sheep shit to the cave where the sheep had been hidden. He felt most proud of the fact that he'd arrested the six men without getting anyone, including himself, injured. Oh, and he'd put together enough evidence to convict all six. Still, sitting in pubs eavesdropping or tramping around fields looking for sheep droppings wasn't the sort of clever brain work one expected from a detective.

He should be the one reciting the names of tests for poison.

"What are you grinning about?" Patrick demanded.

"Nothing important. There's a messenger boy at that club. I'll send word to you at Mr. Sloan's if I can. You're going back there now?"

Patrick gave a sharp nod.

Colm caught up with Quade as he approached the narrow, treacherous staircase. "Me first," Colm said. "These stairs are hazardous."

"You don't need to protect me any longer."

"I go first, Mr. Marrill. Sir."

"I'd forgotten how under your gentle air, you're far more mulish than I ever was."

"Truly, and don't forget again."

"Stubborn dictator."

"Indeed, yes." Colm set off down the stairs, his steps clanging. "I expect you to obey my orders." He knew his face had gone red—the things they could get up to, alone, with him giving orders, ha. Good thing that his back was to Quade.

They walked out into the sunny day, and Colm stopped a moment to let the warmth wash over his face, though he still didn't close his eyes. He was on duty.

The club was less than five minutes by hackney, and it didn't take that long for Colm to discover Quade's plans.

"You think inviting Mr. Grace for coffee will push him to confess?"

"I should be able to see his face change when he knows I know about the coffee."

"Oh? Indeed."

"No need to sound astounded, Colm. I can read emotion."

"You're not so very experienced. I'd say you read 'em about as well as I can read those books of yours. Takes some effort, but there's no catching the meaning right away."

Colm expected an acid retort, but instead Quade said, "Tell me what you think I should do instead."

"Go home. Work. And in an hour, we'll visit Cousin Patrick."

They went over a large bump, and Colm grabbed at the leather strap hanging from the ceiling.

Quade shook his head slowly. "No, didn't you listen to what I said in that office? I have been passive too long—years in fact. I refuse to remain inactive another minute longer than I must."

"Yes, I heard you, Mr. Marrill." Colm wasn't upset, in fact he rather admired his friend's tenacity, but he already understood that a bit of salt from Colm wouldn't bother Quade. "Happens I know that's not what you'll do, but you did ask what I thought."

Quade's laugh was a sharp bark. "Fair enough. If I don't want to know, I shouldn't have asked."

And before they had a real answer about the plans, they were at the club.

When Quade and Colm walked in, the porter looked as if he'd seen his worst nightmare cross the threshold.

"I want to speak to Crispin or Melton, if they're present," Quade said before the porter could send for the manager. "As soon as possible, please."

"We can wait in some drawing room instead of the foyer if you don't want us cluttering up the place," Colm added.

The porter almost smiled. "Yes, yes, the guest lounge will work." He led them to a room just off the entrance and shut the door behind him. The room was large and had the air of a rarely used space. Dust motes floated in the air; otherwise, nothing else moved. A large clock at the corner had hands frozen at eleven.

Colm thought of Patrick's remarks about the club as he looked about himself. The floor-to-ceiling brocade curtains with gold cords still seemed luxurious, though perhaps the sofa and chairs were worn, with some horsehair showing here and there. The flowers in the vase had dropped petals to the table, which had a few water stains, and the deer on the wall looked as if it had been attacked by moths at some point in its life, or rather, after its death. The fireplace was full of ashes and bits from previous fires and he knew, from watching the footmen and maids at Sloan's place, that one was supposed to clear out fireplaces daily.

He wasn't a good observer after all, a dismaying thing to realize about oneself, particularly when recalling details were part of one's job.

Crispin entered the room a moment later. "Hallo, Marrill! We had just held our meeting! You must have heard. Welcome back to the club." He caught sight of Colm and stopped. He coughed that sad imitation of a cough. "Ah. But we're writing in new rules about guests."

"Are you?" Quade stepped back and looked Crispin up and down. "And allow me to make a wild guess. You are placing further restrictions on the list, hmm?"

Crispin's over-large eyes widened so they looked as if they might fall from his face. "The club is a place established for gentlemen to feel comfortable. No ladies, of course. And other elements, though, of course, not that we object to anyone at all." His aimed his fixed false smile at Colm. "Live and let live. Quite understandable, hey? We don't mean restrictions three hundred sixty-five days a year, not at all. We might have exemptions for events. Fights, for instance? Eh, planned ones I mean. Ha-ha. So it's just day-to-day affairs we want to keep for people, well, for gentlemen. You understand."

Quade made a low noise in his throat, an actual growl. "Are you bloody bastards restricting Mr. Kelly because he's Irish?"

"Now there's no reason to grow hostile, Marrill. We are not talking about anyone in particular, hardly a personal matter."

Quade's hands formed fists, and wasn't this a familiar moment, Colm thought as he hastily stepped forward in front of him. "Sure, sure. And I'll be moving along," Colm said soothingly, but couldn't help adding, "You're not the first to be afeared of people who are different from you."

"It's not fear or dislike, I assure you. It's a matter of comfort. The club is more like home to many of our members than their actual residence—and you don't invite just anyone from off the street to your house, do you?"

Quade looked ready to spit out an obscenity. Colm said, "We won't keep you, Mr. Crispin. I wonder if Mr. Grace is on the premises."

Crispin touched his mustache again. "No, I haven't seen him since the meeting."

"Oh? He was part of that anti-Irish movement?" Quade asked.

"It's not anti-Irish," Crispin said, not looking at Colm. "It's simply putting up clear parameters. It is our duty to establish what our members require, a place to gather with members of one's own set." Now he turned his gaze on Colm and actually smiled, showing all his brownish teeth. "I hope you'll still consider my proposition to put you up for a fight? No? You could make some fine money and—" He glanced at Quade. "You have my card if you're interested."

Quade gazed thoughtfully at a painting of a horse above the fireplace. He wore the expression he usually had while messing about with words. "Crispin, old chap, I seem to recall that we've had some Irish members."

"What? Oh, ah. Yes, an Irish earl, I believe, but he was, ah, not of common stock. Educated at Eton."

Quade shook his head. "I know I'm right. In fact, I'm sure of it. If you let me look at the club book."

"But that's for members…"

"You said I'm to be reinstated. I'm as good as a member." He turned to Colm and gave him toothy smile that looked predatory. "We'll get to the bottom of this."

"But the idea is ridiculous, Marrill."

"No, not at all. I know I'm not wrong."

"Mr. Marrill is likely right," Colm said. His Quade had a mind for tiny facts.

"I insist that you allow me to prove myself right, Crispin. Shall we place a bet?"

That interested the man. He promptly said, "All right. A tenner says you are wrong, we've had no Irish members." He paused a moment and boggled at Colm. "Ah, I apologize. Stay here, hmm? Wait here would you?" Crispin's tone was that of a harassed man speaking to a jumpy dog. "I shouldn't leave you alone but—"

"It won't take long," Quade said impatiently.

"I won't leave this room, not even if the building should catch on fire," Colm said solemnly.

"Oh, I say, that is a bit thick," Crispin said. "If there's an emergency—"

"He's pulling your leg," Quade said. "I want to see that book and win my bet. I know there was an Irish member about twenty years ago," Colm said. The two gentlemen left the room, and Colm moved about, looking at the heavy leather volumes on the shelves.

Twenty minutes later, they returned.

"I was wrong," Quade said briskly. "No trace of anyone other than that Irish earl. No common or garden Irish members at all."

"It does seem odd, but there we are." Crispin clutched the ten pounds and seemed to be trying to look grief-stricken, perhaps for Colm's sake? Not such a terrible person altogether, Colm reflected.

Crispin said, "I suspect it would be waste of your time trying to buck the system, Marrill. Our club is just not up for that sort of change."

At the door, he shook hands with Quade and gave Colm an awkward nod. The porter escorted them all the way to the pavement.

After they left and strolled down the street, Quade seemed to melt a little, or at least his shoulders didn't appear to be hunched up to his ears. He wore the most peculiar expression. His lips were pressed tight, but his eyes were bright as if he'd won a bet, not lost ten pounds.

They walked in silence for a few minutes.

"I'm sorry to be the cause of trouble again," Colm said. "I mean you having to leave the club."

"I'd rather belong to a club devoted to the law or history at any rate," Quade said.

"Will you go back? Mr. Crispin said you might."

"Never."

"It's unfair you must leave a place you enjoy."

"Bah. I shall regret nothing other than the venison stew, which they didn't offer often enough anyway. I joined only because my family have been members since it was founded. My brother Mark vouched for me, as did my cousin."

"The second cousin? Dunne?"

"Yes. Odd, isn't it? It attracts younger gentlemen and doesn't seem his style at all. I think he pays membership at several clubs and generally only goes to the Explorers."

"If it's part of your family, does your father belong?"

"Certainly. He hasn't gone for decades and maybe his membership lapsed? I have no notion."

"Why didn't your da put you up for membership?"

"Our relations haven't been cordial for a number of years."

That was hardly a surprise. Colm didn't like the grim set to Quade's mouth and hoped they weren't about to pay his father a visit.

"It seems strange to me your cousin continues to pay dues to a club he doesn't attend."

"Yes, isn't it odd." Quade gave a peculiar laugh. "He is wealthy, after all. And he might go on occasion."

"How does one join? Can a gentleman just walk in off the street?"

"No such thing."

"So only when a member vouches for someone." Colm recalled what Melton had said in the pub. "Yes?"

Quade gave a distracted hum that was probably yes.

Colm, out of habit, looked up and down the street. Guarding Quade was difficult in the crowded, shop-filled area.

They stopped at a street corner, waiting for several coaches to roll past. A flower seller with a basket tugged at Colm's arm, and he bought a boutonnière from her.

Colm thought about giving it to Quade, but that seemed cheeky. He attached it to his jacket instead with fast, impatient fingers as they made their way through the shoppers.

He risked walking next to Quade to ask, "Are you upset that you were wrong about the Irish member?"

"Oh, that—no. I made up the story."

"What? Why? You lost ten pounds!"

"I needed to look at the club records and was tired of Crispin's dithering. I know he can't resist a sure bet."

"So much money," Colm marveled. "But why?"

"I wanted to find out facts about Mr. Grace, such as where he lives. He isn't far from the library so it is hardly a surprise that we would have seen him there. It's a shabby little street with rooms to let, if I recall. Hardly the sort of address I'd expect a clubman to live on." He walked a little faster.

Colm trotted to catch up. "I thought being a member was a matter of breeding and knowing the right people?"

"Yes, certainly. But the dues at our club are about one hundred pounds a year."

"One… One hundred pounds?" Colm swallowed. "A year? Every year? British sterling?"

"Yes. I expect most clubs cost at least twenty pounds, though I've never bothered looking into it. Clubs are not ridiculously expensive—gentlemen often move into those places when they finish university and don't want to set up their own housekeeping."

"Twenty pounds a year." Colm gave a whistle. "D'ye know, I made twenty-five shillings a week and was that proud of my pay? When I made over a pound, I felt rich. It would take me half a year's pay to join any regular club and just about two years to make the money to belong to your club for one year." He stopped on the sidewalk. "That man, Mr. Grace. His clothes, and now you're saying his address, he couldn't have that much to spare every year."

Quade shot him a gleaming smile, an odd response. He said, "Well, perhaps his regular club is less?"

"Ach. We went over that. Crispin and Melton said he joined your club. That was just a story he told you, perhaps to entertain himself."

Quade gave an odd laugh. "Oh yes, I know."

He led Colm around a corner, onto a quieter street. "I'm like my father, I have become such a distrustful person of late."

"We know you have reason to be. The bad fortune haunting your family—I believe at least some of those deaths were murder."

He waited for an angry answer, but when Quade spoke, he sounded as calm as a man discussing weather. "Yes, so do I. Do you have ideas about why?" he demanded, as if he knew the answer—the tone of a priest quizzing a child.

Colm studied a narrow alley that was empty save for a horse tied to a post. "People have been murdered for money. And your family has a great deal of it. I cannot think of another reason to destroy you all. Do you know who would get the money if your father, you, your cousin, and second cousin died?"

"You mean who gets the money if Dunne survives my father and me? No, I don't know the terms of his will. It's best that we go visit my cousin. He'll give us answers."

Colm lifted his hat to a passing lady and, then scanned the street ahead. "If you wish. But you're acting peculiar, Quade."

"Am I? It's just that I'm figuring it out."

"What?" Colm demanded.

"We'll go speak to my cousin. That's the ticket."

"What shall I do? Stand quiet in the corner while you confront him?"

"Not at all. You be as pushy as ever you were as a constable in Ireland, all right? We're nearly as close to his house as we are to Grace's." He shook his head. "Such a small world we inhabit."

Vast London, Colm thought as he hurried after Quade, who'd picked up speed.

Quade didn't barge past the butler, not exactly, but he wasn't content to wait. "I know where to find him," he told the man, then went straight to the room full of antiquities, Colm trailing after him as usual.

Quade stepped into the big room with a hearty greeting. "Here you are, Cousin Wilbur. We meet again."

Dunne, who'd been leaning over a desk, straightened with a huff of air and took a step backward. "You startled me. I can't talk. I'm just on my way to visit a friend," he began.

"Just a few questions," Quade said. "But perhaps you'd like to start, Mr. Kelly?"

Colm cleared his throat. He knew Quade had something very specific on his mind, something that had sent him here like a shot—and that he hadn't bothered to tell Colm about.

But he'd go along with Quade and, trying to sound apologetic and official, picked up a point that Quade had mentioned. "We are still investigating some facts. We need to know who is your heir."

Dunne's worried face relaxed a little. "The Historical and Explorer Association. And a few stipends to servants, of course. Now, if you gentlemen don't mind, I'll—"

"You're a still member of the United Conservative Club?" Quade interrupted.

"Well, I believe so. I never go."

"Yes, I know. Here's what else I've discovered. You've vouched for someone other than me recently." Quade wore a wide smile. It was one Colm had only seen as they walked from the club to Dunne's house. He'd suspected it spelled trouble, and now he knew why.

"Quade, of course not. Pray, let us depart, if you have nothing else." He pulled out his watch. "I shall be late for a meeting."

"Mr. Grace is a new member. And you vouched for him. Interesting, isn't it? You can't have forgotten something that happened very recently. Why would you lie about that?" Quade wore his tooth-baring, predatory smile.

Was Quade guessing? No, of course not. He'd been hunting through the book. He'd admitted as much, and this information must have been his goal. Enough worrying about Quade—Colm turned his attention to Dunne.

He was caught by Dunne's start, the tiniest motion. Colm wouldn't have noticed it if the light on the face of Dunne's watch hadn't shifted. A shiver of surprise.

"Mr.…who?"

Quade still stared, that wide smile fixed in place, so Colm took over. "I believe you heard your cousin, sir. The name he gave was Mr. Grace. Though I don't think that's his actual name. I wonder, do you even know what his real name is?"

Wilbur still clutched the watch. He seemed to wake up and shoved it back into his waistcoat. "Really, Quade, is this manservant of yours always this intrusive?"

"He's a friend." Quade took off his hat and put it on a table. "And he's an investigator. Didn't I make that clear before?"

Colm thought back to the times he'd had to root around for answers in Ireland. When in doubt, one should push, then pour on the butter. "I know that Mr. Grace is far more ruthless than you, Mr. Dunne."

Colm gave a silent node of approval. All right, if he was on the right track, Colm might as well push into unknown—nay, invented—territory. "Your partner in this crime, he's a dangerous person. You're a man of learning and only care about finding the truth. Did he come to you with the idea?"

"What idea? No, no." Wilbur Dunne rubbed his hands together. He rushed to the bellpull and gave it a hard tug. "I'm getting ready to go out now and…"

"We'll walk with you," Quade said.

"I'm ordering a carriage."

"Ach, such a pretty day and you'll drive?" Colm said. "I suppose it's a fine day for that as well. We'll be glad to drive with you."

Wilbur made a small whimpering sound.

Quade apparently got into the spirit of the thing. He adopted the same light tone Colm used. "Wilbur, shall we go to visit Mr. Grace first?"

"Don't be an ass, Quade. These accusations are idiotic."

"Oh? And aren't you even curious about what I know?"

Colm considered raising his hand and admitting he was more than curious.

The butler appeared. Dunne said, "I'll need my carriage, and I want you to show these two gentlemen out."

"No, not yet," Quade said. He ambled over to a statue and picked it up. "Clay, is it?" Dunne was on his way to the door when Quade called after him. "Would it make a dreadful mess if I smashed it on the floor?"

"Sir!" The butler started forward.

Dunne shouted, "Stop!"

The butler froze, but no one else did. Colm went to Quade's side. This was absurd, but he'd follow Quade's lead.

He noticed a heavy wooden walking stick in the elephant foot umbrella stand and reached for it. If either Dunne or the butler should try to attack him or Quade, he'd be ready.

"We shall talk, Wilbur," Quade said, smooth and calm. "Now."

"I have nothing to say to you beyond *get out of my house*. Now."

"Shall I summon the police, sir?" the butler pleaded.

Quade said, "Certainly, and if they interrupt this conversation, they'll probably even arrest me because by then I'll have smashed this little item and…" He walked over to a table and picked up a piece of what Mr. Dunne had called bas-relief. "This one as well."

"Don't! Not the police yet!" Dunne looked frantically around the room. Colm decided to help him focus by lifting the walking stick and holding it over the top of a statue. "'Tis marble," he said mournfully. "But that pottery thing next to it might smash beautifully too, don't you think?" he asked Quade and brought the stick's end to hover over it.

"Hmm." Quade's eyes glittered with something, either malice or pleasure. Colm tried to feel more appalled, all these threats to innocent antiquities. He didn't succeed.

They all needed to calm down. Perhaps he'd get another telling motion or expression from the man with a question. "I say, Mr. Dunne, will you offer us a cup of tea? Or perhaps…*coffee*?"

The man only looked puzzled.

"All right, that might be an answer of sorts," Colm said to Quade. "Either your coffee is fine or Mr. Grace didn't bother to tell him about the plans for you."

He smiled encouragingly at Dunne, who clutched a figurine to his front. "Did you know about the coffee?"

Dunne glared back. "What are you talking about? What will get you to leave me alone, you uncouth heathen?"

"I believe he's talking about your Irish Catholic roots," Quade said. "The subject arises over and over, Colm. How wearisome for you."

"Not at all, not at all. At any rate, we're not here to talk about me," Colm said. "We're here to discuss your cousin's part in the plan to kill off the Marrill family."

Dunne's mouth dropped open, and a small sound came out.

"Now, if you'd had a real heir, Mr. Dunne, we might have considered going to talk to him, or her. It's peculiar enough to suppose someone would go after so many people to gain riches, yet it could be possible. But you're the last possible person with that reason, because if you die, your money goes to some society. I don't think they'd be that ruthless. And it has to be about the money, don't it?"

"We have no need to go anywhere else," Quade said. "I have figured it out."

Had he? With some evidence? Did he think Colm was doing more than guessing? Colm wanted to ask but knew better.

"None of this has anything to do with me," Dunne said, but his protest sounded fainter than it had.

Marrill only smiled.

Colm decided to take up the attack. "Well, now, sir, that's not what the letters from that dead valet say," he said.

Dunne's lips moved, but no sound came out. "Which letters?" he said. "What are you talking about?"

"Ah. Don't you mean to ask 'who are you talking about'? Interesting that you seem to know who I mean when I mention a dead valet." Colm made a tick in the air with the end of the walking stick as if he were marking a scoreboard. He smiled at Quade. "That's another fact in favor of staying on to get more, don't you tink?" He couldn't help laying on the accent a bit. He shouldn't have pointed out the fact Dunne was asking the wrong questions—the man might shut up—but he couldn't help gloating.

"You seem to think you have hold of evidence of some sort that would make me appear guilty of a crime I know nothing about." Dunne was regaining his equilibrium, and that wouldn't do.

"Oh yes, there is evidence." Not really, but Colm was ready for the next bit of intimidation. "Say, you butler, it is time to summon the police, an' you must contact an Inspector Welch." Without lowering the walking stick, Colm fished the card from his waistcoat pocket and tossed it onto the table a few feet away. "We promise not to hurt any of your master's precious objects if Welch is the policeman who joins the party," Colm said.

"No, no," Dunne said.

Quade gave that harsh laugh again. "That's right, Welch has interviewed you, hasn't he, Wilbur? Would you rather have Mr. Granby?"

"I'd rather you leave. Say your piece, then get out."

Colm wondered if it would be worse to guess all the wrong things than to say nothing at all. If he could only come up with some suitably mysterious phrases, he might draw Dunne into somehow displaying his guilt. They should wait for Welch, but in the meantime, he could make himself look like he wielded some actual power in London.

Colm adopted his most authoritative manner, an imitation of his grandmother that had helped him in his old job. "I am entirely serious. Your butler will send a messenger to Mr. Welch immediately. Pick up that card and send your fastest footman at once. Immediately," Colm ordered.

“No,” Wilbur Dunne squeaked. But the butler had already picked up the card and left the room. Clearly, the idea of bringing in actual police to deal with the matter suited him.

Dunne sat in a chair and stared miserably at Quade. “You will spend a great deal of time in prison for this, Quade. You have invaded my space and threatened my possessions.”

“Not as much time as you’ll spend in prison, cousin.” Quade raised his hand and, with all his force, smashed the small clay statue to the floor.

***

Colm’s protest was almost as loud as Wilbur’s, but Quade had had enough of civilized behavior. He only wished he could have smashed the statue on his cousin’s shiny forehead.

And now he had their attention. He picked up another geegaw. This one was also marble, but he might manage to harm it.

Colm stared at him wide-eyed, and Quade knew it was time to explain. His friend had been patient, had gone along with questioning Wilbur, and had done it perfectly.

Keeping his gaze on Wilbur, Quade spoke to Colm. “Soon after my brother Jack died, Mr. Grace joined my club. *Joined*, Colm. He lied about his presence—there was no other club for him. Perhaps when he was younger, he was a clubman, but he has no money now. Do you know who sponsored him? It says in the book, Wilbur Dunne. Not just a voucher for his good conduct. Oh, no, no. There’s a small notation that Dunne paid Grace’s dues for one year, but only one year.”

He stopped for a moment. Time to pay even closer attention to Wilbur. But his cousin only goggled at him without a word. And, very good, Colm stood entirely still, his attention focused on Wilbur.

Quade went on, “Here is Wilbur Dunne, a man who has not even visited the club regularly for years, suddenly showing all sorts of interest. Even Crispin remarked on it when I made an offhand remark. ‘Oh, look, my cousin sponsored Mr. Grace? And paid for him?’ Yes, and apparently Mr. Dunne even promised to put funds toward buying new wallpaper for the smoking room if they let his dear friend Mr. Grace join.”

Quade wiped his hands on his trousers. "Your dear friend? The same gentleman you're pretending you don't know? Why is that, Cousin Wilbur?"

He walked across the room, his shoes crunching the last of the clay statue into dust. Carefully replacing the marble statue, he eyed the other items on the table, then scooped up another piece of a clay tablet covered with hieroglyphics.

Wilbur raised his hands over his ears. "No, no. Stop it. He came to me!"

CHAPTER FOURTEEN

Wilbur looked so pale and drenched with sweat, Quade wondered if he would keel over in some sort of apoplectic fit.

"I need something to drink," Wilbur said.

"Tea?" Colm suggested.

Wilbur gave him an offended sneer. "Brandy, over there. Quade, damnation! Put down the tablet. It's nearly three thousand years old. Put it down."

Quade shoved the clay thing into his jacket pocket, then nodded. "Brandy is fine."

Colm walked to the far corner of the room and poured a glass of brandy—all without taking his gaze off Wilbur for more than a second.

Wilbur drank down the full glass and coughed until his face flushed dark red. He just needed to add a bit of blue and he'd be his own Union Jack.

"Mr. Grace came to you," Quade prompted, close to losing his temper again. "Did he tell you he wished to murder my family? *Our* family?"

Wilbur flinched as if he'd been hit, but he didn't deny it. "It wasn't like that. I know him under his old name. Redding, he was. Cecil Redding. And I knew his story, and had met him here and there. He's a gentleman, of course, and we went to the same school." Wilbur gazed into his snifter as if wishing it would refill itself. "Now you know his real name, surely you understand the truth, for all your father tried to keep the business quiet."

"Keep what quiet?"

Wilbur put down the glass. "Ah, yes. You were just a boy at school when it happened."

"A girl," Quade said, "and Jack." Rumors had reached all the way to his boarding school, and he should have paid better attention. That girl named Grace. "Grace Redding."

"His daughter. Redding said it was ravishment, and I've heard that it was seduction. Jack is—I mean he was—a very good-looking man, and a gentleman who came from wealth. He could have any girl. She was pretty enough, but hardly gorgeous."

"Go on," Quade said.

"There is little more to tell. She was not tempting enough to marry. You know as well as anyone that he required a bride with funds." Wilbur glanced at the nearly empty snifter across the room. "I need more brandy."

Colm jerked his chin at the tray and raised his golden brows at Quade in a silent question.

"Whatever you think," Quade said.

Colm walked to the tray and fetched the bottle. "Go on, sir," he said.

"Everyone said it was an attempt at entrapment because she wanted him. Right after the seduction, she was quite upset, or so Redding told me."

Colm took off the stopper and handed Wilbur the open bottle.

"But, then she, ah…" Wilbur poured and drank off several fingers. "It all got much worse."

"What are you trying to say?" Quade had had more than enough of his cousin and wanted to get to the matter. "Come now, tell me."

His cousin drank down more brandy instead.

"Here's my guess," Colm said. "Miss Redding discovered she was increasing after the event."

Wilbur made a tutting sound but didn't interrupt with words. He nodded.

Colm went on. "And Jack Marrill claimed it wasn't his. Tell me, did he have friends who'd say they'd been with the young lady?"

Wilbur nodded again. "Among others, Jeremiah Marrill claimed she threw herself at him."

Quade sat down heavily on the stone sarcophagus, cold horror filling him.

"A sad situation all around. So very gratchic, tragic, I mean." Wilbur gave a discreet burp. "Miss Redding killed herself. Her mother followed several months later, a broken heart, which is Redding's account, though I might recall talk of another suicide. I didn't know the details. I didn't have time to care about these things. But Redding lately informed me that before the women died, your brother Jack had enlisted the aid of your father and, as I said, your uncle. They were going after Miss Redding legally. Claiming defamation, I think. With all those friends of Jack's as witnesses." He paused to drink down more brandy. "This is the story I heard from Redding, and he is sadly changed, poor man, no longer the very pleasant gentleman I knew. I believe he calls himself Grace to honor his daughter. But it hasn't much to do with me. Why are you dragging me into this matter? You should speak to your father about the matter of Miss Redding."

"Oh, I will," Quade said. "But there are others matters as well, and other deaths. Let's not forget them, Cousin Wilbur. Jack, my uncle, his son Cyril, Phillip, and Mark."

"There is no connection to me." Dunne seemed to be relaxing. That wouldn't do.

Colm jumped in. "Really? When the police examine your accounts, or perhaps Mr. Grace's, they will see that money has exchanged hands."

"Don't be silly." Wilbur made an attempt at a laugh.

Colm gave him sympathetic shake of the head. "We already have seen that you paid for his club membership. Was that to allow Mr. Redding to get closer to Quade?"

"No such thing. I-I felt some responsibility for what could be seen as my family's actions to speed his poor daughter to her grave. You see, you must understand." Wilbur's voice slowed as if he felt his way along an unfamiliar path and had to make up a story as he went along. "Such a tragic, sad…tragedy. I wanted to help him where and when I could. So I, uh, sponsored him for my club and…and other things. When I could."

"Nonsense. You paid him to kill off my family members, hoping to gain a fortune for yourself," Quade had been sickened by the truth, but this addition of mealy-mouthed Wilbur's story sparked a flash of rage. "You know what he has been doing."

Wilbur put down the glass with a loud clunk. "What? What? Not at all. Why would I?"

"I suppose Redding could have told you it was an investment scheme and left the details vague." Colm aimed his warmest, friendliest smile at Wilbur. "And despite paying for his membership, you are in need of money in the long run?"

"Yes, that's it!" Wilbur jumped on the idea as if it were a fabulous gift.

"Your work is expensive, I suppose. Important work," Colm coaxed.

"Yes, to fund the exploration we are planning…" Wilbur's voice petered out. At that moment came the sound of doors opening and closing, and Welch's voice floated to them.

Quade strolled closer to Colm. "It was kind of you to offer him a story about investments. Now he won't even have to think of a way to defend himself against accusations of murder."

"He just admitted he needs funds."

Quade supposed so. He suddenly felt as if he'd come to the end of long and terrible fever only to wake up and discover his family had died of the same disease—a contagion his brother had brought into their world.

Welch briskly entered the room, though his steps slowed almost immediately. "What do you think you're up to?" He glared at Colm.

"Catching your criminal," Quade snapped. "My cousin and his friend, Mr. Grace, planned to murder everyone in my family standing between Wilbur and what he thinks of as his fortune."

"Oh, I say!" Wilbur stumbled to his feet. "It was nothing like that. That wasn't… I mean to say, I was just trying to help an old friend."

"Mr. Grace is actually Mr. Redding. Does that name sound familiar to you, Welch?" Quade asked.

"Well. Ah. Yes, yes, it does. Was just reading up about him in the late Cyril Marrill's file again. But we never found Mr. Redding to be of any interest. He didn't have the money or resources for a vendetta."

"Now you must," Colm said. "Hang on a moment, and we'll tell all."

Quade felt empty. He wanted to go home and pretend that he had nothing more to think about other than his work. The weight had come down heavily for some reason, and his body dragged.

Colm went to the open sitting room door. He looked cheery, like a man who was about to start whistling. More than that, he looked rather maniacal.

Welch said, "You're not going anywhere, Kelly. The servants here said something about threats and destruction, and they mentioned an Irishman."

"I'm staying right here," Colm agreed. "We're going to talk all about Mr. Redding and Mr. Grace. The same man, as it turns out."

He leaned out into the corridor and called, "Hallo," to someone. He held a private conversation with someone Quade couldn't see.

A moment later, the butler entered the room with a new, full decanter of brandy and several glasses, but before he could cross to the table, Colm took the tray from his hands. The butler looked stunned, and no wonder. Not only was Colm doing the man's job, this wasn't the time of day or the circumstances when one expected to drink brandy.

After pouring a measure for Mr. Welch, Colm poured a great deal more into Wilbur's glass. Welch frowned at the snifter in his hands but didn't put it down.

"There we go." Colm sat on a sofa near Wilbur and gave him a friendly salute, as if they were about to settle in for a delightful chat. "No need to tell Mr. Welch the sad tale of Miss Redding. He knows. Hardly a big shock her father would be an enemy to the Marrill family, yes, Mr. Welch?"

"Yes, or I mean no."

"And you would have looked into that matter earlier?"

"He wasn't of any interest to us," Welch said reluctantly. "Mr. Redding had no money left. He seemed a broken man and had moved to the country. It would take funds and dedication to follow the Marrill family for years and make the gentlemen's deaths appear to be accidents or unconnected."

"He had the dedication, it seems," Colm said.

"So you have a man for your crimes." Wilbur beamed at Welch, regaining some of his confidence in more brandy, apparently. "Ask anyone at the society. I have a terrible cough, and an aversion to violence."

Quade felt such a surge of anger, he gasped with it. "You only provided financial backing, didn't you, Wilbur? He needed money, and Redding got what he required for his campaign against our family from Cousin Wilbur. It's that simple. He's a coward, letting a more ambitious man manipulate him."

Wilbur, who was just taking a swallow of the brandy, tried to interrupt—and began to cough.

Quade turned to Welch. "My cousin's fortune is comfortable, but he could use more. Add my branch of the family's resources, and Wilbur should be set for more expeditions and perhaps building a museum for his collection."

Wilbur pulled out a handkerchief and wiped his streaming nose. In a voice hoarse from choking, he said, "You have no idea what you're talking about."

"I believe that if you help the police with their enquiries, you'll be saved from hanging," Colm said brightly, as if offering a treasure to Wilbur. "Not my deal to make, of course." He tipped a hand at Welch as if inviting him to address the room.

"No, indeed, it is nothing you can promise," Welch snapped. He put down the glass he held and glared around the room. "Mr. Dunne, I think you need to come with me."

"I feel unwell from that—that drink. If you'll excuse me a moment." Wilbur got up. He carefully tucked away his handkerchief as he walked unsteadily to the door.

He opened it, and without a look back, he raced off, his heavy footfalls making a racket on the hardwood floors.

The three remaining men in the room looked at each other. The sound of the front door slamming reached them.

Colm jumped up. "Christ, Welch, get moving. He's running away." He bolted after Wilbur, shouting something that might have been Irish. There was some more shouting and slamming, and that was enough for Quade.

He remembered to take the small clay tablet from his pocket and put it carefully on a table before he ran after Colm.

The butler and two footmen stood by the front door as if blocking it. "Mr. Dunne had to leave in a great hurry," the butler said. He looked a bit roughed up, as if a strong and determined Colm Kelly had shoved past him. "He said we should bid you wait here. He'll be back any minute."

"Get the hell out of my way," Welch roared. The three servants did.

Colm was on the pavement, pointing after Wilbur's figure that was disappearing about a corner. Welch pulled out a whistle and blew hard.

"I'll make a try to catch him," Colm called over his shoulder as he started off. "Tell your men to follow me, Welch, but don't let them throw me to the ground. Tell 'em tackle the running fat man, and not me." With that last shout, he lengthened his stride and bolted.

He ran without effort, arms pumping. His hat flew off, and he didn't so much as turn to see it go. His hair shone in the sunlight and his face glowed with absolute joy. Did he like going after bad men or did he simply enjoy running? When they reunited, Quade was going to have to ask him.

"That Irishman is a maniac," Welch said. "Although from what I understand, you're no better. The two of you tearing about London, butting your way into police business."

"Do you mean you believe I'm mad as well?"

They trotted briskly down the street. Quade glanced back to see the two footmen standing under the portico, not even pretending to be busy, merely staring after them. The small boutonniere Colm had just bought lay trampled on the cobblestones. That wasn't a good sign. Quade stooped to pick up Colm's hat, a dented and dusty bowler.

Another battered hat. Likely Colm would always wear hats that looked as if they'd been stepped on. Quade looked forward to finding out. That passing thought provided a nice ray of sunlight in a dark episode.

A seduction or perhaps even rape, a horrific attempt to cover it up by his own family, deaths followed by more murder, and even the sin of his own cowardly determination to go on with his work and pretend nothing was wrong. So much sin, and what he and Colm did together was nothing compared to that.

Yes, Colm was a far more pleasant thought. Quade was growing used to the notion that he and Colm might be together as if they were a real couple. If he'd never had a chance to witness real sin, he wouldn't understand how innocent their time together truly was.

Welch was talking. Something about his memory of the Grace Redding episode. "I wasn't on the force at the time, but I know Mr. Redding made a great fuss about the incident with Jack Marrill and his daughter. Most gentlemen in his position would try to hush up the matter or perhaps arrange a match to save the poor girl's good name. My captain thinks Mr. Redding helped the girl into her final desperate act by allowing news of her disgrace to spread."

"I suppose her father didn't think it was her disgrace but my brother Jack's."

Welch waved a dismissive hand. "Anyone with any knowledge of the world would know how the whole thing would go for the poor female."

"Yes, we are a far more civilized world these days." Facts about the history of law popped into Quade's mind as usual. "In the 1400s, there were hundreds of rape claims in the Midlands, and not a single one led to a conviction at least for the first thirty years. Nowadays, even a prostitute could bring a case of rape."

Welch slowed and stared at him. "Eh, what?"

Quade realized that gentlemen didn't speak of such matters, which, perhaps, was part of the problem. "Nothing of import," Quade said. "But we were speaking of Miss Redding, and I assure you, I heard nothing of that scandal other than a rumor, which I ignored. But I expect even as a child, I worked hard to stay ignorant of the world outside books."

Ahead of them, Colm tore around the corner.

They took up the trot again, and Quade kept talking, as if Welch were forcing a confession from him. Yet now he understood his father's behavior better and wanted to tell someone. "I expect my father resented my obliviousness." Quade sped up, then pushed his hat harder onto his head. "Or perhaps he thought I mocked him every time I asked why would anyone hate us. I don't understand why he would think me guilty when there was Redding, who had a real reason to loathe us all."

He glanced at Welch, who was slightly out of breath.

"I wonder why you didn't consider Redding?" Quade asked.

Welch slowed to a brisk walk. His face had gone red, but he spoke without panting. "We looked at him, of course. Redding had seemed to give up, vanished from London." He gave a breathy grunt. "If you're going to speculate wildly, perhaps your father believed you knew about Jack's exploits and you were punishing your family for all that had gone on. You have the reputation as a prudish monk, you know."

"No," Quade said. "That is to say, you might be right about my reputation and my father's position, but I don't think that's why my father might have thought me culpable. Blast it all, I should have pushed harder to find the evidence. Did he tell you about some incendiary letters he claims I wrote?"

"No. Your father answered our questions with as few words as possible and didn't volunteer a blessed thing. What are you talking about?" Welch demanded.

"The reason for the imitation of my hand by Pennick—or perhaps by Grace, who then placed that evidence in Pennick's room. I should have tried harder to find out what my father believed I'd written. Refusing to discuss some facts might be a family trait." A trait that was now broken in Quade, since now he babbled like a brook after a thaw to a man he barely knew.

He walked faster. When he rounded the corner, the first thing Quade saw about two hundred feet away was a groaning man in the gutter—Wilbur. Colm stood over him, hands on knees, disheveled and smeared with something red.

An instant later, Quade understood that the red on Colm's face and clothes was blood. Quade ran at him, wanting to scream, putting that horror into his speed. He slowed only when Colm calmly straightened and strolled toward him, smiling.

"Colm's fine." Patrick Kelly walked over to join them. "On the other hand, you look like you've seen a ghost, Mr. Marrill."

"I'm all right." Now. Quade was dizzy from the short sprint. He'd never run so fast in his life, or perhaps it was the panic that made him close to falling over. "But you captured Wilbur. Good for you. Who could have guessed that stout, near-drunk man could run like the wind?"

Colm's grin broadened, showing the curves bracketing his eyes and mouth, though it seemed fiercer now. "Desperation makes a man fleet."

Quade knew that well enough. His heart still pounded after the sight of blood on Colm. He tipped his head at Wilbur. "You needn't have beaten him."

"I didn't. Dunne tripped over a pug dog and fell. The dog's owner bludgeoned him with her reticule. I had to protect Dunne until my cousin appeared out of nowhere." He touched his eye and winced. "She got me when she was hitting him. The lady's bag had some heavy objects in it."

He wiped his dirty hands on his trousers. The three of them watched as Wilbur was hauled up by two sturdy cops in uniform while Welch shouted orders. "Kelly!" he shouted.

Patrick Kelly waved. "Let's assume he means me, but don't you go wandering off, Colm."

He trotted over to join Welch.

Quade handed Colm his hat, and they stood in silence with the other gawkers, watching Wilbur get dragged off.

Quade asked, "Do you think he is guilty of everything we accused him of?"

"Indeed, I do, and he'll tell all to save himself from the noose."

"All out in the open at last." Quade turned away from the sight of his cousin being hauled away.

"Are you all right?" Colm asked.

"I am fine."

Colm licked blood from the corner of his mouth. He still had that light in his eyes, a man ready to do battle. "Let's go, then."

"Your cousin said to stay there."

"So he did," Colm said complacently. "I expect he'll find me again soon enough. He'll know where we're going."

"And you're not telling me because…?"

"Turnabout. You didn't tell me about the club records, recall. But I believe you can guess where I think we need to go."

They walked in silence for a time. Colm led the way, striding briskly.

"No longer acting as my guard?" Quade called after him.

Colm slowed his steps. "I think that part of my work is finished. But by Jesus, I am not done at all. No, I am not."

Quade, who did indeed have a sinking sensation that he knew where there were headed, said, "You need to clean up. You're a mess."

"Soon," Colm said, his smile savage and his eyes so bright, Quade wondered if he'd been hit on the head.

"I say, Colm, do you have a plan?"

"Yes." He rushed ahead, and it was all Quade could do to keep up with him.

He'd thought that Colm had no notion of how to find his way around London.

They'd walked more than a mile.

"Do you know where you're going."

"I think so." They went three streets more until the man suddenly stopped and pointed at a dingy red-brick structure with lace curtains and a pasteboard that read "rooms for let" in a front window. "There. That's where Mr. Grace lives."

Quade noticed the signpost at last. "How do you know?"

"You told me his address. I asked my cousin Patrick how to get here."

"What do you propose to do?"

Colm raised his brows. "I assumed you didn't want to wait. You said you are finished with allowing others to take action on your behalf."

Quade looked at the dingy building. Somewhere nearby, a woman scolded. A wagon trundled past; a cat trotted along with a mouse hanging from its mouth. Otherwise, there was no signs of life on the dark stretch of street where they stood. "I am not going to confront him."

Colm crossed his arms. He paced in a small circle.

"Now what are you doing?"

"Cooling m' blood. I itch for a fight with the man who tried to murder you."

"This is nothing like your usual manner, my friend."

He stopped walking to glare at the house. "So I would have thought. But I'm ready to kill, Quade, truly I am."

"Don't be foolish," Quade said. "Leave that sort of fury to other men with more bile."

Colm rounded on him. "Why aren't you angrier?"

"I can't help thinking of my mother."

"What? Why?"

"I wonder if she knew what Jack was. The attack and counterattacks by Redding couldn't have gone on as they did without her finding out. She must know. And she didn't want to. Hiding from the truth, although truly, I'm the last person to cast so much as a pebble," he added even more quietly. "I wonder what she would have done if she'd been in Grace's shoes. Mr. or Mrs. Redding's, I mean."

Colm jerked a chin at the house. "He wanted to kill you. Or to cast you into prison for the crimes he'd committed. That's what he did, and I have no interest in pitying him."

Quade watched his friend, roused and ready to take action. That was precisely how he'd felt less than a half hour ago, with his own cousin Wilbur, before he'd learned the truth about Grace's family history with his own family. The whole thing had become too muddy to retain that glorious outrage. He said, "We'll keep watch but leave it to the authorities."

Colm muttered something dark in Gaelic, but nodded.

Quade moved to his side. "I am touched that you should become fierce in my defense." He expected that he appeared stiff and more formal than usual. He must grow used to expressing himself better. Colm Kelly deserved that much honesty.

Colm's laugh sounded almost as forced as Quade's words. "I didn't know I could be so angry."

"It'll be done soon," Quade promised.

"I should be the one lending comfort. The treachery has been aimed at you."

"I'm reassuring us both. I think you and I have finished our part now. We'll leave here and relegate this episode to my cousin, and Mr. Grace to the past."

They didn't have to wait long. Welch and two more policemen soon appeared around a corner along with Patrick Kelly.

Welch strode over to them, moving so quickly, his breath came in little gasps. "I knew you two would be here."

"Then congratulations, you followed clues at last," Quade said waspishly before Colm, still in that rare angry mood, could say something cutting. Only one of them depended on Welch's good opinion, and it wasn't Quade.

Instead of growing annoyed, Welch gave a bark of laughter—of course he'd be in high spirits. He'd managed to solve a case without the aid of Granby.

He turned to the two policemen who'd followed. "You two come with me." He pointed his pipe stem at Colm before tucking the pipe away in his pocket. "You stay here. Do you understand? Do I have your promise, Mr. Marrill?"

"Yes," Quade began before another torrent of Gaelic came from Colm. He'd spoken more of that tongue in the last day than ever before in Quade's presence.

Quade interrupted. "Yes, yes. Go do your job, Welch." He put his back to the grim boardinghouse and its tattered lace curtains. He didn't want to see this after all. He longed to return to books and work. He'd never appreciated indices and lists of dry facts more in his life.

Eventually, he must learn every bit of the truth. Soon enough, he would have to speak to his father and mother…but not today.

Patrick moved to stand next to Colm. "If I'd known this was why you wanted those directions to this street, I wouldn't have told you. And Welch wouldn't have had to threaten Dunne to get Grace's address." He paused. "Redding's address, I should say."

Colm brightened. "I wish I'd seen that. I suspect Mr. Marrill would have enjoyed it too."

"No, I bloody well would not," Quade said. "That idiot is my cousin. I always rather liked him and his enthusiasms. He wanted me and my family dead. He happily shoveled a number of us into our graves."

Colm walked around Patrick to get to him. Mindless of Patrick or anyone else, he hauled Quade into his arms, pulling him as close as he could without knocking off either of their hats. "I'm sorry," he said, his warm breath on Quade's ear. "That was thoughtless of me."

"No." Quade pulled away. He fumbled out his handkerchief and blew his nose. "You had nothing to do with this mess except help clean it up." He lowered his voice. "I have no desire to burst into saccharine tears, so your kindness must cease."

"And if you do, I might follow with my own wails," Colm said. "Heavy weather for both of us." He sounded more like his normal, light self.

Patrick said, "This is interesting but Colm, I'm not sure you should be groping your employer on the street."

Quade said, "I'm not his employer. You are."

"So I am," Patrick said. He pulled a notebook out of his pocket. "We must wait anyway, left out of the action."

"Thank God, or I'd rip that Redding to shreds," Colm muttered.

Patrick went on, "As your employer, I demand you tell me everything that you know about this situation."

"Not yet," Quade said. A shout rose up.

More men shouted. A woman screamed.

Seconds later, a tall, thin figure raced from the house, straight into the arms of a stout policeman waiting by the front entrance. "Another runner," Colm said. "Where do they suppose they plan to go?"

Quade didn't want to move closer, but when Colm and Patrick trotted over to the crowd gathering around the policemen and Redding, he trailed after them.

Redding had stopped struggling, but when he saw Quade, his face drew into one of those strange smiles. Why had Quade ever thought them a sign of good will or a pleasant manner? The man was snarling, and always had been.

"Good day, Mr. Marrill!" Grace said as if they'd met in the front hall the club.

Colm called out, "What did you put in the coffee? Why did you destroy that picture of the brothers?"

At least he didn't shout out names, but Mr. Grace had no such compunction.

"Why did the Marrill family destroy mine?" Mr. Grace still sounded perfectly reasonable. Truly, he had to be mad.

Quade wanted to step back from that palpable look of hatred, but he didn't so much as drop his gaze as he answered, "I don't know. I didn't know what had happened to your daughter."

"If you had known, what would you have done? Hmm? Nothing. You would do nothing."

Welch stood behind him, scribbling notes. Quade almost wanted to tell Grace to shut up, to say nothing until he could speak to a solicitor.

The policeman started to pull at Grace's arm, but Welch barked an order. "Stay."

They all froze, a little group on the pavement in front of a miserable group of buildings. And of course, by now a new group had formed around them, the usual street urchins and servants.

"What did he do?" a kid called out.

"I worked for the cause of Justice," Redding's voice rang out. "I'd wipe out the slime and leave only the guiltiest party to bear the burden. But God saw fit to remove him before I was ready."

"That would be Jack?" Patrick muttered to Colm.

Colm's answer was quiet enough, Quade didn't have to listen.

He couldn't look away from the skeletal Mr. Redding, but Redding was done talking. He seemed to wilt at last. He bent his head, his gaze fixed on the cobblestones, and wouldn't look at Quade or anyone else again.

Colm came back. Quade didn't need to look over at him, because he could feel that comforting presence standing next to him as if it were a ray of warmth.

"Come, Mr. Kelly," Quade said. "Let's go home."

Patrick held up a hand. "If you're talking to Colm, he should probably come with me and file a report. We are almost certain the man who wanted to kill you is under arrest."

No. That wouldn't do. He couldn't stand the thought of going back to that apartment alone.

"A word with him first." Quade didn't wait for an answer and pulled Colm by the arm to walk a few steps away from Patrick. In a low voice, he asked, "You'd go with your cousin? Is that what you want? To stay at Mr. Sloan's house instead of mine?"

Far too many seconds passed. Hours, weeks moved along while he gazed at those serious green-gray eyes until he got his reply. "No."

One short syllable meant the world settled exactly the way it should and Quade could breathe again. Once the man he wanted had said that simple word, Quade could stop worrying. In fact, it dawned on him that this began something more interesting than anything he'd had in the past.

But for once, he would dot his i's and cross those t's in more than just his work. Time to apply the thirst for details to something more than research in books. Time to bring it to his life as well.

He glanced over at Patrick Kelly, who wore a peculiar grin. Quade decided to ignore him and turned his attention back to Colm.

"Tell me exactly what you want."

"To go with you."

"And then what?"

"Oh, I expect you know," Colm said with a suggestive smirk.

Quade's interest sparked to life, but he'd meant more than the next encounter. He hesitated because, after all, gentlemen didn't beg, his father's voice told him. Wait. They also apparently didn't express anything of importance—and that was absurd.

"I didn't mean to ask about your immediate wants and plans. I meant in the longer term. I meant…" He made a circling gesture with his hands. "Tomorrow. The day after that. A fortnight from now."

Colm looked taken aback. His lips moved. Was he praying? Counting the numbers of days they might have left together? He fingered his cheek, which was slightly swollen from the brief fight he'd had with either Wilbur or the pug's owner. "I hadn't thought."

"No, I don't suppose the idea would occur to anyone. That you might stay on with me. Or that you might want to. Or that I'd want you to. I assure you that I would like nothing better, but you needn't—"

He felt like an idiot, but that was better than feeling like a man who was afraid of indignity. He'd had enough of that for a lifetime.

"You, hush." Colm reached out and laid a forefinger on Quade's lips, a bold and intimate move. His finger was shockingly warm. "I was going to say that I hadn't thought that you wanted me as much as I wanted you. I'd be honored to go home with you, Quade Marrill. And I'd stay as long as you allowed me to."

CHAPTER FIFTEEN

Two weeks later

Colm had his notebook out, but he didn't need to look at the words he'd jotted during the meeting with his cousin and Welch.

Quade was laughing so hard, Colm thought he might choke. "I don't know why you find this so amusing." Colm sat on the arm of the chair where Quade worked.

Quade wiped the tears of laughter from his eyes with his palms. He twisted sideways so he could look up at Colm. "I was pushed into action, became absolutely certain crimes had been committed, because I thought I was being poisoned. And now you're saying it was all my imagination. Ha, after begging him to test the cigar and now the coffee as soon as possible…" He laughed some more before finishing. "Hemner will think me a lunatic."

"It was more than your imagination. Welch sent a man to interview the grocer, who admitted that he'd spilled some kind of liniment on the green coffee beans and hoped the disgusting stuff would roast out."

"I shall never purchase from him again." He pulled out a handkerchief and blew his nose. "What else did you learn?"

"Grace didn't want you members of the Marrill family talking to each other, and he had already sown seeds of discord. He'd sent two short letters to your father, from you in your hand, cursing him or something of the sort. Your father burned the letter and hired a caretaker to watch over you." Colm pressed his mouth tight, suppressing a smile. "There had been some mention of deviant behavior in the notes about you."

Quade's mouth trembled as if he were going to start in laughing again. "And when you read that, you took that to mean something more interesting than murderous intents. Why the hell didn't my father say anything?"

"I don't know."

"And I suppose I do," Quade said. "It falls under the category of staying quiet because a gentleman doesn't express weakness."

"As to that," Colm said. "There is a point to staying quiet. I suffered back home in Ireland because I opened my fool mouth when I shouldn't have. Though I suppose too little talk is not good for the soul."

Quade grunted. "A polite way to put it. I'd say it was more a sign of weakness."

"Ach, now, that's—"

Quade interrupted. "My family is composed of cowards, pretending that their lack of heated conversation was some virtue. Just after my brother's funeral, my father said something about how I had expressed strong feelings and enacted drama, and I had no notion what he was talking about. I should have pushed harder to discover what he meant."

Colm bent close and kissed him. "You're speaking now, my brave friend."

"Mm." Quade deepened the kiss, then pulled back to murmur. "Your mouth is warm, and your scent is of summer."

A polite way to say he smelled bad after he'd rushed back from the meeting with Patrick. His Quade could be tactful on occasion. "Do I? Sweat and what else?"

Quade reached up and stroked the nape of Colm's neck. "Sweat and clean air."

Colm hoped the touch might lead to something very interesting, but Quade let his hand drop and started asking questions. "What else did Patrick and Welch say? Did they learn more about Redding's actions? How did he kill Jack?"

"It seems he didn't kill Jack. Mind you, that came clear after some persuasion, is how Welch put it. Redding wasn't willing to talk, even after he heard that Dunne was talking volumes."

"Cousin Wilbur had much to tell?"

"A great deal. He had no hand in hiring Pennick or killing him. That might be the truth, because much of what he said seems to be true, including the fact that he'd cut off funds to Redding after Jack's death. And Jack really was killed by a bee sting."

"The police believe these two things on what evidence?"

"The first, because they can see that, yes, indeed the bank payments to Redding ended. The second because Redding hinted of his whole scheme to Dunne, and to us, and it was clear he hadn't targeted Jack for murder. Jack was supposed to live and be miserable."

"In prison, I suppose?"

"Yes, and Redding reassured Dunne that the money would come to him eventually, because even though Redding didn't plan to kill Jack, he'd die within a couple of years. He planned to have Jack be found guilty of murder of everyone in your family and be sent to prison. Jack was supposed to suffer, watch his family perish one by one over years, and, then be hanged. That was the point of the ex-valet's clumsy job of putting the blame on Jack."

Quade's eyes went wide. "So even though the coffee wasn't part of his plan, I was to die as well?"

"Likely, yes. You and your father together, I think." And very soon, since the evidence against Jack had already been planted by Pennick, but Colm wouldn't bother pointing out that chilling fact. "When Jack died unexpectedly, Redding's plans had to change at once. When he begged for more money from Dunne, he said he needed another target to take the aim away from Dunne and himself."

"And I think I know who he picked." Quade put the notebook on the desk, all signs of amusement gone, though he was remarkably calm.

"Yes, you were to be the guilty party—he'd already set you up as a hostile man with your father. He'd tried to make the police interested in you with the dead bird, but they didn't take his hints because they had spotted Pennick. He was growing desperate and even more stupid by then. He had broken into your house to find some more ways to make you look insane. He wanted to make it look as if you were the one who damaged the picture of your family. It was to look like you were crossing them off one by one, though I expect he got some pleasure from the act. The broken glass was a mistake, but he was startled and fled. As we saw when he ran you over."

"He did seem the sort who liked to set the stage. He could make it appear I had slain my father and then killed myself. That's what I would have done if I were planning to implicate someone for all those murders. That would leave only my small cousin, who might meet with an accident later on."

"You seem unbothered about this. I'm not sure I could be."

"I suspect I'll lie awake and imagine what might have happened."

"Then you must wake me so I might distract you." Colm sighed and shook his head. "You were so young when this all started."

"Young, but not really a small child. I wonder if he's the reason I have such a reputation for a bad temper. I don't really. I'm the mildest of men, well except for you, of course, but you're a saint."

Colm laughed at his earnestness. "Holy Colm the saintly buggerer," he said.

Quade's mouth twitched. "To think you can joke about that now."

"Far better to do it, don't you think?" Colm said. He knew he blushed, but that would never stop.

"Indeed, I do think that." Quade pulled him down onto his lap.

THE END

His Irish Detective

Look for these titles by Summer Devon

Solitary Shifter series:
Taming the Bander
Revealing the Beast
Releasing the Shifter

Single title
The Private Secretary
The Gentleman and the Lamplighter
Sibling Rivals
Goodbye Phillip
Tail of the Dog
Goodbye Phillip
Must Loathe Norcross
The Hanged Man's Hero
Hot Under the Collar
The Hanged Man's Hero
His American Detective (book one Victorian Gay Detective)

Titles written with Bonnie Dee

Seducing Stephen
The Gentleman and the Rogue
The Nobleman and the Spy
Sin and the Preacher's Son
The Psychic and the Sleuth

Summer Devon

The Gentleman's Keeper
The Gentleman's Madness
The Professor and the Smuggler
The Shepherd and the Solicitor
Mending Him
The Bohemian and the Banker

***Victorian Holiday Hearts series*:**
Simon and the Christmas Spirit
Will and the Valentine Saint
Mike and the Spring Awakening
Delaney and the Autumn Masque

His Irish Detective

Titles Written as Kate Rothwell (m/f romance)

Somebody Wonderful
Somebody to Love
Someone to Cherish
Thank You, Mrs. M
Seducing Miss Dunaway (free novella)
Protecting Miss Samuels
Powder of Sin
Her Mad Baron
Love Between the Lines
Mademoiselle Makes a Match
The Earl, a Girl, and a Promise

Made in the USA
San Bernardino, CA
27 March 2018